I0763484

CASSIE SWINDON

ISBN paperback: 9798864696873

ISBN hardcover: 978-1-7373469-5-1

Cover Design by: BZN Studio Design

Naked Hardcover Design by: Raven Pages Design Studio

Interior Formatting by: Jennifer Laslie

Editing by Kristen Breanne

<u>Dedicated to:</u>

All the women who once upon a time dreamt of being mermaids, witches, and rulers.
You're already one.

ALSO BY CASSIE SWINDON

The Linked Trilogy

Scorched

Severed

Shattered

The Golden Chains Trilogy

Break the Stone

Hunt the Storm

Stop the Clock

The Fairy Tale Flip series has other gender reversal stories such as Beauty and the Beast, "The Phantom Ink," and Peter Pan "The Pixie Window"

ACKNOWLEDGMENTS

Different people support me in different areas of my life. However, all my book-related shout out must first and foremost go to Anna Cackler. When I had moments of wanting to give up, you so cruelly and sarcastically suggested throwing away my characters in the dump. That gave me a rude wake-up call that tossing these stories to the curb will never be an option. Fellow new authors know how competitive it is out there and how hard we work to be seen by so few. Writing is not a very rewarding career in the beginning. Yet, when Anna helped me reprioritize what matters, it's so obvious that creating is the key to joy. So, dear reader, no matter what your passion is, just continue, whether five or five million people experience your craft. Keep going!

CHAPTER 1

Eribelle

A well-intended compliment can still drown a soul.

Even when it's your own father making the comment.

I shift uncomfortably on the make-shift stage, rocking on my ridiculous stilettos. Only flip-flops or bare feet are meant for the shore on a summer day like this.

"Give it up for my gorgeous daughter, Eribelle!" My father's booming voice projects out to the crowd of millionaires on the sand, half risking sunburn while the other half hide beneath tents.

They clap, as expected, but these potential yacht buyers

stay focused on Dad's exaggerated gestures as he commands the stage next to me. I ignore his words as he rambles on using sly marketing techniques and instead give my attention to the sound of the waves crashing beyond the pier. The sea teases the sand, with waves ready to seduce a fool to their death, but I'm not that fool. I know the dangers that haunt the waters of the Below.

The ocean stands as a barrier between me and freedom, otherwise I'd already be long gone from this island.

If only I could run from this ridiculous auction. For a moment, I imagine dashing through the decorative banners and leaving their shreds in my wake. My father has counted on me for the success of his business. My face is his brand. He doesn't need to know this is the last time he'll ever show me off.

I've helped him for long enough. Now, it's time to live my life on my terms—as a painter—far away from here.

Soon. I can flee soon—I just have to keep faking a smile until then.

Men in the front row click their tongues at me, distracting me from my dreams of escape. One gestures as if he's spanking an imaginary woman, his gaze slowly traveling up from my ankles. Ugh, creeper. Despite our three suns shining warmth, a shiver racks my spine as his eyes roam higher up my outfit, which fits the required sailor theme. My shorts are cut too high, and my top is too low in the front. At least I don't have to wear a three-piece business suit. These yacht collectors all must be sweating bullets.

"...and the winner of our auction this year will also get three hours aboard my lovely Eribelle," Dad says into the mic.

My ex, Trey's voice rises above the laughter as he shouts, "She's already been boarded by me and half of Coendriel!"

Thankfully, my skin is already flushed from the heat. I use every ounce of energy to keep my shoulders straight and refrain from crossing my arms over my chest. I will not hide from these piranhas.

More entertained hoots and whistles mix with the testosterone swirling in the summer air. These men deserve to be dragged to the bottom of the sea.

Dad's foot hits the microphone stand, sending a high-pitched squeal into the group. If he feels any protectiveness toward me about Trey's rude statement, he masks it with a forced grin. "I *meant* the winner will get three hours aboard my personal *yacht*, named after my beautiful daughter, Eribelle."

A round of applause infects each boat enthusiast, and many nod in approval—either at the harbored yacht or at my figure. My cousin, Brooks, sweeps into the crowd and hauls Trey from the event.

My mind wanders across the violent blue waves to the distant coast that holds my future. A boat is my only means of freedom. At this point, even a damn canoe would suffice. I'm almost desperate enough to consider swimming, despite the merfolk stalking the waters.

Threatening gray clouds rumble from afar, prompting every millionaire's head to turn toward the sea. Instead of worrying about what the harmful sky carries toward us, I mentally snap a still-frame image in my mind to later paint this ominous storm. Which gray will I use for the clouds? Steel or platinum? Or how about slate? Walrus gray? Maybe silver, as sleek as the legendary trident of the sea.

"A toast!" Dad's voice jolts me back to attention. He doesn't need to yell for his words to vibrate deep within my bones. The men raise their glasses in unison as he says, "To salt, sails, and sweet beauties."

When Dad winks at me, I try to unclench my muscles. Why couldn't he have said "sweet creativity" or "sweet cunning," or honestly, anything that isn't about my appearance?

"Okay, men, good luck bidding, and don't forget to tip the bartenders." Dad points to the women in sailor outfits.

The crowd shuffles into clusters. Finally, I'm granted a moment to breathe. Dad walks toward me on the stage, his auburn hair the same shade as mine shifting in the breeze.

"You could've at least washed the paint off your hands for once," Dad scolds with one glance at my violet-tipped fingers. "Sweetheart, I'm sorry about Trey. I'll make sure he doesn't receive an invite next year."

Dad's strong arms wrap me into a rare hug, and I nostalgically ease into his embrace. If only things were different. Dad isn't aware that he'll promise one thing yet turn his back on me as soon as it benefits him. His words and actions have never matched. No matter what he says, I'm convinced he only sees me as one thing, a marketing strategy—a product to entice men to buy boats.

"Don't worry, Dad." I float down the stage steps in my outrageous five-inch stilettos. "Trey is allowed to be bitter that I broke up with him."

Dad's gaze works the crowd of colleagues, boat club members, and politicians. "Trey never deserved you anyway. I won't have anyone sour your name and drag your reputation through the mud."

Yet, ironically, Dad will parade me around the richest men of our nation, in an outfit that barely has more fabric than a bikini. I've let this go on for too long, and another useless conversation with him about my hopes for my future won't change anything. I'm done being used and trapped.

A moment of relief from the scorching suns finds me as I

move under the shade of a vendor's tent. I swipe a bottle of water, and the beads of condensation drip down my fingertips as I bring it to my lips. I pull it away; fuchsia pink rims the top of the plastic.

"If you want to punish Trey for anything, it should be for how ugly his hat was." I pretend to laugh and point at a stranger. "Look, that guy over there looks like he's going to a funeral."

"These men are not a joke, Eribelle," Dad hisses. "You are twenty-one years old, damn it, so start acting like it. Go cozy up to Arnold Strinden over there. He needs some extra coaxing."

Nauseous. I'm physically nauseous. The man who prides himself on having raised me doesn't even know me. Why can't he ever ask about my current projects, or what inspires me to paint?

"I'd rather go back to my studio. Why don't you recruit someone else for help?" I ask.

"It's not like I have your brother here." His face softens again. "You're all I have left."

And there it is. The guilt. My mother left us when I was a baby, and my brother died in a boat accident a decade ago. No matter how much I hate my dad's behavior, I still love him. That wretched love is what has delayed my escape. But I'm done waiting.

I grind my teeth and face him. "Dad, I need to talk to you. Tomorrow, I'm going to —"

"Let's chat later, sweetie. This isn't the time for one of your fairy tale dreams." He finally spots whoever he is looking for and waves the man over, then kisses my forehead and whispers, "I'll be right back. Please, be good." The titan of a man who gave me half my genes stalks off to his colleagues.

A knot ties tight in my stomach. Be good. That means

stay quiet, agree, and smile. When did it get this bad? How have I let myself stoop to such a level? All my past work only accumulated to this demeaning job. Fuck this.

I let out the breath I've been holding and remind myself—just a little longer, and I'll be out of here.

A young man with aristocratic cheekbones walks through a group and locks eyes with me. Jordan Idros. His smile charms every other woman on this island, but to me, it resembles a snake slithering up his cheeks. In my teen years, I welcomed his pursuits, but now my body stiffens when he approaches. Jordan reaches for my hand, and I have half a mind to ball it into a fist, but instead let him kiss the back of my knuckles.

"Good day to the most popular redhead of Coendriel." Silky secrets line each of Jordan's syllables. "How are you, my princess?"

A sour taste coats my tongue, and I hold back a gag. We may have linked our Taj99 devices as teens, but I've ignored all of Jordan's recent messages. Apparently, he hasn't taken the hint.

When Jordan smiles, his teeth are brighter than the dusty white sand lining our coast. But his eyes aren't right. They mirror the sharp edges of a fishing hook. My gut squirms and flashes warnings.

"Enjoy the auction, Jordan. I'm headed home." I turn toward our estate right behind the party.

Sweat drips down my back and slides over each vertebra as I spin away, and it feels like the entire island holds its breath. Don't follow me. Don't follow.

"Wait, Eribelle." Soft footsteps skid on the sand-coated pavement. "What's wrong?"

"I'm…" I glance out at the sky and think of the first thing Jordan will believe—a damsel in distress. "I'm afraid of storms."

He nods and holds out his arm. "Well, at least let me walk you home."

"No, it's okay. I can walk the treacherous two minutes. The landscape artist is right there at the edge of the garden. See?" I point to one of Dad's dozens of employees.

One of Jordan's eyebrows angles so high I picture a new painting project, but instead of the face of a man, it would be of a sly eel. I've spent a lifetime being fooled by men who only wanted to use my looks to their benefit.

Even Trey had only dated me to use my connection to Dad's empire and show me off at the gala downtown. With Eribelle Erickson on his arm, he was given many job offers. I had felt him slipping away, had ignored my instincts that the words of commitment Trey had whispered into my ear for months had all been fake. Stupid. I'd been naïve and stupid.

"Stupid, stupid…" I mumble as the bottom of the sky falls out.

Jordan shields his eyes from the tropical rain and shrugs off his jacket. "Here, take this."

I poke a finger into his chest, completely out of patience, and ask, "Why?"

"Excuse me?" His smirk battles between confusion and entertainment.

Rain soaks my hair, plastering the fiery red onto my drenched shirt. "*Why* are you giving me your jacket?"

Jordan bites his lip, his eyes dropping to my mouth. "Because it's the gentlemanly thing to do?"

"No." I step forward. "Your brain thinks my eyes are symmetrical, my boobs are the right size, and my hips can bear children. And for some insane reason," my voice rises, but at least no one else is this far from the party to hear, "those qualities make you think you deserve the right to claim me as yours. This jacket is a cage. Do you want to imprison me?"

Jordan shifts on his feet uncomfortably.

"You've been asking me out for a year but know nothing about me or whether we're compatible. Maybe that woman down by the docks is your true love." I point to a stranger climbing into a fishing boat.

His jaw drops, and rain splatters down his face. "Eribelle, I simply wanted to buy you steak and wine."

"I don't like steak."

Leaving him in the fresh downpour, I splash through puddles and stomp my way up the grand staircase of The Erickson Estate, where my studio beckons to me from the highest floor. If I had it my way, I'd live in a one-bedroom apartment, far from all this unnecessary extravagance.

This time, Jordan doesn't follow. Thank the goddesses above.

The front door is too heavy to slam, but I try anyway. A large moan sounds when the ancient door grinds against the floor. I slump down on the other side of the threshold, and a groan explodes out of me from somewhere deep in my core.

"Well, aren't you a sopping mess."

I don't need to glance up to know the owner of that magical voice, my best friend and makeup artist, Sampson. My head falls further between my knees as I try to catch my breath. Sampson tiptoes over the slippery marble. He squats, not letting his designer jeans touch the water pooling around me.

After a heavy sigh, Sampson loops a wet strand of my hair around his finger. "Oh, darling. Did they make you do the photo op?"

When I finally meet his eyes, tears begin to fall.

"Oh, tell me. What's wrong?" He collapses to the floor next to me, designer pants and all.

My hands shield my cheeks. "I can't do this anymore, Sampson. I'm not a doll."

He nods and strokes my back. "Dolls are creepy as shit."

I gulp down a half-chuckle but let it all out. "I'm not some *thing* for my father to parade around."

"Parades are disgusting." Sampson rolls his eyes. "So many germs. Everything gets sticky, let me tell you."

Tension begins to ease out of my shoulders. "And Trey made a fool—"

"Oooh! I'll kill that hat-wearing bitch." Sampson cranes his neck to the window. "Which way did he go?"

I let myself laugh this time and lay my head on his shoulder.

He winks. "I bet Ozaron is on pins and needles awaiting your arrival."

Across the sea, in Ozaron, artists of all kinds will meet for the biggest conference in the world in a few weeks to network, swap portfolios, sign up for classes, apply for scholarships, offer mentorships, or sell their creations. My entire future depends on my ability to be there.

I move my finger over the pattern on the floor, drawing invisible lines like the rays from the spectacular three suns.

"Whatcha drawing this time?" Sampson's gaze follows the pattern of my finger across the pristine floors.

"Nothing."

Sampson stops the movement of my hand, calming me. I stare at the floor. It's so clean that my reflection bounces back, red curtain bangs framing my skin. Right in the middle, my rare blue eyes stare back at me. Eyes that have made the front page of Coendriel's local paper a record number of times because only merfolk have my cyan blue.

Maybe that's why I feel so different. All I see is a lost girl who wants to be seen—truly seen—and understood for who I am. Only Sampson appreciates my art and passion. Which is why I'm so glad he has agreed to leave with me. Except, I can no longer wait until tomorrow to start our new life.

"Come on, let's go," I say as I rise off the slippery floor.

"Is it time to poke holes in Trey's face in that old scrapbook?"

I tug him up and sweep us around the corner. "No, we need to pack."

"Pack for a sleepover on our last night here? Where will this wild adventure be? The Criggin Cove?" Sampson trips over his own feet, but I pull him faster. "Let me guess. We're sleeping under the stars? Ew, no, bugs. I don't do bugs. Actually, let's take a pause and rethink these shenanigans."

"No, we're going to Ozaron…now." I pause but don't dare look over. "You'll still come, right?"

"What are besties for?" he says enthusiastically, all in.

Relief swarms in my gut. We scramble up stair after stair, finally reaching the fourth floor of my dad's mansion. Sampson staggers into my room shortly after me.

"Do we…have to…*run* to the piers?" His hand leans against the doorframe. "Because…darling…I simply won't survive." Sampson shakes his head dramatically. "And what if the merfolk drag me Below. I'm too delicious for them to resist." He folds in half, catching his breath. "But seriously, how…will we manage…to make it…across the Barrett Sea?"

"I have money saved up from teaching at the studio and someone willing to break the rules for a piece of my cash."

"Bribes. I like it." Sampson scratches his chin. "Why not steal some money from your humble Pops too? It's not like he'll know the difference."

"No. I'm not relying on him for anything else."

"I hate to tell you the obvious, but your face is plastered on every other billboard down the coast with 'Erickson Yachts' proudly written above that bright red hair…" Sampson's eyebrows knit together adorably like a little puppy's. "Your father's connections can't be underestimated.

If anyone sees you board a boat at the festival tonight, they'll rat you out."

"Then I guess we'll need a disguise."

His eyes light up brighter than the chandelier hanging proudly above us. "Done and done. Give me approximately three seconds to find my bin of wigs."

As Sampson disappears into my closet, I survey my room for the last time, memorizing every detail from the well-worn smocks hanging on a towel hook, to the three easels by the bay window. Instead of custom wallpaper, my paintings cover the walls from floor to ceiling. The lowest ones show my skills as a teetering toddler only able to reach a couple feet from the ground. As I grew, the details morphed from stick figures to detailed sceneries and profiles of various people. Dad's cleaning crew calls my work beautiful, but someone should erase that word from the dictionary.

Each swipe and stroke of color isn't meant to be pleasing. That's too easy. My goal is to allure viewers with my art's uniqueness. I want them to dig down deep to discover the feelings my pieces evoke. Every caress of the paintbrush onto the canvas has a purpose. Periwinkle in the sunsets highlights the poetry of falling in love. Crystal blues in the scene hung above my nightstand portray epic friendship. The colors battle each other on the canvas for the right to stamp a memory on one's heart. And the trident gray of storms is for the women who crave true freedom.

I stare at my favorite. The cyan eyes that haunt me in my dreams. Masculine. Raw. And hungry.

"Eribelle, sweetie," Dad calls from the hallway.

A bolt of lightning flashes through my muscles as I jump into action. At least I hadn't started packing yet, so there's nothing to hide. I wasn't expecting him. There's no reason for him to have left all his business partners at the auction.

"I'm busy," I say as I gather up my best landscapes for my portfolio.

"This is too important to wait." His broad frame fills my doorway. "I have the most excellent news."

Before I can open my mouth, Dad pulls out a tiny box from his pocket. With a quick flick of his finger, the box opens to a sparkling ring—my mother's ring. I don't even remember what she looked like, and Dad has always refused to talk about her, but this one piece of her has sat on our mantelpiece my entire life.

My frenzied heart pounds even faster. "What are you doing with that?"

"Jordan Idros has asked for your hand, sweetie! It's a match made by the Sky Goddess!"

My heel smacks into the foot of my bed, and I tumble back onto the messy sheets.

"Eribelle, my goodness, I've raised you to be more poised than that." Dad rushes forward and pulls the ring from the box.

I wrestle with the mound of pillows trying to swallow me whole.

"Come out of there, child." He fluffs the blanket, only for the other side to parachute up.

Eventually, I fall out from the cotton suffocation pile and find myself on the cold floor.

"Congratulations, baby girl, you're engaged!"

"No! Dad, you can't marry me off like that. It's the sixteenth falcon year, for sands' sake! Arranged Partners are from centuries ago."

"He's a sturdy choice with a steady income. Wealth creates power, you know that." Dad pats my shoulder. "You'll be doubly taken care of this way, trust me. No merfolk will ever lay their hands on you. I won't ever have to worry about your safety again. I'll never lose another child." He marches over, waiting for me to hold out my finger. When I hide both hands behind my back, Dad says, "Don't be silly. Put out your hand."

For now, Dad needs to think he's in control. Otherwise, my plan will go to shit. So I hold out my finger. Mother's one-of-a-kind ring fits my finger perfectly. Just like that, the restraints tying me to this island pull a bit tighter.

CHAPTER 2

Eribelle

As the town's bell tower strikes midnight, Sampson and I hide behind the corner of a popular bakery where vines climb the brick exterior. The scent of cinnamon buns wafts through the night air like magic. My mouth immediately waters, and I recount the food items in my backpack to make sure they'll last across the Barrett Sea. Soon, I'll be free. That's all that matters.

Sampson peeks around the wall into an alleyway. His long, curly wig covered in a bandanna resembles an outfit worn by a rock star, and I've never seen him wear such tall boots. Any other night, this might be comical, but my nerves are on high alert.

I adjust my oversized neon opera mask meant for a rave and cross my fingers that no one will recognize me, even though I'm carrying a rather large portfolio case. Anyone else awake at this hour will hopefully assume we're just another tipsy couple meandering toward the dock for an epic masquerade.

Sampson tiptoes across the street like a gazelle taking ballet class. His shadow flickers under one of the streetlamps until he finds a new spot behind a bush. No matter how many times I wear heels, it doesn't make it any easier to walk on these cobblestones. My boots clickity-clack as I follow in the shadows.

Faint music streams from a nearby bar, but no one spills out of its back door—yet. We have to hurry.

Quietly, we slip behind an abandoned ice cream cart, wait, check both ways, and then dart across another alley. The hypnotic call of the sea intensifies with each step. I twist the Commitment ring on my finger nervously. I couldn't leave Mom's jewelry behind.

Ahead, the pier is quiet as boats rock gently side to side.

"Look." I point to Dad's yacht, and Sampson's gaze follows. "That's who we're meeting. She's Jordan's ex and also leads my dad's security."

Sampson nods. "We need code names. I'll be Oegnus, and you'll be—"

I cut him off by jogging the short distance between shadows, knowing he will follow. I hope we don't scare the woman, but I can't risk anyone else spotting us.

"Hey there." I sidestep Sampson and stagger into the light, hoping the woman will respect our plan.

"You're late. I almost left," the sailor says.

"Aye, matey." Sampson's fake pirate accent doesn't fit his rock star vibe, and I wince as he pretends to fall over. "We need a toilet foooor a captain who drank a wee bit too much rum."

The woman rolls her eyes and connects a little ramp from the dock to the boat. "Get on before I change my mind."

I've been taught to fear the endless ocean and its power after my brother, Ben, died years ago. A part of me has always wondered what it'd be like to embrace the frigid waters and jump in without worry. Instead, I shuffle onto the yacht and listen as our accomplice unties us from the dock.

"Can we trust her?" Sampson whispers. "Do you think she'll give us the keys or will she turn us in?"

"I'll go talk to her."

On the wall, I catch sight of a familiar framed picture hanging; a young Ben standing next to our father. I still miss my brother in the same way I'd miss a severed limb. Since he can't have the future he always longed for, I'll make sure I live enough adventures for the both of us.

Slowly, I check for signs that the sailor has betrayed us and called a dozen of Dad's security to drag us back home. There are no other sounds besides the soft waves lapping against the shore.

"Looking for these?"

I jump and swivel around. The woman holds the yacht's keys in her hand, and they dangle together to create music in the night.

"Thanks for helping us. I'm surprised you recognized me in this costume."

"You're the most famous face on this island, Miss Erickson," she says and steps closer. "The only human I've ever encountered with blue eyes. Did you really think I wouldn't recognize you?"

When I'm close enough, I lunge for the keys, but she swipes them behind her back. I study her stern expression and say, "I have the money we agreed to."

All she'd have to do is radio in to a guard and everything would fall apart. They'd be here within a minute.

"Do you love *him?*" The look in her eyes can't be mistaken. Hate. But is the hate focused toward me or the man she's referring to?

I pause, waiting for her to elaborate. When her gaze drops to the ring on my finger, clarity dawns. Jordan. She still cares for her ex. She shifts uncomfortably until her face is under the light-post beam. With cheeks that flushed, I'd bet she's still in love with him.

"No," I say without expounding.

"I'll still help," she says, "if you never return, and never speak to Jordan again."

I nod, thanking my lucky stars that we might complete the impossible, and she'll hand over the keys. I suck in a breath. Am I really doing this? I'll make Dad look foolish in front of all his comrades. That isn't my intention, but if we're successful, he'll wake up with his boat gone. Whoever won at the auction won't have this yacht for a prize and news will spread that his remaining child abandoned him.

"I'll give you a two-hour head start before I raise the alarm. I can't lose my job for you." She lifts the anchor from the water and attaches it in place on the yacht. "Now go. I don't want to see you ever again."

I stare at the keys in my hand and mutter, "Thank you." When I look up, her silhouette is already moving away.

I rush toward the helm. Adrenaline pumping, I check behind my shoulder, ready for someone to pounce, but no one is there. Quickly, I turn the key in the ignition, and the engine roars to life. I push on the gas, and the yacht slowly drifts in the calm shallows before I direct her toward my future, toward Ozaron, a new life in a different world.

CHAPTER 3

Axton

My mom used to say, 'The only way to lose yourself is to be afraid of getting lost.' Fear doesn't belong in the royal marine guard, or RMG as everyone knows it by, nor does the luxury of getting lost. For someone in my position, the only option is to protect the crown.

Princess Gia's birthday festival is in full swing in the royal courtyard. A pod of dolphins joins the merchildren, out-swimming them easily. Their powerful tails, shining scales, and flowing hair only add to the beauty of Nerida. Everyone's dressed in costumes, from fins to tails, at the princess's request. Even though she's turning thirty this year, she loves her themed parties. Our citizens tend to indulge her outlandish requests since it's well-known that the legendary trident drove her to insanity once upon a time.

A merman bumps into me and I grip my spear tighter.

"Smile much?" He laughs, obviously drunk, and swims away.

My muscles remain tight since the queen and her daughter are swimming out in the open, more exposed to threats from Above. My entire purpose as second-in-command is to make sure they stay alive. Some irrational humans still believe our mere existence poses a threat to them. Because of fables and their fear, fishermen and sailors from Erickson Harbor have been trying to eliminate our kind for years, and they've gotten too close recently. First, a fellow guard died after being trapped in a net. Then a merchild was speared with a hook. Another poisoned. All dead. Because of humans.

And then there were my parents—dead for an entirely different reason, but I won't let history repeat itself.

Queen Rayna swims away from the crowd and toward her castle doors. She passes each of her guards but stops in front of me, as usual.

"Any word from the surface today, Axton?" She meets my eyes, a rare honor.

"Yes, my lady. Two more human kidnappings by Criggin Cove," I whisper while keeping my eye on the crowds swimming nearby. Someone here might be the criminal who is putting our kind at risk by capturing humans against the treaty's policy.

"Damn it," she hisses but keeps a smile plastered for the public. "Do we know who's to blame yet?"

"No, my lady. The criminal is probably a human from Coendriel. Don't worry, I'll catch whoever it is."

Queen Rayna's glare could cut through the skin of a walrus with one slice. "Yes, you will." She drifts closer as the current pushes her body. "You and your head officer will meet with me at high tide tomorrow to discuss your plans to put an end to these crimes."

"Yes, my lady." I bow slightly as she wades past me through the castle doors.

I finally let my shoulders loosen. My grip on my spear relaxes, and I stare up at the magnificent castle. Sharp black and navy rocks form the outline of the tower, blend in with the deep-sea hues. Coral grows off the façade, a natural reef, and fish swarm in schools near the windows. Unique seashells decorate the front door—a project by an elementary class of merchildren last year—some hanging crooked.

"What did my aunt have to say this time?" My best friend pokes my back and tries to grab my spear. I twist toward Lena faster than she can poke again. Even for mermaid's standards, she's striking with dark brown skin and long black braids. Her fangs sparkle like diamonds when she smiles at me wickedly. I know that look—trouble.

"What did you do this time?" I ask.

"Lighten up," Lena says.

As the queen's niece, she has always given me a hard time for being too serious like the soldiers who used to guard her as a child when we played among the reefs.

With one swift motion, I twirl my staff and pin my best friend to the side of the castle. A few guards glance our way, but I nod toward the public crowd. They understand and disperse, following my silent orders immediately.

"Did you go to the surface yesterday?" I ask.

"Why would I do that?" Lena winks and pushes against my weapon fruitlessly.

"Just tell me you weren't at the cove where the humans were captured."

Playfully, her fist collides with where my fin meets my

stomach, and she tries to push me toward a trench. We wrestle. Hard. With more energy than we have for years. Lena somersaults through the current and punches me in the face.

"Lena!" I growl. "Stop fighting me and talk."

"Of course I went to the surface." Lena's eyes sparkle. "You can't blame me. It's as if you expect me to sit back and let one stupid creep ruin the years of peace my aunt has created."

"Lena, it's not safe up there."

She waves me off. "I'll be fine."

With an exhausted groan, I ask, "Did you at least see the kidnapper?"

"Yes, but he wore a mask."

"Tell me about him. Any detail at all will help me find the culprit."

"Maybe I'll keep my secrets this time," Lena says. "It's not like you can wrestle them out of me."

She launches at me once more. I block my face, expecting another brutal slap, but instead, she jumps on my back and pokes my sides. She's the only soul in the sea who knows my tender tickle spot. I squirm, but she jabs me again, laughing.

Fierce little fingertips point at me and wag up and down. "You can't defeat *the claw,* Axton! I dare you to try!"

I roll her off my back. My armor feels stuck on itself and heavier than usual. I wade to the right. Dart to the left. She chases me into the trenches. For a moment, I let our childhood game erase all my problems, but my most important duty—the Queen's safety—my priority can never be swiped from my memory. At least I have an army of loyal guards to rely on, all of whom would die to protect the Crown.

I hide in the shadows, but an octopus has claimed the spot and flails its tentacles.

"Oh, sorry, bud."

Lena bounds around the corner and the momentum of her wake makes me stagger back. "So, what did Aunt Rayna ask you earlier? I saw you two talking." One of her long braids floats in front of her face.

"I swore to her that I'd find the one responsible for taking the humans."

"I'll help," Lena says, "If we don't, a war will start."

"No, I can't risk it. You're my evil little shri—"

"Shrimp," Lena finishes. "Till the day we die."

Death is always a possible outcome in my job. As the queen's number-two guard, I run the risk of not living to see my twenty-ninth birthday next year. At least Lena doesn't have to live in constant danger. I hold her gaze as a thousand visions flood my mind.

Lena and I daring each other to dive into the darkest part of the Barrett Sea. Racing turtles through the tall sea grass. Rescuing an injured lemon shark we named Fart. Cleaning up pollution at our annual teenager retreat.

No matter what choices Lena has made, I'll always protect her. "Don't worry, Lena, your aunt will never know about your mistake Above."

"It wasn't a mis—"

"And your carelessness will *never* happen again. If I hear about you going to the surface again, I'll personally make sure there isn't one piece of you left for me to give to the queen. Got it?"

She tilts her head to the side. "Did you know that the left side of your jaw twitches when you try to be serious?"

"Lena!" I throw both hands up. "This *is* serious. Don't do

it again. I don't care if the Sea Witch herself casts my name in a curse to threaten you. Don't play the part of a hero alone, or I'll—"

"Okay…" She lowers my arms slowly and wraps her hand in mine. "Okay, fine. I promise, Ax, I won't do it again without you by my side. But you better come up with a plan, and soon."

Octopus ink squirts out behind us and mixes in the water like a painting.

"Ew, did he ink us?" Lena laughs, then pulls me up the trench as we glide through kelp like the old days.

My sleek breastplate clatters against its neighboring shoulder pad, but otherwise, we swim side by side in comfortable silence. Once we arrive at the courtyard again, Lena swims away to help the remaining volunteers strip down the banners and signs from the festival. She looks over her shoulder and sends me a little wink.

Now I have my own duties to fulfill after such a monumental evening.

A group of merteens swim by laughing and I wonder if maybe the youth of our seas know the gossip about who is to blame for the humans disappearing, or maybe one of them is the criminal behind abducting the humans. If so, what's their motivation?

If I had chosen to pursue my rare magic and had studied with the Sea Witch for the last few years, I might even know a spell to read their minds, but after the deaths of my parents, I knew that magic wasn't the path for me. Protecting others is all that matters, and I have a well-thought-out plan to maintain safety in this kingdom. It's flawless and once my senior guard retires, everyone will implement my new rules, regardless of whether merfolk consider them too strict.

I head toward my quarters but shadows curl around the moon light streaming from the surface. Within seconds, the last rays are swallowed whole, and the navy blue alters to a devastating darkness. A fast boat approaching holds the potential of wrath in the form of a wind nymph carving at the tip of its bow.

A skitter rattles my spine, and my gut coils tight.

Suddenly, a metal device drops into the water. *What the...?* Sinking. Lower. Deeper. I squeeze my spear and swim toward it. Tiny holes flip open on the contraption, and little metal pieces zoom out in all directions. One hits the side of the castle and lodges into the stone. Another barely misses a fellow soldier.

"Swim away!" I wave toward the remaining citizens. "Go!"

Where's Lena? My team forms a barricade against the castle. I use my arm as a shield against the impending blast, but nothing comes. Heart pounding, I loosen my clenched jaw and glance around at the others taking cover.

Thankfully, the attempted attack has failed. I swim up to find the source. Fast. Murky shades slither around my heart in desperation. I suck in a deep gulp of water, then break the surface to search for the crew responsible for the attack. Waves thrash against my cheek, and I know I only have a minute until I need to dip back down to gulp more water. For now, I stare at the gray clouds that suffocate the lightning-riddled skies, both enticing and deadly.

With the strange sensation of wind whipping my face, I squint. Water splashes fiercely, and I can feel the wet contrast against my skin. I've been Above hundreds of times, but the other-worldliness always shocks me.

Rain batters the top of my head in droplets. A massive yacht rolls over the angry waves. Its murderous captain sits atop that ship somewhere, probably sipping a damn martini. Rage pummels through me. How dare the humans drop a weapon on our queendom.

Lightning streaks create a pathway as if guiding the

monstrosity straight to me. Thunder crashes and sends a jolt of adrenaline through my veins. I'll never get used to that booming sound.

I need to see the name of the ship, then gather my team to track it. When lightning cracks again, letters in cursive form a word on the side— *Eribelle.*

I duck below for a gulp of water and shout at the top of my lungs, "Fuck you, Eribelle!" cursing the wretched Above. The name tastes like poison on my tongue.

When my face hits the foreign air again, a red light contrasts with the endless gray. My mind searches for the term again. What's the word? *Burn.* "No…fire."

My tail works harder in the raging current as I gain on the boat. The fire flows chaotically in the air like a ribbon. Hair. The ribbon is red hair attached to a woman. She dances with absolute freedom, her hands raised toward the rain assaulting the ship. Her total abandon seems as if she summons the lightning and thunder through her spirited movements.

A magnetic pull draws me to her, but I can't last much longer without breathing water. I lower, suck in another gulp, then rush up to see her once more. My heart pounds against my ribs and I pull myself up a ladder on the side of the boat that leads to the deck. We don't have these Below, so I have to use my upper body strength to hang from each rung.

When I peer over the edge, the rain slows, giving me a better view. The woman could be a sea goddess herself, with porcelain skin, freckles smattering her shoulders, and soaked hair that smacks against her waist as she twirls and laughs.

"Sampson!" she yells in an accent. "We did it! We're free!"

This woman dropped a weapon on royal grounds and has no right to feel so carefree. Plans start to form of what orders to give my team. Half of the soldiers will need to stay and protect the castle while the other half trails this boat to its dock and gathers intel.

My lungs burn for water, so I start to lower myself from the ladder, and just as I hit the welcoming water, another lightning bolt splits the sky. Something splashes in front of my face and vanishes quickly from view. I lower to see the helm sinking fast. What is that? More splashes. Bits and pieces of metal splatter all around me. The boat has been struck.

"Help!" a muffled voice screams.

The yacht breaks in half and fills with water. Deadly fire consumes one side where the woman grasps onto a railing.

"Sampson!" she screams.

I follow her gaze to the other half of the boat, where a man teeters on the deck on his knees.

"Sampson!" The woman reaches into the air, voice shaking. "Sampson!"

When his side of the boat tips, he slides over the edge and into the depths. The luscious ocean swallows him, its mouth open wide. In a few seconds, I could save him. All I'd have to do is scoop him up from the devious current.

But the woman loses her grip too.

Beams and sharp debris float and sway around me in the waves. Terror drives a harsh hook through my heart and I rush toward her still body descending at the side of the boat. The shape of her wild hair spreads like seaweed as she bobs under a plank. Boards sink, dragging her low. Finally, I reach the woman and try to pull her to the surface, but she's much heavier than she should be. That's when I notice her long hair is tangled in rope.

I have to handle her roughly to get her loose.

Twist her.

Jerk her body quickly.

Yank.

Once I tear her free, she's as light as a merchild. She needs air. I shove her face above the surface. Her body stays slack and limp in my arms. Eyes closed. Lips gently parted.

Wake up! I beat her chest with my fist. Again. Hit. One. Two. Three.

Suddenly, she gasps for air. I thank the powerful Ulsa Below for helping. The woman's eyes fly open, and shock racks my core. The woman's eyes are mystical, bright, and entirely marine blue.

CHAPTER 4

Eribelle

Freezing. So wet and cold. My body rocks and sways.

Where am I? What happened?

A rich baritone shouts something in a Neridian accent. That's not a good sign. If a merman is close by then I'm doomed.

Wait, why does my head throb? Rain splatters the top of my face, but it hits my cheeks instead of the top of my hair. Something's not right. My eyes peel open with difficulty. Devious gray fog blocks my ability to see far until I realize I'm staring up at the sky. Fangs of lighting bite the surface of the ocean again and again. Orange flames streak, making my heart race on overdrive. A fire.

When my body jerks in confusion, water splashes. I'm supposed to be on Dad's yacht. Every time I try to move, my muscles resist, exhausted.

"I've got you. You're safe," a deep voice hums with a liquid texture, smooth as paint. "Relax so I can swim faster."

What in the Abyss? Realization clicks into place that I'm being carried like a baby by a merman. I can't get a good look at his face before he submerges his mouth. The front half of my body is above the surface while my back is underwater. And his arms have me in a tight hold. Shit.

This merman wants a calm, easy meal? Fuck that. There's no way I'll be a corpse at the bottom of the sea. A thousand skeletons probably line the seafloor, a graveyard of past meals for these repulsive merfolk. I refuse to be the next dish.

I still can't see the merman's face. Rain strikes my head like bullets. And his arms imprison me against his hard chest, so I can't escape. Thrashing, I dig my nails into his flesh. Push with all my might. Sink my teeth into a wrist. His grip loosens for a second, and I take a chance to swim from the scaly predator.

How far away are we from land? I need to warn Sampson of the threat. Wait…Sampson!

Images slice through my mind of Sampson flying overboard. All the missing pieces finally connect. No, no, no, no. Where's Sampson? Maybe he found a plank to float on nearby.

I stroke hard and fast, shoulders tired, legs sore, and head still throbbing. Why is this happening? I suck in air and desperately search for any raft or scrap to clutch onto. My clothes have absorbed too much water and weigh me down like an anchor.

Waves collide with me. They knock me under again. A cyclone drags me. It flips me toward a boulder. I brace myself for impact. Instead, the merman shields me from the collision and scoops me into his arms again.

"Stop fighting and let me help," he says, then lowers his head underwater again while keeping me Above.

The dolphin-esque swipes of his tail undulate, and this guy has the obscene strength to hold me over the surface while keeping his head low.

"Sampson!" Brutal waves splash into my mouth, making me cough. "Sampson?" My throat scratches raw. "Where is he?"

The merman resurfaces and says, "The man sank."

Impossible. I whip my neck in each direction. Sampson is going to enter Ozaron's conference next week. He has plans to rise to the top and become a makeup artist for runway shows. Plus, Sampson never finished our game. The last thing he said was '*Never have I ever been on a fifth date.*' So it's his turn to take a sip of the cabernet. He was beside me, alive and excited for the future. He can't be gone. He must be fine. He *has* to be.

"Where is he? Where's Sampson?"

"He belongs to the Below now."

"Liar!" I flail in the merman's arms, kick his body, and struggle against his iron grip. "Liar!" Water covers my mouth again, and I choke for a few seconds. "Go back!" I claw at the merman's wrists, etching crimson lines in his golden skin. "Go back!"

"He's dead."

"No…" I'm unsure if I said it aloud.

"Okay."

Okay? Just…okay? Oh my goddess, he can't be dead. Sampson had his whole life ahead of him...and how am I supposed to go on without him? My rock. The one person I looked forward to seeing. The one person who accepts me.

A shudder rips through my body until I go limp. The rain dies alongside my hopes of surviving this ordeal.

The merman's face finally peeks through the curtain of haunted drizzle. His square chin leads to a rigid, masculine jaw. Dirty blond stubble frames his cheeks and matches the long hair that's thicker than the strands of my favorite paintbrush. It twists into a bun at the top of his head. What surprises me is the royal seal on the metallic band circling his forehead like a crown.

"You're a guard for the queen?" I writhe in his grasp.

Silence.

I have yet to meet his eyes. I have to convince him to go back to the shipwreck.

"Where are you taking me?" I ask.

"Be grateful. This ocean has a crueler embrace than mine."

I have no intention of thanking the enemy anytime soon. He swims for miles or inches, hours or minutes, I can't tell. My fingers probably resemble raisins at this point or have turned robin-egg blue from the freezing temperatures. My toes have gone numb, so maybe they fell off.

Exhaustion takes over.

"So, why haven't you eaten me?" Delirium and hypothermia must be settling into my bones—but does anything matter anymore when my entire world is twisting inside out?

"I'm a vegetarian."

Fabulous. I've been captured by a smartass.

"But I know some sirens who enjoy salmon dip with redheads." His large hands loosen from my legs, and my heart rate doubles, preparing for him to chomp into my thigh.

Instead, my body turns vertical, and my feet hit soft sand. I stand in shallow water, but deep enough to slosh over my waist. He dips under the surface, probably breathing in some much-needed water again. Why am I not running?

Frozen to the spot, I glance around. Stars have chased away the gray clouds and speckle the obsidian sky. Pivoting, I try to steady my shaking legs. Every little bit of me begs for a bed. I stagger in a circle. The famous Erickson lighthouse isn't visible. Where am I? My toes catch on some sort of plant. I trip. The momentum sends me crashing to the sand.

"Why couldn't you wait three whole seconds for me to help you?" His voice is quiet behind me.

On my hands and knees, I fight back the tears threatening to add to the endless sea.

I try to keep my voice steady while whispering, "Leave me alone." Slowly, I crawl until there's sand coating my shins. My hair drips like a leaky shower head, forming tiny holes in the sand.

"Rest on that log," the merman says while pointing.

"Why did you bring me *here*?"

"Don't assume I'm a hero."

"Well, you *are* wearing a RMG crown. What's your name?"

His eyes narrow and I wonder if he'll refuse to answer but then says, "I'm Axton, second in command of Her Royal Highness, Queen Rayna of Nerida." His low voice is despicably pleasant, in an unfair way.

"No last name?"

"Merfolk don't have last names. We all have a unique first name, like our eye color. No two of us have the exact same pattern of our eyes. Think of it like a human fingerprint." Yet he still hasn't looked at me.

"Well, then let me see *your* eyes."

"No." Axton moves further away where the water slopes deeper. "What's your name?"

"Why?"

"I need it for our log. We record each damsel we're tempted to eat. For taxes."

He's not funny. "It's…Gertrude."

"Liar."

I frown. My body weighs so much and I feel like I'm in a fog, already falling in and out of sleep. So tired. I hear splashes as the Axton jerk swims away without another word. Finally. Thank the Goddess almighty.

"Well, bye, then, I hope a shark eats you," I say, then collapse onto the sand like a starfish, arms spread wide, and stare at the Moina Constellation in all her glory. An ache throbs in my chest as I think of my best friend, but I push it away again, not ready to deal with my fears.

"You'll want to bandage that." It's *him* again.

Ugh. Why didn't he leave? I squeeze my eyes shut and count to ten silently. Maybe if I play dead, he'll float back into his salty depths. Or a whale could swallow him whole. Yes, I really do prefer that option.

"Whales don't eat merfolk."

"Seriously? Can you read minds now?"

"No, you're talking out loud. I think you're in shock." Warm skin brushes against my side and then seaweed wraps around my scrapes on my forearms and thighs. "This should help, but I can't stay here with you."

"Darn, my loss."

He coughs. "I would if I could, but this air—"

"I'd rather walk on a plank of stingers than spend another moment on this beach with you."

"How touching." He nudges me. "Open your eyes, human."

"I don't want to…so tired."

Wheezing sounds startle me, and my eyes snap open. I meet Axton's gaze for the first time. The rare color of hope stares back. Not one master painter could ever capture the color of his gorgeous eyes. An azure base magnifies the cyan speckles that circle his pupil, and outside, rings circle like rain rippling into a pond.

The exact same radiant eyes from my dreams—wicked blue.

CHAPTER 5

Axton

When *not-Gurtrude* looks me in the eye for the first time, I arch away. There's something wild and unnatural about her gaze, a look I'd never want to get lost in. A woman with such a strong spirit can take care of herself. At least Grams taught me that much growing up. So there's no need for me to stay here any longer.

I turn and wiggle like a ridiculous seal in the sand, creating more distance from the woman, belatedly realizing I should probably warn her about the dangers of staying near the water. When I turn back, though, she's nowhere to be seen. Smart girl.

I squint, unaccustomed to the air stinging my eyes. It's impossible to tell where the woman's footprints lead once they hit the treeline. Where did she disappear to? I scan the area, wishing for once that I had feet. I shouldn't care. I don't.

A loud crack snaps from up high. A squeal follows and then a thundering thump. A tree branch falls onto the beach.

"Take that, Trey! And your ugly hats deserve to be shredded into a thousand pieces." Within the tree, she tries to snap another branch, while swinging her legs in the air. "You couldn't survive a minute in the wild, *doll*," she changed her voice to a mocking, low rumble, imitating a man. "You'd die within minutes, *sweetie*. Your looks can't save you in a jungle, darling Eribelle."

Eribelle. It fits her, even if she's like a sharp splinter buried under my skin. The way she's speaking is definitely characteristic of shock.

"Well, look who's still alive!" she screams into the endless night. "Me! That's who!"

Eribelle's damp hair is twisted into a long braid and her shirt is no longer completely transparent. Little scratches line her bare arms and smudges of dirt streak her skin. Or maybe that's her makeup smeared. Her eyes are red-rimmed, probably from crying over her friend.

My heart skitters in my chest when she climbs higher in the tree. What if she falls? With a blade in her hand, she begins hacking and sawing at another branch. Is she collecting wood for a fire? I may actually stick around to witness fire in person.

The moon's light catches on the sharp edge of the blade and the royal symbol detailed on the side is proud and clear —the same one as on my headset comms. I grope at my belt, and sure enough, the sheath is empty. Damn-sands! The girl stole my best dagger. How?

Another branch collides with the earth, and Eribelle

raises both arms in victory even though her body shakes from fatigue. Sitting on the branch, she wraps her arms around her knees with her head tucked between them. Sobs wrack her body. Her crying grows louder as I swerve around coral. When my stomach brushes against the shallow floor, I halt, unsure what to do.

"I'm sorry, Sampson." She seems oblivious to my presence. "I'm sorry. I'm sorry." A strangled cough spurts from her chest and she shakes with the violence of a shark. "I'm sorry."

Her agony feels like a boat crashing into my skull, automatically draining me of all safety protocols.

"Eribelle…"

She gasps and almost tumbles off the branch. "Witch's tits!" A twig scratches into her arm, oozing fresh crimson. "Don't sneak up on me like that! I thought you left."

The scent of her blood is so purely human I almost gag.

"Why are you looking at me like that?" When she scrunches her nose, the freckles on her cheeks dance. She follows my gaze to her injury, then covers it quickly with one hand. "You promised you wouldn't eat me."

I hold back a smile, and grumble, "I'm no monster."

"That's not what I've been taught." Eribelle climbs down the tree anyway, which helps my heart rate go to baseline again.

"Is that why you dropped a bomb from your ship?" I ask, "To kill us monsters?"

Her jaw drops. "What? A bomb? I don't know what you're talking about."

I've been able to accurately read body language and facial expressions my entire life, which is one reason I rose in the guard ranks so quickly. Everything about her eyes, her body position, and her tone tells me she's telling the truth, but the sincerity in her expression shifts to frustration in the blink of an eye.

"*Your* people have killed three of our fishermen," she says, fear lining her voice. "And maybe our yacht wasn't destroyed by the storm. Maybe *you* demolished our boat and took Sampson for yourself! How am I supposed to trust you?"

My teeth grind together. "I didn't wreck your ship, and it's illegal for merfolk to hurt humans. We also don't eat them or suck their blood like in the twisted legends. Our kind has pledged an oath to respect the Queen's treaty with the humans. And we would never drown one of you unless attacked first."

There's only been one exception in the last decade. Those of us guards sworn to protect the throne and serve the Queen and her daughter take their royal secrets to the grave —that someone lives within the castle grounds that shouldn't be there, someone the humans can't ever learn about.

"So, you've never eaten a human?" Eribelle starts drawing an image of a castle in the sand. The shape of the structure is undeniably the Castle of Ozaron across the Barrett Sea. Is that where she was headed?

"No, we don't eat people, but listen, you have to hide." I don't want to scare her about the chance of tree nymphs living here so only relay part of the truth. "I need you to hide in the forest tonight, but don't go too far in, but also don't stay on the sand, just in case."

"In case what?"

"There's an unidentified merman out there who wishes humans harm. I need to find out who it is, then I can help you return home. Eat. Stay hidden. When I come back, I'll have a solution. I hold out my hand. "I'll need my dagger in the meantime."

"If you return…" Her laugh makes the hairs on my arm stand upright. "Then I'll challenge you for the weapon."

"Fine."

I dive headfirst into my sanctuary and suck in a lungful of relieving water. My chest stops burning with need, but for some reason, my nerves don't calm. The Queen won't like the report of my interaction with a human. She's more than I bargained for. Witty. Resourceful. Maybe I'm dealing with a half-mortal from ancient legends. Or maybe she's a wind nymph in disguise.

As I swim away, moonbeams shine onto polyps and a group of Crown of Thorns stars. A herd of seahorses float above macro algae. Creatures of the night awaken with each flitting moment, and I keep my eyes peeled for anything ready to pounce. Neeks, especially, have never been pleasant to me, all of them holding resentment against Lena and me for the ways we tortured them as kids. Lena—my best friend. Just like that Sampson guy was Eribelle's best friend, and I left her alone.

"Shit, shit, shit."

I can't just abandon her. Maybe I could ask Lena to watch Eribelle for a few days and catch her some fish while I hunt down the criminal. Just as I'm about to call Lena, my comms sing with an incoming message. I push the symbol and a hazy image of Lena pops in front of me. At night, the live feeds are much clearer in the dark water.

"Axton? Where are you?" Lena's face is tied into knots.

"Um, I'm about twenty nauticals West and coming home."

Lena glances behind her, tense. "Nice way to avoid my question."

I gulp, hating to keep information from her.

"Are you actually West?" Her image becomes fuzzy again, as if she's moving quickly instead of staying in one place like we're supposed to when sending comms.

"Yes, you're the only one who has a connection to my tracker other than the Guard. Check it."

"I did, you moron." She zaps in and out of focus. "Your tracker says you're on land."

My dagger…

The tracker is in my dagger with Eribelle.

"Um, right. Don't worry about that right now," I say.

"You don't…Crcrcrcrcr…have much time."

"Why? What's wrong?"

"Didn't you get the message from the Queen?" Lena asks.

Another alert pings my headband and flashes before I can even prompt it to start. An automated voice speaks while I swim.

'From Her Royal Highness, Queen Rayna of Nerida, as of 01:00 hours on this sixteenth falcon year, Axton's position as second in command for the Royal Marine Guard is hereby terminated.'

I stop so fast that a fish slams into my back. "What?"

'Axton has been accused of breaking the treaty by murder of the human species and is required to turn himself into the palace before dawn or a bounty will be issued for his immediate capture.'

"No!" I tear off my headband and shake it hard. "I didn't do anything."

Pressing the royal symbol, I try to reconnect with Lena. All my access has been removed. Shit. Shit. Why would the queen think I killed a human?

I need to clear my name.

CHAPTER 6

Eribelle

My legs shake from exhaustion and any rational thought has been swept away by the wind. That doesn't stop me from heaving this stubborn log. I haul it to the pile of litter I've found scattered by the tide. My bare feet crunch over old plastic and I bend to pick up frayed rope. An impromptu raft doesn't have to be pretty to be functional. How far is it to back home? Even the highest branch of the tallest tree couldn't show me any land nearby in this darkness. I'll have to wait until the suns rise to map out a course. Just a few more hours.

There's a chance I might be able to create a raft that won't fall apart. Maybe it'd be more successful if Dad ever taught me to sail. Sampson always thought Dad withheld information on purpose, intending to keep me trapped. Oh, Sampson—I never should've asked him to come with me.

A strange smacking sound alerts me to movement on the beach. What if that merman returned? No, he's a RMG; the last thing on his mind is coming back to help a human. Why did he save me in the first place? They hate our kind.

I step lightly on weeds and peek around a palm tree. Something moves by the shore. What is it? I creep forward. Ahead, an animal is bent, eating a meal. My heart rate speeds, and I plaster myself to the trunk. If it's a jaguar or panther, my plans of building a boat are pointless.

It turns toward me. I grip the stolen dagger in my hand and hold my breath until moonlight shines on the fluffy face of a beige mutt. It's just a dog. Apparently, I'm not a threat because the mutt lowers its head again and bites into a second fish.

Despite the sickening smell of the raw fish, my stomach rumbles with hunger. I should've eaten at Dad's auction yesterday. Standing on his stage feels like a lifetime ago. In one night, I've left my home, lost my best friend, and met a merman. I didn't ask for any of this. The only thing I wanted when we stole Dad's yacht was to make it to Ozaron.

"Damn sea." I sit on the pile of trash I've collected and the dog wanders over. "I hate the ocean. How about you?" As if I've known the dog since her first breath, I pet her soft fur. "What should I call you?"

She sniffs my hand, then licks my wrist. Her floppy ears perk a bit when I raise my voice, but otherwise, she's chill, a soft spirit at heart. The dog's vibe reminds me of abstract paintings, smooth and flowing, the strokes blending into one another—naturally overlapping.

"How about Overlie."

She flops to her side and sneezes.

"No?" I rub her belly slowly, my hands trembling from fatigue. "Abstract paintings are blurry. I could call you Lury."

The dog shakes her head.

"Don't like that one? Okay, let me think. You're such a calm girl."

Her nose nudges my hand and I pet her snout again. "You're right. I shouldn't tell you who you are and aren't. I've had my share of that to reach the end of the Barrett Sea and back."

More painting terms clash together: line, texture, form, color, tone, brush, contrast, balance, chaos.

"Oh, that's good. I'm calling you Chaos, girl, because you don't have to be boxed into a label. Who am I to judge you? You're probably a little dynamite at heart."

Her tail wags as she closes her eyes and rests her chin on my leg.

"I'm not good at having a pet, Chaos. Trey once said I'm not good at anything. But I can paint, I swear. He was wrong to judge me, and Dad was wrong too." I sigh and submerge my hand deeper into her fur. "Sampson is the only one who believes in my art. He'll love you…I mean..."

Sampson. Ugh. Even if I do make it to the art conference, how could I face a future there without Sampson by my side? Maybe this whole disaster is a nightmare and I'll wake up to my best friend smiling, but the harsh reality strikes a savage paint stroke on my mind. I'm alone.

As exhaustion washes over me like a wave, I wipe a tear from my cheek and close my eyes for a moment of peace.

Rays of light pour down from the Above and shimmer off my scaly tail. I swish my hips and glide behind a coral reef. Mangroves, anemones, and sponges block my face from my pursuer. My heart races with excitement, knowing my partner will find me soon. I count down the seconds until his blue eyes lock on mine and he snatches me into his chest. The one who owns my heart trails a fingertip down my neck and his lips hover over my collarbone. I suck in water, frozen in time, desperately waiting for his mouth to cover my skin. As he lowers further, I hear shouting that doesn't belong here.

"Where is the soldier?" a deep voice shouts, followed by a dog barking.

Wait, dogs can't be underwater. My body jerks awake, with drool dripping down my face. Where in the Abyss am I? A forest? Right, I survived a shipwreck.

Stars still shine, but they have traveled across the sky. It won't be long now until the suns rise with dawn. My entire body mirrors the weight of an anchor, cementing me to my little nest among the weeds.

"Little dove! Wake up!"

The voice is real, someone is here. I don't dare move a muscle.

"Where's the soldier, m'lady?"

"Tell us or become breakfast." Another male voice, closer this time. "Where are you meatiest?"

My heart runs wild. If I stay away from the water, the mermen can't reach me.

A snake slithers from the beach through the weeds. I hold back a scream as my every muscle tightens. Suddenly, the snake launches at my ankle, and twists around. Instead of scaly skin, it's frayed and rough. A rope. How is it moving? I kick fiercely but it yanks my leg hard. Pain tears at my hip and a phantom power drags me. Hard. As. Fuck.

"Aaaah!" I dig my palms into the rough terrain and try to sit up.

The enchanted rope pulls faster. Twigs scrape against my

back and the bottom of my legs. Everything is clenched. I fight. Roll to my stomach. Grapple at any roots and branches available. Out of breath. Then I hit the water. The tide rolls in, soaking my clothes again in seconds. From the beach, Chaos barks like a deranged beast but she doesn't step one foot in the water.

"Wait. This isn't a commoner, Striker," one says, but they're all masked, so I can't tell who spoke.

"I know this girl. It's Finley Erickson's only child." A fair-skinned merman with one eye and long scraggly hair grins, showing off his missing teeth.

I scramble against the taut rope which only locks me in place. The one named Striker reaches from the water and runs a long fingernail along the arch of my restrained foot. His leathery skin has aged from being at the surface in the suns too much for his kind. "We do love some treasure, don't we, boys?"

The others all grunt in agreement and nod, slithering closer, bellies almost flat against the shallow floor, their remaining teeth sharpened into wolf-like fangs. Chaos growls, jumping on her hind legs while baring her own teeth.

"Leave me alone!" I kick Striker's face with my free foot and feel the satisfying crunch of his nose breaking.

"Ulsa-almighty!" Striker's hands fly to his already-bloodied face. "We've got a cute fighter."

My breaths come in raspy breaks.

"What was that, dove? Are you already begging for your life?"

Shaking my head, I claw at the sand in any attempt to gain distance from the water. Sweat drips down my back and my vision turns spotty.

"She's got a wild look to 'er, Striker. Maybe we should get this over with fast."

"Trident take you!" I curse and crumple into a ball, hyperventilating from my failed efforts.

They all laugh, mocking my attempts.

"My father is the richest man in Erickson Harbor. He'll give you whatever amount you want. Take me to him."

I regret my pleas the moment they leave my mouth.

Striker smiles. "You're mistaken, little dove. Mister Finley Erickson hired us. We have plenty of money."

Everything goes still for a moment. The waves stop crashing and my muscles go slack. It isn't possible. I don't understand. Dad is working with mermen? No, they're just lying to confuse me.

Striker snaps his fingers. Immediately the rope binding my ankle tugs me closer to the creep.

"Wait, don't eat me." I boldly glance at each one circling me.

The group laughs in unison. One picks at something in his teeth but still looks at me like I'm a meal. I slowly reach for the dagger in my belt loop.

"You know what I'm thinkin' boys?" Striker licks his lips. "Every game needs a pawn."

I think of the Taj99 device tucked into my shorts pocket with Jordan's contact linked to my account. He'd help without asking questions, but I'd rather not rely on any man to save me.

"How much is my father…how much is Finley paying you? I'll give you double to leave me alone."

Another chorus of mocking laughter sends a shock of nausea through my gut. I gulp down the terror.

"We've got enough money to swim in gold," one snarls from behind. "That's not what we're after."

Quickly I swipe the dagger out and slash at the rope binding my ankle. I miss. Striker grabs me, making Mom's ring dig painfully into my skin. Bruises will form bright as blueberries by tomorrow. That is, if I'm still alive.

Striker wiggles his finger, that long nail curling like a coil. "Now, now, dove. You wouldn't want to anger us."

I gulp and despite the fear raging in my veins, I meet him square in the eye. "If you don't want money or my life, then what do you want?"

"We need that guard's location. The one who owns that dagger in your hand."

"Why?"

"Have you heard of the Sea Witch, Ulsa?"

Of course I've heard of the most powerful Sea Nymph in history, but what do these men want with her? And what does she have to do with Axton?

CHAPTER 7

Axton

The soft, majestic dawn blinks her eyes open. Everyone back home will awake soon. I must swim straight to Queen Rayna to explain what truly happened last night.

A herd of sea lions challenge my speed, but I only focus on the growing silhouette ahead, a single mermaid armed with the distinct shape of a halberd. She's alone and blocking my path. I won't let anyone imprison me against my will. I didn't kill anyone and will fight the charges at all costs.

"Axton!" Lena's familiar voice yells through the water and the details of her face become clear.

I relax my shoulders and swim toward her.

"Axton!" Worry lines crease Lena's face and she crashes me into a hug. She casts me a knowing look demanding to know what happened. Her halberd lowers to her side and I suck in her familiar scent. She releases me from her embrace and both trembling hands clutch my arms. "So, you know about the bounty?"

I nod as she searches my face, gaze stopping on my empty forehead where the royal symbol no longer sits. It broke off automatically when I got the message and sunk to the depths.

Lena tugs my wrist. "Come on, I have a cottage on the border of the Barrett Sea that no one knows about. You can hide there for a few weeks until we find another option. Let's go."

"Wait." I stop our momentum as a bale of leatherbacks coast by. "I'm not running."

Lena's eyes bulge and she studies my face again, then quick as a dolphin, she makes up her mind. "Okay, we'll fight this. I'll do some research in the library downtown for legal support."

"Leeeena, look at me. Lena…"

"Someone may know a law that could—" she rattles on.

"Lena! Take a breath." Gliding toward my best friend, I place her hand on my chest. "Is my heart racing?"

She shakes her head, but fear still plasters her expression.

"Everything will be okay. I'll get my position back."

"How?"

"By explaining to the Queen myself. Eribelle might also back up my story if I can convince her to—"

"Who's Eribelle?"

"She's a human."

"What? Have you lost your goddess-damned mind? The very last thing you need right now is to be associated with one of them."

I start swimming in the direction of the castle anyway,

despite Lena's attempt to yank my tail the other way. I don't have time to fight. With a simple swish, I flick her off my scales and hear a grunt behind me.

"Ax, this is suicide. What if Queen Rayna changes her mind and issues an immediate kill at the sight of your face if you approach the castle?"

Her forearm brushes against mine as she swims past and tries to cut off my path. "Your entire future is at stake. Everyone has been offered a reward to hand you over to the authorities. It's not just other guards looking for you; the entire town is on watch."

I dodge around her, gaining speed, and ask, "How much am I worth?"

"You don't want to know."

At the brief humor in her voice, I let myself smile. "Why don't *you* turn me in? You could buy that sword you've always wanted."

Lena flips her halberd around and smacks the handle of her weapon against my back.

"Ow! Damn it, Lee! That hurt."

She spins it around again and slashes the sharp end until it stops only inches from my face. "You think *that* hurt? What do you think they'll do to you if they capture you? The queen doesn't react well to her guards dismissing her royal decree."

"I didn't kill anyone!"

"I know, but they have video evidence proving you're guilty."

I pause, certain I heard her wrong. "What?"

Lena pushes a button on her belt and a video projects into the water. Distorted, it shows the lightning storm, Sampson sinking, and...what looks to be me smashing Eribelle's head against the side of planks, when really I was trying to release the tangled hold of her hair on the ropes.

"That isn't what it looks like," I whisper as it replays.

"I believe you, Ax, but no one else will. From this angle, it seems pretty clear that you purposefully rammed the woman's skull."

"But I have no reason to kill Eribelle."

Lena shuts off the feed and runs a hand over her braids. "Think about it. Someone recorded that. Whoever took that video was not only nearby and didn't help, but tried to make you look like a villain."

That makes me pause even longer. "Who? I don't have any enemies."

"Well, you have loads of them now." She follows me around the corner of a reef. "They're saying you are the one who has been dragging humans off the beaches."

I stop and stare at the coral swaying. Maybe she's right and I do need a better plan.

Quickly, I divert to the left and head toward Grams' house. Lena's gaze scorches into my back, but I know she'll follow. We've swam this route a thousand times and despite her hating the risk, she'd never abandon me.

Soon, the scent of Grams' potions wafts through the current but before I glimpse her cottage through the pearled gates, covered in sea ivy, her pet neeks slither from the shadows. The sharp horns atop their slimy heads could puncture bone, but it's their slithering tails that send shivers up my spine. As Grams' personal security, they're necessary because my grandmother is the infamous Sea Witch of Nerida, the most powerful nymph in the Eastern ocean.

"Answer one question..." one neek hisses unnaturally. I never bothered to learn their names. It continues, "...to prove your identity and you may enter our mistress's domain."

A shudder rips through my spine again. "I don't have time for this."

"Why are you in such a rush?" The second neek circles me, skimming its slippery skin against my arm.

I grind my teeth.

"Should we give him an easy question this time?" The first neek speaks in such a high pitch, I curl my shoulders to my ears.

I cup my mouth with both hands and yell. "Grams! Please let me in!"

The second neek screeches, then wraps its long body around my throat. "You sound like a threat to our mistress. We will not tolerate threats."

I count down from ten in my head, using every bit of effort to not grab my spear. Then, slowly, I fill my lungs with water and ease my body calm, then wait silently until the neek releases its hold.

They hover next to each other again and ask in unison, "Now, for your question, child…who killed your parents?"

"Are you shittin' me?" Lena jumps forward, ready to slash each in half, but I restrain her with both arms. She writhes and screams, "Is this some joke? Ulsa would *never* ask that."

"Ah, little wench. We ask the hardest questions before one may enter."

My jaw clenches tight as nightmarish memories swarm my mind from years ago.

My father wore the uniform of the top RMG position. He smiled down at me. I was only a merteen but already knew I wanted to be like him in every way. On a rare excursion to the surface to keep the peace with the humans, we were gifted the strength to breathe air for ten full minutes. Eight minutes into the negotiations with their leader, something felt very wrong. I blacked out for only a moment and awoke to the man yelling curse words and my father shielding me.

Then suddenly, the human waved a trident in front of my father's face. The blues of Dad's eyes turned gray and cloudy.

"Dad?" I shook his arm. "What's wrong?"

"I have no son. Get off me, boy."

"You will contain the powers of the Sea Witch in these orbs and return them to me," the human commanded my father, who nodded in return.

"Dad! Wait!"

He threw me aside. "Go away, kid!"

Strange liquid leaked from my eyes and tasted like the ocean's salt. Tears. Yes, I was crying for the first time. Father dove into the sea, leaving me Above but I couldn't chase after him since I still had two minutes remaining to breathe air. Dad could hold his breath for that long, but I hadn't mastered that skill yet. Trapped Above I cried harder as the remaining humans taunted.

"Poor little merboy," one human mocked.

"You stupid-fish people don't know what's coming," another joined in.

"How is he crying? Merfolk don't have feelings," the first said.

I shoved my head Below, but my lungs burned when I tried to gulp water. Rising again, I clenched my fists into balls and swore to myself I'd help Dad.

"Maybe we should curse the kid too, sir, as a backup."

"No, this merboy can be our witness. Go, child. Tell your people we are to be feared, not dragged Below. Spread the word that a new age has started, a time when we take your kind from the precious sea. Warn those who dare to breach the surface that they'll never taste saltwater again."

Finally, my lungs needed water. I plunged, feeling abnormally cold as I readjusted to the temperatures. Dropping lower, I trailed Dad's scent to Grams' cottage. Threats echoed and loud crashes boomed from the other side of the pearl gates.

I hid behind a reef, shaking as the shouting continued. Something burst the side of Grams' cottage apart. Every instinct screamed at me to go help, but a strong arm wrapped around my waist. I turned and met Lena's eyes.

"I promised your Ma to not let you in there, Ax. You have to stay with me." Lena's terrified voice whispered in my ear. For only fifteen years old, she was so strong.

Ferocious shadows curled and bounced within the cottage window.

Ma's voice shouted, "Hans! No! Stop!"

Then both Ma and Dad flipped out of the cottage, fins over heads. Grams' two neeks chased them out. Blinding light shot from their eyes and into Ma and Dad's chests. They both convulsed, then stilled. Their bodies were sprawled like a starfish, flat, then started sinking. Sinking to the Abyss.

My memories of Ma fade year after year, but it's hard to forget Dad's features when I look just like him. For years, his expression has haunted me in the mirror. If only I had been able to protect them from the neeks' shock, they'd still be alive.

Lena shakes my arm gently, bringing me back into the present moment. It's been more than a decade since my parents were murdered, but their loss still haunts my nightmares. Grams argues that her security pets aren't the ones to blame, but the human man who hypnotized Dad with the trident. It's a good thing that weapon hasn't been seen in ten years. With the ability of mind manipulation, whoever wields it would be unstoppable.

"Axton?" Lena whispers uneasily. "We need to hurry, answer the neeks."

I clear my throat. "You two. You two killed my parents."

The neeks hiss. "You may enter."

The pearl gates open slowly, and a cluster of crabs skitter off. Despite visiting Grams' cottage a hundred times, the unsettling magic still sends a chill up the back of my neck. The sea grass remains still, defying the current of the ocean, and most creatures have the common sense not to venture beyond the pearl barrier. Darkness envelopes her cottage. Her home has a living, breathing heartbeat from deep within. The place that was once my sanctuary has rotted into a festering pile of bitterness after the witch lost her only daughter, my mother.

"I'm very busy. What do you need?" Ulsa's thick white hair protrudes from behind her shelves of orbs. Each globe glows a different color, as if a painter designed new vivid shades that the world hasn't been introduced to yet.

Grams turns, bright lipstick popping against the ghostly color of her pale skin. "Hello, Grandson." She could be anywhere from age sixty to six hundred. No one knows the truth about the witch's past. Some say her father was a sea god. Others say she is a demon who has masked herself in a violet cloak of skin for the last century. I've never asked, because to me, Grams is the one who taught me how to mix basic potions, how to make my bed, and clean my scales. Monster and mentor in one, she holds my heart in her rare smile.

"I need your help," I rush out my plea.

"You're here to save the poor, unfortunate soul in distress," she says, with a smirk.

"No, I need to clear my name. The queen has issued a warrant for my arrest. She needs to understand that I'm innocent."

"That's not what you need." Grams wiggles one long, skinny finger and points to an orb.

A vision inside shows a human woman thrashing in the shallow waters, a rope tied around her ankle with masked mermen circling her.

"Is that Eribelle? Do something! Save her!"

Her dark eyes narrow. "You know I can't do that, young

one. Magic demands a trade, a balance. Something needs to be given in order to receive."

"Fine! Let her die!" I yell, hoping Grams would never consider it.

She eyes me intensely. "Why do you care about *this* girl?"

"I don't. I care about being a guard. And whether or not it's my duty, I'll protect each and every soul, whether they have fins or legs."

Grams swims to the cauldron and mixes something boiling inside. "Tell me, Axton, would you want to help this human soul if her skin was burned from head to toe? Or if she had a prosthetic leg? Or had a mole the size of your palm on her face?"

"Of course. I'd help anyone in need." I chew the inside of my lip, needing her to hurry. Soldiers could be on their way here right now to arrest me. I check behind me only to find Lena hovering by the door.

Grams crosses her arms, making her look more like Ulsa the witch, than the caregiver who made me brush my teeth twice each night.

"Don't look at me like that." I tap my fingers fast on my side. "I'd protect *anyone* in need. No matter what they look like."

A little tsk clicks from her tongue. "So you weren't entranced by the woman's beautiful curves?" Grams' voice rises. "Why did you save *her* and not her male companion during that storm?"

My mouth drops. How did she know that? Was Grams behind the video that the queen sent out? I pull out my spear and glance to the back of her cottage for soldiers to jump out.

She eyes my weapon like it's a joke. "Was the life of the man not as important as the girl's?"

"You're trying to corner me into saying I did something

wrong." I ram the sharp end of my spear into her floor. "Did you want me to let her drown, *Ulsa*?"

"Don't speak to me with that tone, boy." She makes my spear dislodge from the ground without touching it and lets it clatter to the floor. "Admit you saved the girl because of her beauty."

"FINE!" I threw my hands up. "I've never seen anyone with a face like hers, but that doesn't mean I'm a villain for noticing her beauty."

"Then prove it. If you don't care what people look like, then sacrifice your sight as magical payment for your request."

"What? No! I need my sight to be in the guard. They rely on me to read facial expressions and body language. No one else has my skill."

"Don't you remember, you're no longer a soldier?" Grams studies my face, not giving me any inkling of how she feels about my new situation.

I swim back and forth in her cozy cottage, considering her offer. If losing my sight is all it takes to clear my name, it may be worth it. Blindness doesn't have to be the end of my career. Plenty of merfolk are blind and still achieve their dreams. All it would take is some extra training and some adaptive equipment, then I'd still be able to do my job.

"You'll only help me clear my name if I sacrifice my sight?" This is taking too long. I tap my fingers on my thigh at a faster tempo.

"Yes, that is what I said." Grams nods. "And if you ever want your sight back, you need to see the human. Truly see her. AND you need to lose yourself to being lost.

"What?" I shake my head in confusion, trying to make sense of the deal. Sacrificing my sight to prove my innocence is worth it, but the rest doesn't make any sense. Especially because I probably won't ever see her again, blind or not.

Lena chimes in quietly, as if reading my mind. "Keep your sight, Ax. This is a bad idea. We can go back to that beach together and tell the human girl to testify on your behalf to the queen, then the problem is solved."

That could work. If, and only if, Eribelle agrees to be brought into the depths. I don't have a way to give her gills. I don't have time to think about this. Guards know I'm related to Ulsa. They're probably already on their way.

"Yes, okay, I'll give up my sight for my freedom, but I need more information about the rest."

"You'll understand when the time comes." She smiles all-knowingly and claps her hands together. "Excellent, and when you get back, we need to talk about transferring the rest of my powers to you."

What? Powers? What is she talking about? I already chose a career in the Guard over a future with magic. Before I can argue, Grams grabs a heavy orb and chucks it at my head. Instead of crushing my skull, it stops mid-air and oozes liquid metal into the water, which then morphs into the shape of a new crown. The water around us spins and whirls into a cyclone, vibrating all her belongings in the cottage. I bear down, digging my fingertips into the plant-wall. What is she doing?

"Picture what you want most!" Grams whips her hands wildly in the water. After her expression changes, she asks, "*That's* what you want? To save the girl?"

Unable to speak, I shake my head frantically in protest through the devastating current. No, I want freedom from false accusations. Yet, Eribelle's face keeps jumping to the forefront of my mind.

"The bargain is sealed within the gem in this new headpiece," Grams shouts over the noise. "You may contact me one time with a question."

Cold metal wraps around my forehead, with the power of

the Sea Witch's deal inside. My muscles clench and I let out a roar. Magic swirls through my head, my shoulders, my elbows, my stomach, my knees, my feet. What the fuck! Why do I have feet?

Through the chaos, I frantically glance at Grams, whose frown arches deeper than the sea's trenches when she says, "You have two weeks until the spell runs out, then you'll be blind forever."

She nods as Lena grabs my arm and pulls hard. Then everything goes black.

CHAPTER 8

Eribelle

The enchanted rope turns my ankle raw and red. What kind of curse is this? No matter how hard I try to crawl toward the sand, the rope holds me in the water.

"Leave me alone!" My throat burns from screaming at the mermen. "You'll regret this!"

"Oh yeah? Who's gonna get you out of this mess?" one of them snickers with venom similar to that of a deadly squid.

I can't even threaten them with my father's wrath if they're working for him. Nothing makes sense anymore. Maybe someone else's influence would scare the gang. A different powerful face pops to the forefront of my mind.

Jordan Idros. Maybe my *'intended'* has a way to eliminate these monsters, not that I'd want to rely on that man to rescue me.

"Master Idros will butcher you for this." I splash one in the face and he laughs, rotten teeth on display.

"Who?"

Shit, they don't even know his name. I guess Dad's perception of Jordan's influence isn't as accurate as he had thought. What other leverage do I have to get out of this situation?

A sudden buzz of energy strums through the water, zipping to the shallows. I squeeze my eyes shut as a blinding light covers us all. When I open them, all the mermen have vanished. Instead of their obnoxious heckles, only Chaos' nervous barks meet my ears. I spin, searching for the hunters, waiting for one to jump out to scare me. Nothing—they've simply vanished. What in the Abyss just happened? Chaos's barks turn to whines as she paces in the sand.

"I'm not afraid of you, fish boys!" I twist again, scanning the shallows, ready for one to attack.

The quiet lapping of the water near Chaos' paws slows my racing heartbeat. The ocean glistens with rays, but not a splash arises in the distance.

"Where'd they go?" I eye the dog, who sits and pants, tongue drooping out. Well, she seems to be the only soul around for now. Tension remains in the air, as if the forest inland is holding its breath.

I quickly check my injuries. Scratches line my skin and a few bruises will form tomorrow, but otherwise, nothing feels broken. When I reach to tear the rope off, a scalding heat still scorches my fingertips.

"Ouch!" Recoiling, I shove my blistered fingers into the water, letting the salt sting my skin.

The rope doesn't glow with any magical hue, but it definitely must be cursed. Fan-flippin'-tastic.

Morning rays shoot up from the horizon. Despite the promise of a sunny day, there's an eerie sensation hovering around me, like a hollow vibe from the island itself. If I squint into the trees, their branches don't sway in the breeze naturally but seem to gesture like arms and hands.

I shake my head, needing to focus on what's real. The mermen might return any second, so I need to hide as deep into the forest as possible. Chaos has survived here for who knows how long, so fresh water must be close by.

Legs shaking, I push off the shallow floor and stand. Gravity plays games and snatches my balance for a moment, but I swing both arms in the air to steady myself. I scan down the length of the beach, following the trail of a thousand shells washed up. Whelks, bonnets, scallops, and clams of all colors sprinkle the white sand like a painting.

My head throbs and my vision goes in and out of focus for a second, but when things clear, a large lump drifts in the water ahead. The strange clump of beige undulates in the waves.

"What is *that*?" I squint, expecting the distinction of a walrus or seal, but the shape doesn't fit either animal.

Chaos runs toward it, sniffing the air, but she doesn't walk into the shallow water. She barks once and turns in a circle then barks again, pawing at the sand. When I grow nearer, I gasp.

One of the mermen remains, but unconscious, face down in the water. He is deadly still and his arms are flopped like a broken doll. Good, he deserved a violent death. The tide rolls him in further and I clutch my heart at the unexpected sight of legs.

He's human! I move closer, stumbling as water sloshes

against my shins. Even from here, his skin smells of fish but what worries me is the lack of any movement.

"Shit!"

I untwist his arms. A shimmer of light reflects off a silver crown, his only article of clothing. Chest pounding, I try to lug him to where it's more shallow. He's as heavy as a ton of bricks. Chaos barks with each of my strained attempts. I heave. Suck in a breath. Drag. We barely move inch by inch. Pull. Harder. After my muscles constrict for an eternity, the man is at least halfway out of the water where I can finally flip him over.

I shove him over to start chest compressions.

"What the fuck! Axton?" How can a merman be a human —a very naked human? I may be hallucinating it all, but I straddle him, hands clamped together, and push my palms into his sternum again and again.

Down. Release.

Down. Release.

Sweat drips down my temple.

I push. Harder. Faster. Up. Down. Up. Down.

Axton spits water straight up like a fountain, and immediately rolls to the side, tossing me off. All I can see is his sculpted back as disgusting sounds of gagging warn me to keep my distance. How does he have legs? That's not possible.

His seaweed filled hair is tangled into such a ratted mess that I can't tell if it's dark blond or light brown, but it doesn't matter because I'm captivated by the intricate tattoos claiming his back. Swirls of black inked shapes and detailed characters of another language crawl over his broad muscles. I'm definitely dreaming.

He sucks in gulps of air, shoulders rising and falling fast. When he hunches forward, the arch of his spine sends a ripple through his muscles all the way to his neck. The sand

and water droplets coating his tattoos are art themselves. If only I had a paintbrush.

Axton grumbles something I can't understand and drops his head even further. I wait. One. Two. Three seconds. He doesn't turn, move, or acknowledge me, but stays still as a statue like I'm invisible.

"What did she *do* to me?" he mumbles and his fist punches the water. "What. Did. She. Do?"

Okay, so if he's talking, he must be real, and he's definitely pissed. Slowly, I wade backward trying not to make a splash, but the water feels too real. Too wet.

"Who's there?" He twists toward me, arms out as a shield.

Chaos whines and I have to agree with her nerves.

"How are you human?"

"Fuck! I can't have fuckin' legs!" he yells so loudly that Chaos runs and hides.

Yup, he's very real—and unstable. Instead of using precaution, I rise and race away to the sand. The moment my foot attempts to cross the barrier from wet to dry, the rope around my ankle catches on fire.

"OW!" The rope snaps tight with such force I drop to the water on all fours. I try to crawl out of the shallows, but the rope attaches to me like a leash on a pole.

"Tell me where the fuck I am and who are you?"

"I'm nobody. We're dreaming. This is all a dream," I repeat frantically, "It's a dream, a dream or I'm dead," I say, eyeing the titan of a man. I glance between Chaos and him, back and forth, then run a trembling hand over my forehead.

His face angles straight at me but his bright blue eyes act like I'm a ghost, focusing above my shoulder. Their royal blue color sends a shock through my veins. So very blue.

"Wait…your voice…Eribelle?"

I drop my gaze to his gladiator legs, resisting the urge to look at his dick. He tries to stand on the legs that match the rest of his body, but his knees wobble in and out like a baby deer.

"This is so messed up. I recognize your voice," Axton says, "but I can't picture your face anymore. I remember last night and our conversation, but I can't imagine what you look like." His hands grope over his eyes, rubbing them so hard I'm worried his knuckles will pop one out. "I'm not supposed to be here. What did she do to me?"

What is he talking about? I'm right in front of him. Swaying like a drunken pirate, he manages to straighten to an enormous height, probably six-foot-five. His arms extend in front of him as he totters one weak step at a time.

"Are you drunk?" I ask, hoping there's some valid reason for his madness.

"Eribelle..." His fists are clenched. "Are the mermen still here?"

"No, but why are you looking over there? Can you not *see* me?"

"I can't see anything. Keep talking so I can follow your voice." His footprints leave large marks in the sand.

"Stay away! You have legs. You must have been cursed or I…I don't know!"

Axton reaches in front of him and staggers forward. "I'm not cursed. Well, I don't think."

"This is some sort of dark magic. I don't want you near me."

I wish I could run away into the forest but the rope attached to my ankle doesn't let me leave the water. Fears crash over me as I scan his tattoos peeking over the back of his wide shoulders. His body is a weapon in itself.

"I said, stop coming closer." My breath hitches with each of his unstable movements toward me.

"I'm not going to hurt you, Eribelle. Where are you?"

"I'm at a castle ball, hoping my prince charming will

sweep me off my *feet.*" I press a finger into my temple. "How…how do you have *feet?*"

My entire body tightens when Axton's toe stubs into my leg. He drops to his knees and his hands hover over my body.

"May I?" he asks.

"Excuse me? May you what?"

"Check if you're hurt."

I splash at his face. "I'm fine. Don't touch me. Back off, demon spawn."

"Demon spawn? So clever."

He sits back on his heels and a tiny smirk pokes at the corners of his lips. My eyes deceive me again and descend. Lower. So many questions I've never considered before run through my mind. Do mermen have penises? If mermen do have them, where are they hidden inside their scales? This penis is all human and right in front of me.

"Eyes up here, miss."

I jerk in place and my attention snaps up to another devious half-smirk. I smack his shoulder and say, "I thought you couldn't see."

"That's correct. I exchanged my eyesight for…it doesn't matter. So, what happened after I left?"

"I'm not answering your questions until you answer mine. How are you not a merman anymore?" Another slap to his shoulder makes Chaos jump out from behind her hiding place and start barking.

Axton's head whips to the beach. "A dog? You've been busy in the few hours I've been gone. Where did it come from?"

"Oh, you know, Chaos chooses its own path."

"Is that a famous philosopher's quote?"

He doesn't move a muscle. So, it's now or never. I test his vision and lift my shirt, flashing my top half. I bounce my bare breasts around. No response. Damn. How in the Abyss is a blind man who doesn't know how to walk going to help me escape from this deserted island?

"Why are you blind?" I ask. "What happened?"

"My Grams has some special *skills*. I traded my eyesight for something I needed but apparently, she had other plans." He sighs and hesitates. "My Grams is Ulsa."

"What?! You *casually* tell me that you are a descendant of the most powerful Sea Witch?" I shift in the water. That mermen gang mentioned the Sea Witch. Maybe Axton doesn't need to know this bit of information quite yet. I have to keep control to know what we're up against.

"That's not all," he admits.

"Obviously." I scan his legs again. "The legs are a bit greedy, don't you think?"

"I didn't ask for these. Believe me, this is not what I asked for. Grams is *not* getting a birthday present from me this year."

When that deadly smile plays on his lips, I swear the birds in the palm trees sing a harmony. For a moment, we simply share the silence. The expressions on his face are like watching a newborn experience life for the first time. Every time the breeze blows a new scent our way, Axton's eyes widen to saucers, and he sucks in the wind. Water slaps into my stomach and I push away the strangeness of being next to a nude mermen-human who's wearing a tiara. I snort at the thought of him playing tea party.

"What's so funny?" he asks.

"Nothing." I glance back at Chaos who has lain down, still unwilling to join us in the water. "We need to get you some clothes."

"I think fresh water and food are the priority over clothes," Axton says, "unless you have something you'd like to take off and give me to cover up."

"Actually, I already did. You missed it."

He pauses, jaw clenching. "Liar."

His hand finds the silver crown wrapped around his forehead, but it's different from the typical uniform of the RMG that we've studied in history schoolbooks. He tugs at the crown but it seems magnetized to his skull.

"You don't like your tiara?" I ask.

"Grams sealed our deal in this headpiece." His hand rubs over the bright gem.

Great. I'm attached to a cursed rope and there's dark magic literally wrapped around his head. I try to calm my racing heart by staring at the clouds.

"I've seen Grams do this before. The stones inside the headpiece are connected to the souls who made the bargain. The bargain has been broken when the gem has lost its light." He groans. "Grams sure loves drama, but this is the last place I expected her to send me. How are *you* supposed to be the key to saving my career?"

"Your career? What are you talking about?"

"Nothing." His jaw flexes tight. "Don't worry about it."

"Well, as much fun as this reunion has been," I press a hand to my empty stomach, "you have to find supplies because I'm kind of bound to the waters right now."

"What do you mean?"

"A bunch of mermen were here and they attached some sort of evil rope to my ankle. I can't move out of the water or it burns me."

Axton crouches and hovers his hand over my skin but doesn't touch me. "Where?"

Reading his expression, I give consent. "Go ahead. Maybe you can rip it off."

His fingertips brush against my knee, and slowly skim down my wet shin. The seriousness on his face would be almost laughable if we were in a different scenario. When his hand touches the rope, he staggers back and splashes into the water.

"Shit! It burned me," Axton says.

"Yeah, it's a lovely gift. So, like I said, I'm stuck but we need fresh water pronto. Do you think you can find some?"

"Of course, that'll be easy. Since I can walk and see so well," he says, pointing to his eyes.

"Why did you trade your eyesight? Why not exchange your fabulous sense of humor?"

"Because Grams thought I saved you and not your friend during that storm because of your looks." He deadpans. "Apparently she thinks sacrificing my sight was needed, but on top of that, I can't even remember what you look like."

I'm fuckin' tired of men treating me like an item or like beauty is my only asset. The whole point of escaping home was to start somewhere new, where people appreciate me for my skill and talent and passion. Yet, even during my failed escape mission, I only survived because of my looks. I can't run from it. Rage toward every man on this planet completely consumes me.

I start rambling to myself under my breath. Then louder. I scream so wildly my throat burns. Body tense. Blood pumping. My haunted sounds shriek into the sky like I'm being tortured within inches of death.

Out of breath, I finally quiet, chest rising and falling fast.

A few silent beats pass, and then Axton asks, "Um, are you okay?"

"No, I'm not okay." I hold back hot tears. "My ankle hurts! A bunch of crazy mermen threatened to eat me. I'm stranded on a deserted island with you. I'm hungry, tired, wet, cold, and I smell like fish!" I take a deep breath. "I need to get to Ozaron but I'm trapped. I'll always be trapped!"

The sky steals my breath and packs it between the clouds.

He shifts his stance. "How can I help?"

I hate feeling weak and having to rely on someone else. Everyone always underestimates me because of the shape of my nose or the whiteness of my teeth or the size of my breasts. It's really a sick joke the way men's brains are wired.

I sigh. "I've already tried to get this rope off a dozen times but I can't leave the sea. Can you find some fresh water?"

"You're the angry hungry kind."

"Hangry?! I am not!" My chest thrums. "Okay, Axton, I'm going to let that one slide, because you're probably in shock from gaining legs and all, but I'm sure you know we might not survive the day if we don't find water."

"Right, humans need fresh water. I understand I can do this." He turns toward the forest with his hands outstretched in front of him but then turns quickly. "I don't have a plan. I always know what I'm going into, or have a backup option. I'm literally going into this situation blind, Eribelle. What if something goes wrong? What if I fall into a hole? What if I get lost?"

I manage a smile. "Ya know what, tough guy, sometimes getting lost within my artwork is when I find the real essence of the piece."

"I'm going to pretend I know what that means." He turns away again. "Bye…maybe forever."

I ignore his bare ass on full display and crane my neck to the ever-loving sky. Axton probably doesn't even know how to find a lake or pond. Our non-plan is disastrous, but for now, it's our only option. I cross my fingers that he'll make it back in one piece.

"And bring me back some ketchup to eat!" I yell after him and cross my arms. "I can't eat rocks without ketchup."

CHAPTER 9

Axton

What in the Abyss is *ketchup*?

Even if I could see, there's no way I'd be able to find a type of food I've never heard of. This is the worst plan ever.

With heavy blackness as my only companion, I keep my arms stretched out in front of me and walk slowly. My new legs tremble and sway but at least I am mobile. At any second, I might step into a hole, or I could fall off a cliffside, but there's no going back to the beach without nourishment. Eribelle thinks we might die if we don't drink fresh water soon.

Everything feels different on land. A strange thing with

wings drones and whizzes by my head, reminding me of annoying krill. Some of the other senses I can't even describe, such as a strange scent drifting through the breeze. When my lungs breathe in this thin air, the crisp sensation feels so foreign. I've breathed oxygen before, but never for so long. There's a challenge in the air, as if it has captured my lungs in its claws. Then I smell the obvious magic surrounding us. I don't like it. There's something unnatural about this forest.

Once, in primary school, Lena told me that nymphs whisper their secrets to one another, all planning how to overtake humans. I never believed her, until now. With each step, an imposing presence lurks behind me and I feel watched, like something stalks my every move.

My bare feet crunch over a rough object, not sharp, but rather crackly. I crouch, pick it up, and feel the thin flat material. Raising it to my nose, I suck in through my nostrils. A dead plant, maybe? Interesting. I've never considered a dry plant before. Above and Below the sea truly are two different worlds.

A scurrying sound to my left makes me freeze. Who is here? Fuck. I gulp and clench my hands into fists. How the hell am I supposed to fight when everything is dark? The sounds grow louder.

Louder.

All my muscles tense. How large is it? Are there more than one? I need my damn spear, which still lies in Grams' cottage. This might be the one time I have to hide. Fur brushes against my leg and I stagger back. My side smacks into a tree. Pivot. Trip. Fall.

My hands slam into the ground.

A tongue licks my face, then a wet nose pushes against my arm. Wait, didn't Eribelle find a dog? Against all my better judgment, I lift a hand toward it, waiting for the animal to chomp off my finger, but nothing happens. Slowly, I lay my hand on its head. Yes, it's the dog. Relief floods my veins and my racing pulse slows.

"Hey, boy."

It barks at such a high pitch that I jump.

"Sorry, you're a girl? I got it. Can I trust you?"

She nudges me again as I rise back to these new, strange feet. Once balanced again, I bend over and pet her back to figure out her features. Medium height. Fluffy. Soft. Floppy ears. Long tail. I wonder what color she is. I feel like a fool for taking advantage of perfect vision for almost thirty years. I only have two weeks to gain my eyesight back. The thought of never seeing again is too much to handle right now, but it's not as bad as the possibility of never working as a guard. Enforcing security is my entire purpose in life. I must clear my name, and the first step to accomplish that is to find water. This shouldn't be so hard.

The dog barks and crunching sounds ahead warn me that she's walking off.

"Hey, wait! I need your help."

I grab a stick this time and hold it out ahead to block my face from hanging branches. At least I can go faster this way. If I run into anything, my makeshift sword will get the brunt of it instead of my hands. Soreness already creeps into foreign muscles in my lower half and I yearn to massage them. Instead, I follow the sounds of the dog in this never ending nightmare.

What if the dog leaves me behind? How big is this forest? What if I can't find any food in time? What if I can't find my way back to the beach? Sweat drips down my bare back and panic seizes my chest. Doubling over, I grip my knees. Inhale deeply. My matted hair flops over the front of my face and dangles. I can't do this.

"Dog, wait!"

I need the sea. Breathe in. Need the ocean. Breathe out. Need Lena. Breathe in. Need food. Breathe out. Okay, it'll all be fine. I'm a soldier. At least the panting sounds return and fur swipes against my leg again.

"Good, girl." I stroke her head and she pushes against me for more. "You need a name if we're going to do this together. Hmm, how about something sweet? Gill? Flounder?"

She barks wildly, not stopping for a moment.

"Those don't fit?" I tear off some loose bark from my stick-weapon. "Okay then, how about Storm? Tsunami?"

At my heels, I feel her body turn in fast circles.

"Jeez, you're a bundle of chaos in disguise aren't you?"

She sits on my foot, her bony butt jabbing into my big toe.

"Well, I'll call you Storm until we get back, then Eribelle can name you. How does that sound?"

Something tugs at the end of my stick-sword. "Hey!" My fingertips find Storm's mouth at the end of it, biting between fangs.

"No, it's not time to play, girl. We need food."

Instead of the tug-o-war that dolphins insist I play, Storm starts to walk. Not too fast or slow.

"Wait, what are you do—" My jaw drops open. She's leading me. Holy goddess, Storm must've been trained by someone.

Still taking cautious steps, I hope there aren't any poisonous plants near these trees. Storm tugs me along in a zig-zag pattern. Maybe the dog has no idea where the Abyss she's going. I let Storm lead me through the forest—with this blazing heat, it might be a jungle. Even with the obvious shade from the canopy of branches above, the suffocating heat from the suns bears down. Yes, this must be a jungle. My free hand pushes against my temple in frustration.

I'll have a few intentional words for Grams when I get home. How could she turn me into a human without warning? I think of our conversation, trying to make sense of why the bargain didn't work out as planned. At least those mermen didn't take Eribelle. Later on, I'll need to find the perfect way to convince her to help me. Once the queen sees that Eribelle is alive, then all charges against me could be dropped.

'If you ever want your sight back, you need to see the human. Truly see her. AND you need to lose yourself to being lost.'

How does that have to do with anything? And how will I know if Eribelle feels seen? I can't even remember what her face looks like or the color of her hair. I remember what Lena and the queen look like and all my comrades. But I have no recollection of Eribelle's features. She's like a blurry blob in my mind. Frustration coils throughout my stomach.

The Sea Witch doesn't play games, so what is the point of giving me legs? Now, I only have two weeks to figure this all out or I might be stuck on land. I kick the ground and send some specific curse words to Grams.

Suddenly, Storm barks sharply, and then the ground disappears. I'm falling. Fast. Smash into a layer of hard pebbles. Pain ricochets through my shoulder.

"AAAAH!" I clutch my arm and roll over.

As Storm yelps somewhere above, I slowly rotate my traps and delts. Nothing broken. Not dislocated. Thank the goddesses. How can this get any worse? I can't even see how far I fell. My hand grasps a handful of stones under my bare ass and I hurl them, screaming at the top of my lungs.

A little *plop* sounds. I gasp, crawling forward, pushing the pebbles ahead. More soft *plink plink* sounds meet my ears and, in an instant, all my dreams have come true. Groping forward, my fingertips lower into a small pool of water.

Cold. And moving with a current, meaning it leads somewhere.

"We did it, Storm. We found water."

Cupping my hands, I bring a pocketful to my lips and slurp it, greed coating my tongue. Delicious.

For a second, I almost forget about the pain in my shoulder, the fatigue of my legs, and the hunger in my belly. I stop mid-drink and let it trickle down my chin. How am I supposed to carry this to Eribelle? I don't have any bucket or bottle to carry water back.

"Damn it!" I splash the little puddle again and again. "Damn it!"

A tearing sound above combines with a hearty creak. What the…? *Rip*. I stand and curse Grams again for taking my sight. No matter where I go, complete, devastating darkness traps me in a lonely cage.

Now isn't the time to give up though. With both arms out again, I fumble to the sides of this hole and try to claw a wall. Too steep. How far down am I? Little wisps of wind feather from above, then fabric lands on my head.

"No way!" I grapple with the material and touch…buttons and a…zipper. I'm glad so many similar objects has been carried over between cultures. It's almost as if one day, maybe long ago, merfolk and humans had traded among each other. My fingertips find the hem and trace the outer shape. Pants– now these I definitely haven't worn before.

"Are you a magical dog, Storm? How did you find this?"

I lean against the dirt wall and step into the pair of pants for the first time in my life. Our fabric is made of a different type of material, and these pants are a bit tight so I have to leave the top button undone.

Storm barks behind me. I keep following her whimpers until the ground slopes up like a steep ramp. Left foot. Right foot, then finally, I feel the pup's tongue on my skin.

"Thank you, girl." I hug her close but her neck lowers. When she pops back up, something sharp pokes my neck.

I grab onto the end, expecting a stick, but frown. It's a piece of sleek, heavy metal. Not willing to waste more time by groping the air, I drop to all fours and touch anything close by. Twigs break under my weight. Weeds or long grass tickle my arms. Pebbles dig into my skin. Then I find another chunk of metal. I slip my fingers up, going over the shape and curves of the structure. At first, it doesn't make sense. I repeat the same movements, knowing I can't waste time. The revelation instantly hits me like a crashing wave.

"Storm! It's one of those flight machines, that travels in the air. They must have crashed here." Grasping onto the edge, I circle around the giant piece meant to be airborne and feel the sleek metal of one of the wings. "How long has this been here?"

Quickly, I search for supplies amid the rubble and destruction, staying cautious for sharp edges. My breath turns ragged from the heat and my head swirls from exhaustion.

This would be so much faster if I could see anything. I shake away my cursed thoughts toward Grams and fiddle over something softer than all the rest—a backpack.

"Yes!" The zipper snags on the lining so I flex and pull it with one yank. Stuff tumbles out onto my feet. "What'd we find?"

Storm barks and her wagging tail hits my side. Munching sounds make me spin around and clasp her snout closed with both hands. I feel a plastic wrapper hanging from the side of her mouth, its contents already devoured.

"Drop it!" Only the wrapper lands in my palm. "Don't eat any more. We need some for Eribelle."

My fingertips stroke the ground until a pile is collected: three potentially edibles for humans based on how the wrapper feels—maybe it's ketchup—a canteen like fishermen use on boats, a small box, a knife, and an abundance...of paper?

I toss the backpack on, grimacing when my shoulder throbs. As Storm leads me again, we quicken the pace with a newfound spark ignited. Everything will be fine because we found supplies and Storm is a genius dog who can perform miracles.

Once I return to Eribelle, I'll tell her the situation, beg for her help, and then, the finish line will be to clear my name and reinstate my position in the Guard. Easy. Nothing can go wrong now. I've got this.

CHAPTER 10

Eribelle

Sea foam prods me from all sides, no matter how often I sweep it away. While I sit in the shallow water, foam drifts back and clings to my legs. I've stopped caring how wet I am or trying to reach the sand. Instead, I wrap healing seaweed around my burnt ankle.

I scan the treelines for the fiftieth time, waiting for my naked 'knight-in-shining-tiara' to return. The suns sneak lower on the horizon with a sideways snicker as if it's mocking my trapped state. For hours, an endless cycle of toxic thoughts have been playing on repeat. What if Axton was molested by a wild peacock? Could I strangle the peacock with this demon rope? My heart drops at the image of the merman injured–alone and blind—what an epic first day with legs.

"Stop worrying about him," I mumble to myself into the breeze and curl my knees into my chest. "His kind are our enemy." Even as I say it out loud, something about that statement doesn't ring true. He's saved my life and is risking his safety out there in the wild for me—no, for us.

High-pitched yelps bounce off the trees. I twist, sloshing water with my movements, and squint into the vibrant sunsets. Bright rays blur two shapes, one short on all fours and one tall. I use my hand as a shield to block the light and smile at the duo. Chaos leads the soldier with a stick in her mouth, the other end in Axton's hand. My heart cartwheels at the sight of the backpack strapped over one shoulder.

"Chaos!" I shout and open my arms wide.

"What?" Axton stops in his tracks. "Where?"

"Chaos!" I crawl as close to the sand as possible, keeping my body in the sea. "It's the dog's name."

She drops the stick connecting her to Axton and sprints the rest of the way to me, but once her paws touch a drop of water, she retreats and whines.

Axton trudges forward with gnarly scratches visible up one shoulder. "I'm not your favorite? You're breaking my heart, Storm." His hand finds the top of the dog's head before he collapses to the sand.

Axton instantly lays flat on his back, chest rising and falling hard. Dirt coats his toned legs and his brows pull together tighter than a fishing line.

"Her name is Chaos."

"This dog is the opposite of chaos," he says through struggling breaths, "She's absolutely brilliant and the only reason I'm alive."

I reach forward, hand hovering over Axton's scratches.

"Well, I'll probably only be giving you two stars on my

review. The customer service was a bit delayed in the package delivery." I eye the full backpack.

Axton snorts—an actual snort—and rolls over to his side so his head droops heavily on one propped hand. His gaze lingers over my shoulder. What is it like for him to be trapped in darkness? My world couldn't exist without colors. How could I paint without vision? I'd be completely lost in a void if I were in his position. He must be scared. Yet, he still managed to succeed alone in foreign territory without complaint. Maybe he isn't my arch-nemesis after all, but that doesn't make him a hero either.

"So, you didn't fall in a hole?" I ruffle Axton's hair, then immediately regret it.

Circles underline his eyes that I hadn't noticed before. When was the last time he slept?

"I have good news and bad news," he says as he unzips the backpack and throws me a protein bar. The expiration date passed three months ago. I tear it open anyway and chew into the gooey crunch mix. A twist of sweet and savory flavors melts over my tongue in a moment of ecstasy.

"What's the bad news?" I chew another bite in a rush.

"This is all the food I found."

I lick the wrapper completely clean. "You two were gone a long time."

"Did you miss me?"

"No, I missed Chaos."

"Of course you'd miss Chaos." Axton sighs and rotates to grab a canteen of water.

"Oh my goddess, thank you," I whisper before gulping it down. "Did our little friend get any?"

"Yeah, I heard her slurping at the pond."

My eyes are locked on the second bar in the backpack. "You should have a bite too."

His smirk doesn't have as much life as before his trip. "I already ate five of those."

"Liar."

"I did find something you'll thank me for a million times over." His smirk finally rises higher.

"Oh yeah? Is it paint and a brush?"

He grins as if it's something much better than my prized paint set at home. "No. Put out your hand."

"Is it something that'll bite me?"

"Are you into biting?"

"Axton!" I slap his arm. "If I have to be stuck with you, then keep your mind out of the gutter."

"What's a gutter?" His eyes dance with delight and I simply wish they'd meet my gaze. "Eribelle, do what I say and put out your hand. You won't regret it."

I stick out my hand. He lays an assortment of wildflowers in my palm, some petals already bent or wilting.

"You're welcome." His proud grin plasters over his face as he leans back. "I didn't think I'd be able to find it, but Storm —I mean Chaos, helped me."

I study his face, wondering where the joke is.

The excitement of his features makes him look a decade younger. "I found ketchup! We would've gotten back an hour sooner but took a detour. I remembered a story my mother told me once about humans eating ketchup at a camp cookout. It's so strange how we live in such different worlds." His mind seems to wander again until he finishes. "Go ahead, tell me, how does it taste?"

I stare down at the dying flowers in my hand and can't help but smile. Despite failing miserably, the man had tried. "It's great, Axton. Best ketchup I've ever had."

He nods, seemingly satisfied with himself. I tug some floating seaweed closer and gently lay it over his bloodied scratches. He winces for a moment, then turns his head. I swear for a moment, his eyes lock on mine. I clear my throat and find an immediate interest in the birds soaring above.

"So, your mom is a ketchup expert then?" I ask.

He frowns. "She was an expert at many things, but unfortunately not about ketchup."

I lean forward, basking in his scent: carnal, male, and wild. Is he like my exes, unwilling to truly listen or share? If I asked him what happened to his mom, would he avoid the topic or shut down or change subjects? Why do these answers matter to me?

Instead of having to ask, he volunteers the information on his own. "My mother died years ago."

"That really sucks." I pause, wondering if he'll care if I share a piece of me. "My mom left when I was a baby, so I never knew her. Dad said she belonged to the sea and always wanted to travel. Growing up, I always pictured her as a pirate. She never came home, not even for the funeral when my brother died in a boating accident. Apparently, Dad always likes to joke that she liked ketchup on her steak, but I really don't know much about her or if that simple fact is even true. I mean, I don't even like steak, so the only detail I know shows that we had nothing in common."

"I'm sorry you had to go through that." He runs a hand through his messy, sand-filled hair. "Once, my mom made a scavenger hunt for my birthday. She had probably spent weeks hiding clues and recruiting others in Nerida to participate. It took me hours to find the last clue."

Images of little Axton swimming from reef to reef, looking under rocks and digging between plants, make me smile with warmth. "What did the last one say?"

"The only way to lose yourself is to be afraid of getting lost." Wrinkles form on his forehead, knitting together the emotions threatening to break free.

It doesn't make sense that this self-assured man has ever

felt lost a day in his life. He probably has it all: the respect of his queen, colleagues, and friends who admire his skills as well as a secure job.

"What's your favorite memory of your brother?" he asks quietly.

My heart almost stops. No one has asked that before.

"Every Sunday we'd paint together. He was terrible, but he taught me how to blend colors, the size of brushes, and what strokes to use. Each week we'd find different scenery to paint and surprise each other with the finished project. I still have over a hundred of his paintings stashed away in my studio."

Axton swallows audibly. "I bet you put the two images next to each other and compare."

"No, I burned all mine after he passed."

He opens his mouth, waits, then closes it again.

I crack my knuckles. "Um, so, what else is in that backpack?"

"Just paper and pens."

I bolt up to my knees. "Really? Something to draw on? Let me see, wait, no I don't want to get it wet."

He rummages through the pack and holds a wad of paper, all full of cursive writing and symbols. "It's a bit of light reading. I liked the cliffhanger though, edgy stuff," he jokes.

I'd smack him again if it wouldn't splash the sheets of paper. "Here. Kneel and hold it like this. No, the sunsets are there…" I change the angle of his hand.

Both on our knees, facing each other, I'm captivated by the fact that my width is only half of his. How would any woman ever be able to spoon with this man? Not that I want to, but four of me could fit in all his nooks and crannies.

I crane my neck and skim the material on the paper. Half isn't legible. "Okay, turn the page." Halfway down, I gasp.

There's a symbol in another language that matches the tattoo on Axton's back.

"Turn around!" I try to twist his shoulders, but he's as sturdy as a wall.

"What? Why?"

"Just do it."

As I slide my fingertips over his collarbones, gooseflesh rises on his skin and a little shiver shakes his back. My fingertip traces the shapes, curves, and swirls of ink that all eventually lead to one symbol in the middle.

"What does this tattoo mean? The one in the middle," I ask.

"Nothing." Axton's back stiffens. "Why does it matter?"

"The symbol on your back is on many of these pages."

A beat of silence. Then another. "No, it's not." He swivels around slowly, concern written all over his face. "That's impossible."

"Come on, Axton. Just tell me. Obviously, your tattoo means something."

He crosses his arms, then mumbles, "What I'm about to tell you, can't be repeated."

"I'm telling Chaos."

"Only if her middle name can be Storm." He deadpans.

"Fine."

"Fine." After a few moments of hesitation, working his jaw, Axton finally bends down a bit so his silver headpiece is in my line of sight. "I have magical powers."

"Well, no shit, you're Ulsa's grandson."

"No, not the ones I was born with. It's in the crown. Look at the middle of the gem. Really closely. Can you see anything inside?"

I squint inside the crystal-looking jewel. Sure enough, the center shows the same symbol as on his back. I gasp and point, accidentally smacking Axton in the face.

"Oh, sorry."

He rubs his eye. "I need to teach you how to punch better."

"Yeah, with all our free time, I can't believe we didn't do that first," I mumble as my heart rate doubles. "I saw a symbol in your gem."

"I was afraid of that. The same thing happened to any foolish, desperate soul who has made a deal with the Sea Witch. Part of the sea's powers are bound in this gem because of our bargain."

I lean in, ready to hear more. My brother loved history and dedicated so much of his time to studying other cultures. Hunting ancient scripts and collecting them in our local library was one of his hobbies. Regardless of what meaning was written on all those scrolls, if I keep one, I could bring a piece of Ben's passion with me wherever I go.

Axton rubs his hands together. "Okay, so since I know it's in there, I'm going to try something to free you from the rope. Before I do this, I need to promise that we will destroy all these papers."

"But—"

"Do you want to be freed?" His voice turns as sharp as a dagger point.

"Yes."

"We will bury half of them while the other half the waves can devour. Promise me, Eri."

He called me Eri. No one has ever given me a nickname I've liked—until now. Unsure why my hands start to tremble, I nod in agreement. "Okay."

"Since I can't see, you'll need to guide my forehead to your ankle and make sure the gem touches the rope, but not your skin. NOT your skin, got it?"

"Got it."

"It might hurt for a second," he says with a slight cringe.

"I'll be fine, but how do you know what to do?"

With his head bowed to me, I place my hands on both of his temples. The sharp cold of the silver crown contrasts with the warmth of his skin. A severe jab surges through my veins quickly then stops. The rope snaps off and floats in two pieces, already moving with the current. Jumping, I almost knock Axton straight over but catch him mid-fall.

"Woah, you're heavier than I thought," I say.

"Blame the ketchup."

I choke on my own laughter. He had actually eaten the dead flowers. Oh man, I can't ever tell him the truth now.

I guide him out of the water. My feet smoosh into the dry sand and relief cascades over me. Unexpected, grateful tears fall but I keep them silent so he doesn't have to witness my breakdown. I've never loved land more than right now.

I wiggle my toes in the sand and stare at the palm trees, wanting to hug them all. Crunching sounds behind me are followed by crinkles and more ripping. Axton is destroying all the paper from the backpack. My gut implodes with an instinct to stop this. Yes, I had promised, but something about those symbols seems too important to destroy. I hop on Axton's back, like a little monkey.

"Hey!" He spins and reaches over his shoulders. "What are you doing?"

I swipe a paper from his grip and try to grab for others. "Give those to me. You're making a mistake."

"What? No way, you promised!"

"Why are they so important?"

Axton shakes me off his back and I fall into the sand, panting. Quickly, he drops the rest of them into the ocean and stomps on them. They dissolve and bleed black ink into the water.

"Damn it, Axton! What are you hiding?"

He growls something unintelligible. At least he can't see

that I still have possession of a single sheet. I glance down and try to memorize the symbols and phrases. Too many. If only the Taj99 in my pocket could still take pictures. After the boat crash, it stopped working. I dig in my tiny pocket and pull out the device to try anyway. A little red light flickers in the corner warning me of an incoming message. Wait, no three. The device should still be broken. I hover my hand over the button, then hit play.

My father's voice projects from the tiny speaker. "If you think it's funny to steal my yacht…"

"What was that sound?" Axton turns fast. "Is someone else here?"

"There's a storm coming, sweetie," Dad continues. "Get back home, right now or…"

I skip the rest of that one.

"We're all searching for you, baby. Don't worry," Dad sounds desperate. "Brooks and Jordan have a team on the west and I'll be on the east. Don't give up and whatever you do, don't trust a merfolk."

I wipe away unexpected tears. The familiarity and genuine worry of Dad's voice slice me in half because it mirrors his sounds of terror when my brother was taken by the sea. If this Taj99 survived the waters, maybe by some miracle, it'll still be functional to make a call.

"He sounds *pleasant*," Axton says.

Only at the sound of his voice, do I notice Axton's hand is rubbing my back.

"I'm calling them for help," I say.

"No, wait."

"Why?"

He pauses. "I need you to go Below with me first."

"Um, excuse me? That's never going to happen." I punch in my cousin's number and they miraculously answer in one ring. Why hadn't I thought of this before?

"Eribelle?"

"Yeah, it's me." I hold back a sob.

"Holy fuck, you're alive." Brooks gasps on the other line. "Where are you?"

"At a vacation resort." I wipe snot from my nose.

"Not funny. I thought you were dead," Brooks says. "Sampson's body washed up in the harbor."

I can't respond.

"He's dead, Eribelle. Your dad kept you on Coendriel to protect you but you left! Sampson was murdered by merfolk."

That isn't true, but no words are left in my brain.

"Turn the tracker on your Taj99 so I can come get you," Brooks demands and the call drops.

"I didn't like his tone," Axton growls, "and of course he blames merfolk without proof."

"Their tone," I correct.

"What?"

"My cousin goes by they/them pronouns."

"Well, I don't like the sound of their voice."

"Brooks is terrified and probably hasn't slept," I defend my cousin. "They're confused and worried and—"

"They were hiding something. Come on, we need to sleep. Let's talk about it in the morning." Axton holds out his hand, and in that moment I can choose to trust him or label him as my enemy. He has done so much for me already, but merfolk have always plagued our people with fear. Dad has constantly warned me to stay away from them and the group who threatened me proved him right. I have no reason to fully trust Axton. He won't even tell me the meaning of his tattoo or why he wanted to destroy all those papers. If he's hiding something, there's no chance I'm giving him my Taj.

"Maybe if you tell me your secret, I'll give this to you," I say, testing him.

Axton kneels and pats the sand beside him. "I don't like your infamous ketchup."

"That's not the secret I was hoping for."

Axton's sigh holds the weight of a thousand worlds. "Secrets are hard to unravel."

"Here's mine. I ran away from home and I'm never going back. Even when Brooks comes, I'll force them to take me to Ozaron."

"Then come Below with me first. I need your help with something. Just for a day, then I'll help you get to Ozaron or anywhere you want to go."

I sigh and let sand cover my skin like a blanket. At least Chaos is here to warm me as she curls into my stomach. The suns watch us with knowing eyes. So much has happened so quickly. Sleep isn't a luxury I can afford, but when Axton pulls me gently to his chest, I learn that we might be a perfect spooning fit after all.

CHAPTER 11

Axton

Birds wake me with their chirps, but I open my eyes to heartbreaking darkness. What time is it? The direction of where the suns shine down convinces me that we slept longer than we should've.

I need my damn vision back. I had made that deal with Grams too quickly, without thinking things through. How am I supposed to clear my name easily or capture the real criminals or find a way to get my tail back if I can't see? My entire purpose is to protect the queen, and I don't have time for three-day-long naps with mildly irritating women.

Eribelle surely doesn't seem afraid of being stuck with me. Her back presses against my chest; the soft rise and fall of her breath takes my arm that's draped over her side on a calm ride. Up. Down. Up. Down. I can feel her size and curves in all the places we touch, but what color are her eyes? When the suns splash her hair, does it glitter light or dark? Is her skin the shade of the night sky or a fair seashell?

Eribelle yawns and makes adorable sleepy moans. Her butt barely shifts against my groin, but it still makes my dick stiffen. Crap. I slowly try to back my hips away, but instead of the horrified response I brace myself for, she turns and snuggles closer, her lips brushing against my skin. I keep telling myself the only reason I held her close all night was for warmth. No other reason. None.

"Five more minutes, Trey," she mumbles.

Shit. Fuck. Double shit. Who's Trey?

I clear my throat and roll away slowly, bumping into a furry lump of Chaos behind me. "Um, Eribelle?"

Her body jolts, and then a sudden breeze kisses my skin where her body used to be. A second ticks by when only the birds chirp.

"We only slept like that because it was cold," she says, a dash of panic in her voice.

"Correct." I try to wipe away the layer of sand attached to every inch of me. Pointless. "You were talking about Trey in your sleep."

"My ex? Weird. Sampson will laugh when I tell him…oh my goddess." She bustles about; soft footsteps sound to my left, then my right. Back and forth. "Sampson…Brooks told me they found his body." Her voice increases in pitch and speed. "It's all my fault and I shouldn't have brought him on that yacht, and now he'll never meet his favorite celebrities or go parasailing in Fortrusia, or—oh my goddess, who's gonna tell his mom…"

"Woah, breathe." I step forward cautiously, unsure exactly

how far away she's pacing, and gently take both her trembling shoulders. "Look at me."

She quiets, sniffles interrupting exploding breaths. "Are you looking at me...because I can't see."

Eribelle chokes on a painful laugh and surprises me by burying her face in my chest. Her hair tickles my stomach and a few of her tears drip down my front.

"He's never coming back," she whispers, "Like my brother. They're both gone."

I wrap my arms around her small form, like it's the most natural thing in the world.

"Right before Sampson flew overboard..." she whimpers. "He's never looked so scared."

The pain etched into her every word slices me to my core.

"I'll never..."—sniff—"see his..."—sniff—"smile again."

I rub her back in small, rhythmic circles as the waves batter the shoreline, moving the day along. Time doesn't stop for anyone. Life continues on, even after loss, and I need to get my life under control again.

Eventually, Eri slips out of my grasp and an emptiness replaces where she used to be pressed against me.

"How about we say a final goodbye to your friend?" I lay a soft hand on her shoulder.

I take her silence as agreement, but I still wish I could see her face to know if she's nodding or staring off into the sea, or if she needs a tear wiped from her cheeks.

With my toe, I form a ceremonial circle in the sand, probably lopsided. A merfolk custom, I stand with one foot outside the ring, within the life source, and one foot inside the ring, representing the afterlife. In front of me, I hear Eribelle's movement, maybe she's mirroring me, but I'm not sure of human funeral traditions.

"Thank you to the goddess of mountains, soil, wind, and spirit for giving our realm time with Sampson." I reach forward and accidentally bump my wrist into hers before twining our fingers together. "And may the goddess of the sea and storms bless him with a peaceful eternity."

When she squeezes my hand gently, I bow my head.

Eribelle coughs softly. "Um, I…I'll miss you, Sampson, and the passion you felt about makeup and I'll miss all your jokes, even though they were terrible. I wish we had the chance to register for that internship together. I even had ideas for the décor of our apartment in Ozaron. But…you won't be here to argue about the wallpaper pattern or whose day it is to take out the trash or if we should get a cat." She coughs again. "You always knew how to make me smile. I'll keep your positivity, I'll try to shine your light through me."

A long sigh leaves her, heavy with a thousand memories, releasing them to the shore.

"Tell me about the sky. I want to remember this moment." I blink, but no colors return.

"You don't have to see to remember." Eribelle's voice remains soft. "How about you tell me what you hear and smell."

Stealing a moment, I capture everything close by.

"The sea is trying to soothe us, obviously listening to our conversation. I can taste the salt in the breeze and feel the water spraying my cheeks. I don't have to see to know that the depths in front of us hold secrets, whispering legends to the merfolk. These gentle waves also hold the fury of a cyclone in its claws if it holds a grudge. What I never knew until yesterday is the different types of sand in the Above. Twist your toes, Eri. When I squish like this, I can feel this kind is wet and thick."

"What else?" she whispers.

"Because the suns' heat blasts my shoulder, I know that seagull squawking over there flies north and Chaos is pawing a hole," I say and point, "but amid all of this, the one thing holding my focus is your hand in mine."

A tiny gasp slips from Eribelle. She snags her hand away and says, "That was beautiful, Axton. If I had a paintbrush, I could paint this view from your words."

Someday, I'll figure out how to give her paint. Maybe I can find some blueberries that can be mashed.

"Okay, unfortunately, this isn't an all-inclusive resort. We need a plan," Eribelle says. "I can't go home. And you want to drag me into the sea, even though neither of us can breathe underwater. My Taj isn't working again, so our only option is to walk. Maybe this isn't an island, but a peninsula connecting to the mainland. I can start my life here once I find a village inland."

I don't dare tell her this is indeed the tree nymph island and there's likely no people, but if she wants to walk, it'll give me more time to think of ways to convince her to talk with the queen. Maybe I need to persuade her of how dire the situation is. Do I play the pity card?

I start walking and stub my toe on something hard but hold in my grunt.

"Um, so…" Eribelle sounds unsure for the first time. "Do you know anything about that mermen gang? They were looking for *you*."

"Really?"

"Yeah, they wanted to know where you were and kept pointing to this dagger." She places it in my palm. I give it back to her since she needs the protection more than me.

"There's a tracker in this. If you ever get lost, my best friend, Lena, will eventually find you. Only she and the guard have access to its location."

Long pause. "Did you and Lena ever…" I swear a soft coconut scent drifts from Eri's vicinity, sensual and raw.

I swallow my dangerous thoughts and the ghost of her

skin against mine when she had slept. "Why do you want to know?"

"I don't. You can have *relations* with whoever you want. It's not my business." Her defensive tone is definitely not cute, not even a little bit.

"Don't worry, Angelfish, Lena has a girlfriend named Nolia."

Eri pauses for so long that I wonder if she wandered off. "So, soldier, can you possibly move any slower?" She pokes my side with a stick.

I grab the stick and let her lead me. This time, all my fear and hesitancy from yesterday has been cut in half with her guiding me. It's not like she'll let me walk into a hole. The sand eventually merges with grass underfoot then soil. Shade finally arrives, blocking out the blaring suns, yet after only a few minutes, sweat slips down my back. A soft rustling tells me that Eribelle picked up the backpack. "Let me carry that."

"Why?" She huffs. "It's not like there's heavy paper inside anymore."

I don't care if she's pissed at my choice to destroy those papers. They never should've existed anyway. If the symbols were truly from the ancient nymph language, there's a chance that the papers held dangerous information—the only spell that can steal Gram's powers.

Even if Grams has a controversial reputation, our queendom needs her power. Without it, my species of merfolk might cease to exist. Humans shouldn't know ways to steal the sea's magic. I have more secrets than Eribelle can guess, none of which are safe for her to know, but she needs to trust me at least a little for my plan to work. I'll need to give her more insight to win her over. On this island, bubbled by humidity, we only have each other to rely on.

If the only way to convince Eri to come Below is to get her to trust me more, then I need to open up to her.

"Eri, I have a question."

"The answer is twenty-seven." There's a playful smile lacing her voice.

"Funny, we can do a standup show for Chaos later. Winner of the best joke gets all this island's ketchup."

"Deal." She pulls me to the right. "Watch out, there's a log...yeah, right there."

I step over it and crunch my bare feet into a layer of dead leaves again. "Did you know merfolk are born without a sex organ? As infants, we aren't male or female, we simply *are*."

"Well, I wasn't expecting that info." Her pace slows. "Then, how do you have a..."

I can't help but chuckle. "When we go through maturity around age thirteen, we're given a choice to pick our sex. There's an annual festival in Nerida where each adolescent drinks a potion created by the Sea Witch that starts to transition their anatomy into their sex of choice."

"And you chose male."

"Wait, I did? They must've messed up my paperwork!"

She turns, slaps my shoulder playfully, then continues again.

"Anyway, the festival is one of my favorite times of year, when the leatherbacks migrate. Everyone's in such high spirits and we all share food with neighbors the whole week. Even Lena lowers her scowl and manages the activities and games. It's a major rite of passage that identifies who we are."

"Why are you telling me this?" she asks.

"Well...my tattoo is rare." I hold my breath for a moment, wondering if telling her this secret is the best choice.

"Go on," she says.

Slowly, I let out the breath I've been holding, and explain. "My tattoo is connected to sea magic. If humans learned our ancient language and translated it on those papers, there's a good chance they were looking for a way to kill my Grams. If that happens, there's no one else to create the potions and complete the rituals for the maturation ceremony. If Ulsa dies before training an apprentice, we'd have hundreds of merfolk who can't reproduce. All of Nerida would eventually die off within one generation unless we all migrate."

She pauses as we trudge through the humid woods. I keep cringing when Chaos or Eribelle shuffle, assuming I'm about to run straight into a tree trunk.

"Well, we obviously can't let that happen," she says confidently.

The tension coiled in my muscles releases.

"But aren't there more merfolk outside of Nerida?" Eribelle asks.

"Yes, far away, but our ancient language is applied to all the witches of the different seas. If humans learn how to kill off one queendom, they can eventually kill us all." The soil underfoot becomes more like mud, so I know we're closer to that stream by the aero-tran crash.

"I know there's always been tension between our species, but why would any human want merfolk completely gone?" she asks. "We even signed a peace treaty."

"Yet, humans have been snatched from the shore as recently as this week."

Eribelle slips, making the stick lurch in my hands. I hold on tight to steady her as she curses.

Teaching her about our culture brings me back in time to when I presented on a stage among a dozen classmates, nervous but excited. Lena had leaned over and whispered something about wanting bigger boobs than Karie and I had laughed at the worst time, right when Ma and Dad entered the arena.

"So, I've always wondered..." Eribelle snaps me into reality, "...if your scales reach to your waist, where is...I mean how..."

"How do merfolk have sex?"

She coughs, chokes, and stops walking. "Sorry, just, I swallowed a bug or something."

A full belly laugh erupts from my core. "Are you scared of sex talk, Miss?"

"Oh. My. Goddess."

"This is perfect. If I knew you were embarrassed so easily, I'd have given you a harder time."

"Shut up." Eribelle snaps playfully and stomps forward, pulling me along like her trained seahorse.

"Well, if you can use your imagination and sprinkle in some magic from a Sea Witch, then it's not hard to understand. Our scales shift for sex. Females open, and mine, I mean males change into the shape of a…"

"Stop! You don't need to say it."

Unable to contain myself, I bend over laughing. Sweat drips off my forehead. "This is too good to be true. I wish I could see if your cheeks are bright red right now."

"You're an asshole. Hurry up, you're lagging."

When she begins marching again, her feet create a rhythm that my heartbeat ticks along to and I catch myself smiling.

"Don't you smile at me," she says with more spunk than I've heard from her so far.

"How would you know I'm smiling?"

"I'm not blind, like *some* people, Axton."

"Shouldn't you be looking forward, as our guide? Or am I too irresistible for you?"

An adorable growl rumbles out of her and I roll in my lips to silence myself. Why is my heart rate slamming so fast? The hike is less difficult than yesterday, so I shouldn't feel this sense of adrenaline. It doesn't help that I keep thinking of ways to explore merfolk sex that humans couldn't dream of, but my attempts are only blurry since I have no recollection of what she even looks like now.

"Hey, Eri?"

"Yes, Axton?"

"What do you look like?"

"You don't remember?"

"That was part of the bargain," I clarify, "I have no idea what you look like."

"What if I'm hideous?" she asks.

"You're not."

"You don't know that."

I stop in my tracks and pull on the stick connecting us. Without sight, I know she's looking straight at me. Her energy is overwhelming. So, with the hope that I'm looking straight into Eribelle's eyes, I whisper, "In all seriousness, Eri, you're the third most beautiful person I've ever met."

Her laughter hits the top of the trees and rises to the sky. The sound gives me pelican wings. Immediately, my new mission is to make Eribelle laugh again, and every day forth, as long as I can.

But then she grabs my wrist in a death grip."Oh, fuck!" Her cry rips through the branches and splits my breath in half. "What in the Abyss is *that*?!"

CHAPTER 12

Eribelle

Sharp branches draw ugly scribbles into my skin, but what made me scream are the two skeletons leaning against a palm tree. Debris from a glossy, sleek aerotran crash litters the weeds. Since we're both barefoot, I check for anything sharp poking up from the earth, then guide Axton to a boulder.

"Sit." I push his chest down.

He resists, muscles taut and on high alert. "No. Why did you scream? What do you see?"

Axton doesn't need to be disturbed by the knowledge of skeletons here. Maybe bodies Below don't decompose the same way as ours and it would only confuse him. Or he'd immediately question what killed this pair and demand that we're in danger and leave, but he can't move fast while blind. There's no point in rushing if he'll get hurt tripping over a log.

"Nothing's wrong, I just walked into a spiderweb," I say.

He doesn't look convinced.

"Sit down, soldier. There are thorns everywhere so I don't want to deal with navigating you. I see a backpack ahead so this is probably where you found the other one. Stay put."

I lean forward and guide him to a safe position.

"Whoa, Eri, you gotta be careful getting too close to the gem in my headpiece. Don't let it touch your skin." Slowly, he pats the boulder behind him, then lowers, making those tiny shorts rise a bit on his gladiator thighs. "Okay, how far away is the backpack?"

"Just a bit. You'll be able to hear me the whole time."

Chaos stalks ahead cautiously with her nose high. I join her side, but instead of a sloppy kiss to my hand, a low growl rumbles from her throat. A shiver snakes up my spine at the warning. There's no turning back though, we need to find more food in case I can't contact Brooks again.

"Tell me what you're doing." Axton's palms are positioned on the boulder as if he's ready to push off at any moment.

"I'm only stepping on leaves, Axton, a play-by-play won't be the most entertaining right now."

"I know, but be careful."

My heart races as I move closer to the skeletons. The other backpack sits right between them, and one has its bony fingers over the zipper. I suck in a breath, cringing, and slowly slide it off. Quickly, I snatch the pack. Inside, I rummage through more granola bars, an empty canteen, a few pairs of clothes, half a tube of toothpaste, and a bottle of insect repellent. Those all rest on top of maps, binoculars, and a journal full of messy notes. I immediately rub a blob of toothpaste all over my teeth and swallow the minty taste.

If they had food and supplies, how did they die?

"Well, I found more granola bars," I say, "We will feast like royalty tonight."

"Anything else?"

"Um, some clothes that might fit you better than that diaper."

"Ha. Ha. Ha. You should write that joke down so you don't forget."

"You threw our only pen in the ocean."

Since I'm far enough away that he can't hear my every move, I flip through the journal. My whirling nerves morph into a mass of hope. My heart skitters at the ancient script and symbols scrawled from top to bottom. They might've been researchers or treasure hunters with no intention of stealing Ulsa's powers like Axton had assumed. Since he can't see the writing to read it, his theory before was just that—a guess. Plus, if I keep these, no one will see them but me.

"I bet you didn't know that at home, we have bars, too," Axton starts, "but they're mixed with bits of salmon."

"That sounds appetizing. Do you boil crabs and smoosh some of that in?"

"I'm allergic to crab."

For some reason, that makes me smile. A merman allergic to shellfish, but I guess that makes sense since I'm allergic to horses. Axton could probably crush hundreds of false assumptions I have about merfolk that have spread like rumors across our lands. It makes me question how many lies I've been fed over the years.

I trudge back to him, hypnotized by those crisp blue eyes framed by his wavy, unkept hair blowing in the wind. Will he ever be able to see me? Maybe it's best he never knows what I look like. If his vision returns, he might start treating me differently.

The muggy scent of rain spikes the wind and the trees start to sway dramatically.

"I made something for you," Axton says, both his hands hidden behind his back.

"When? How?"

"Just now, when you were being sneaky over there." His smirk returns, teasing me with his pillowy lips.

"I wasn't being sneaky."

"Oh, Eri. The word devious is written across your forehead."

I lift my fingers toward my forehead, only to stop myself.

"Whatever you're hiding from me is okay, Eribelle. We don't have to tell each other everything."

"I'm not hiding anything."

"You're the world's worst liar," he says.

I cross my arms and kick him in the shin gently. "What did you make me?"

From behind his back, Axton pulls out a short stick wrapped by thin stems that connect a tuft of hair to the end. I glance at his hair again, then at the dagger lying next to him. He made me a paintbrush, with his own hair. Oh. My. Goddess. Butterflies flitter in my stomach. If he wasn't a merman, I'd tenderly brush a thumb over his wrist right now, all the way up his forearm. Instead, I take a deep breath and swipe the paintbrush from him.

I inspect how tightly he has woven the stems, made as if he's an artist himself. "Holy Abyss, Axton. How did you learn to do that?"

"Once upon a time, my hands created fierce spears. I coaxed their points into angels of death."

"How poetic," I chuckle, but stop when I see his expression.

"My dad taught me how to shape weapons since I was eight years old. The only one I'll never have the expertise with is a trident."

"The trident? Isn't that just legendary?"

"No. As children, Lena and I created a clubhouse made of the skeleton bones of sunken ships. We had stashed hundreds of human artifacts that sank to the depths after a shipwreck. The only items I collected were empty wine bottles from every region of the globe, like Ozaron, Khajit, Gonia, and Runlose. Some were full of algae, others corked with a rolled note inside, faded ink splattering the pages. Among the papers, I found an image of the trident. My dad had me practice forging models but I always failed."

Just because he found a picture of a trident doesn't mean it's real. "So you're advertising the terrible skills of your hands?" I tease. He bites his lip—making me stare at his mouth a bit too long. "Well, thank you. This paintbrush is definitely not the *worst* present I've ever gotten."

"I bet plenty of men have given you gifts of admiration." His words strike a spot in my gut that I don't want to explore. "Hey, can we keep walking? This spot gives me the creeps."

I tuck my newest paintbrush in the side pocket of the backpack. "Yeah, let me fill these canteens first. There's a pond right over there."

"I knew I smelled water." He pokes my side with our walking stick. "Can you lead me? I know you said there might be thorns, so I'd rather stick close."

Something about this spot feels unnatural, or Axton's paranoia is rubbing off on me, but I hide my nerves with a smile coating my response. "Fine, but only because you made me a present."

Once we reach the pond and our toes smoosh into the

mud, I fill the canteens, gulp one until it's empty, then refill it. Axton does the same with his.

"Does this mean all I have to do is buy you gifts to get what I want?" The huskiness of his voice challenges me to turn.

"What is it that you want, soldier?"

Slowly, Axton closes the gap between our bodies with the fierceness of a lion. Even though his eyes linger above my shoulder, I know what's on his mind as he presses his bare abs against my skin and pins me to a tree. My mind plays tennis with the decision of where to look—his lips. His eyes. Lips. Eyes.

Holy Abyss. He's going to kiss me. My pulse quickens to overdrive as he lowers his lips and hovers them over mine, Axton whispers, "They're watching us. Do exactly as I say."

"What?"

"Quiet." He yanks the stick from my hand and cages me to the tree with it. Tight against my neck, the bristly bark scratches my skin.

"What are you doing?" I shove him off and rub my throat, seeing tiny specks of sticky red smeared on my finger.

Axton barely steps back, wildness charging his body. His expression seems hyper-aware, as if sinister shadows hide close by, ready to attack. "Fight me."

Gorgeous sunrays shoot through the holes in the canopy, creating spotlights on the forest floor, but the light doesn't match the energy shifting to a ghost story setting. Maybe one day, when I'm old and gray, I'll be sitting around a campfire weaving tales to my grandkids about this island and how a merman gave me a paintbrush, and then got water poisoning from a toxic pond and suffered hallucinations.

"Um…maybe we should sit down and rest, Axton."

"No, trust me," he whispers and tendons stick out from

his neck. "They're spying on us, and they need to see you as strong, someone not to challenge."

The pond water had altered his mind, but then I notice no birds are chirping and the earlier breeze from an incoming storm has ceased. Maybe he's right.

I wipe my clammy hands on my shirt and resist checking over my shoulder for a predator. Heart pounding, I grab a large stick from the ground and smack it against Axton's.

"Come on, then, give me your best," I play along. Maybe this is a merman's version of flirting.

His block proves the years of training he has had with a similar weapon, maybe a spear.

"How can you do that without seeing?" I'm already out of breath.

"There are other ways to see, Eri."

My shoulders stay tight as he swings his stick toward me. I rush back, dodging from his swipe.

"Good, you're quick, use that to your advantage," Axton says.

An eerie hum hits the air, then another joins in harmony. I flinch. Spin around to the threat. Nothing is there. My breaths start to burst in and out when I glance back at Axton. His skin color has turned ashen white. Hair lifts on the nape of my neck.

"Keep fighting me, Eri. Our fight might scare them away." His stick clashes with mine again. Little fragments of bark fly off into a pile of leaves.

When he advances again, I tremble. Lose focus. Drop the stick. He swings through the air, missing me by inches.

"Stop…Axton…I can't…"

"Fight me, Eri!"

I want to run. Flee. Hide. He's lost his mind.

"Fight me!"

I pick up the stick. Slash it through the air. Ram it into

Axton's weapon. Push him backward. Seconds stretch on for eternity. Axton stumbles over a branch and lands on his back. Panting. I stand over him, stick raised high. Sharp end pointed at his heart.

"Stop, child," a hollow hiss snakes into my ears.

Below me, Axton's eyes are wide and his chest heaves with exertion. He mouths, *'Did you hear that?'* but I'm too scared to answer. I hold my breath and turn toward the voice, slow-as-death.

The bark of a tree stretches and morphs into a nasty face. Dizziness overrides my senses, but I keep both feet planted firmly on the ground and aim my stick at the creature.

"Stay back!" I scream.

"Don't you dare command a sacred nymph," it sneers in a crackly voice.

I gasp when a human shape detaches from the bark and walks out. Woodsy brown and green, from head to toe, the creature forms into violent scraps of wood. Its features are distorted by vines wrapped around each limb and its throat as if trying to suffocate itself. I think we found what killed those explorers. Chaos growls at my feet.

"Wh-what do you want?" I stand between Axton and the giant tree creature.

"You stole something from us," it shrills.

I swallow down the panic and clutch the stick tighter. "I d-don't know what you're talking about."

"What's in your backpack, human?" It stalks closer, fungus covering its false nose and sap leaking from the crevices that form eye sockets.

"Flooring for a new kitchen," I say.

"Drei, did you hear that? This one finds herself funny."

Another tree alters forms and a smaller one walks into the clearing, with flowers sprouting from her ears and ants creeping over her shoulders. "Aye, Viera, and she finds herself a thief too."

Sweat drips down my temples and my knees wobble. Drei sidesteps me and lunges for Axton, or maybe the backpack lying by his side.

I scream, "Get back!" then try to aim the stick at its throat but feel paralyzed.

"They're tree nymphs," Axton whispers, barely moving a muscle.

"Nymphs? But those aren't real."

They both cackle, hardcore villain style. These creatures are only supposed to be myths. Terror seizes control of my chest. I'm overcome with the urge to run, but I can't leave Axton behind. He seems frozen with shock—or their magic has incapacitated him. Drei crouches over Axton and scrapes his neck with what looks like a tongue made of cockroaches.

"Wh-what do you want?" I beg.

"The journal. Hand it over," Drei says.

I glance down at Axton. His severe frown could write elegies on its own. As much as I'd love to learn the secrets within the journal, our lives are more important than some ancient scribbles of symbols. I hand it over. The nymph reaches to me with long splinter nails that could slaughter any warrior. "Now, go home, little human, and tell your father we found the key." Viera licks her lizard lips. "And when the time comes... touch the gem to the power source to stop it all."

"Yes," the other smirks, "you will need to touch the power source to the gem."

What does that mean? What would they want with Dad?

"Eri, run!" Axton finally finds the ability to shout and struggles against an invisible forcefield holding him captive.

"Let him go first, then I'll do what you asked," I shout.

Viera shows her fangs, spiked thorns ready to draw

blood. She peers at me from the empty darkness and a snake slithers out. "He doesn't belong to you."

"He doesn't belong to you either!" I stab Viera's bark with my stick and jagged sounds flare like an explosion from the nymph, sputtering and gurgling.

"Sister!" Drei lunges to her aid, abandoning Axton's side.

I haul him to his feet and start to drag him through the forest. That's when I notice he had tied a rope from the backpack around both our waists.

"Go!" he screams.

We crunch over leaves. Dirt coats our legs. Sprint. Collapse, full of scratches. I rise. Rasping breaths. Shaking. Run.

And run. Stumble and run. I'm sure my body will implode from the sharp stitch in my side or maybe from the agonizing shredding sensation up my shins. My chest burns and scratches are all over my legs from bushes whacking against my skin. I don't dare look behind me or slow. The rope around my waist digs into my skin and burns from rubbing. Axton's breaths are labored and every so often the rope goes taut from him tripping on his new legs. When I'm positive I'll die if I run another step, I collapse to my knees, panting. Twigs scrape my legs, but I don't care. On all fours, I gasp in and out, letting my head hang heavy. Axton pants beside me, clearly just as exhausted.

His nose flares and a harried, wild appearance matches his bulging eyes. Tightness slashes my lungs in two and the world closes in on me. I've heard mythical stories of fire, forest, sea, and wind nymphs, but they're not real.

"I n-need Chaos."

"She's…right…there." He points behind me, then lifts both hands behind his head and sucks in deep gulps of air. "Do you see the nymphs?"

"No, but we need to get off this island!" I hurry to his

backpack and dig out the Taj, praying to any deity that it works. "I have to turn on the tracker."

I push the button to signal Brooks but keep my eyes on the treeline. My Taj doesn't work. The red light isn't even flashing.

Axton tries to catch his breath. "I…told…you," he gasps between words, "to destroy all the…papers." He swallows and places one hand over his chest for a few beats, then continues, "What journal was she talking about?"

"There was one in the backpack."

"Why didn't you tell me?"

I throw both hands up in the air. "Oh, like you've been completely honest with me? Why do you need me to go to the Below?"

"I told you not to worry about it," he snaps.

"Then *you*," I push his chest with one finger, "don't need to worry about my personal findings."

"Fine."

"Fine!" I say louder than him.

I don't owe Axton anything and he doesn't need to know I still have one remaining paper in the backpack. I don't feel guilty. I don't. It's now invaluable since a murderous nymph wanted it so badly. Why did she mention Dad? How can I leave my old life behind after these nymphs clearly threatened my father? Should I go back home and warn him? Maybe, first, I should find someone who can interpret the last paper I have hidden, and they mentioned a key. Why does the key do? What does it open? How did they find it?

There's too much to consider, and at this point, all I want is to forget the last few hours ever happened.

CHAPTER 13

Eribelle

"We need to go back," I whisper aloud while petting Chaos.

Her soft fur is like a comforting drug. I lean into it and inhale, breathing in the wholesome scent of dog. There's nothing quite as grounding as an animal in nature. Sure, she fed off our energy and looked a wee bit concerned when tree monsters were attacking, but now that she's out of danger, the pup wags her tail as if no problem exists in this world. How can she turn the mental switch off so quickly and simply just be? Maybe in my next life, I'll be lucky enough to reincarnate as a dog or maybe a sloth.

“We need to go back,” I whisper again. “They had a key. I need to get the key.”

A few yards away, Axton is also mumbling and counting something on his fingers. It’s like we’re both barely holding onto our sanity.

The tall trees sway around us; hopefully none of these come to life. In each direction, greenery surrounds us. Maybe the nymphs have an army at the ready. Are nymphs only palms or could they come out of any species of plant life? How many tree nymphs are there? Do they only live on this island? How have I lived a lie of a life, completely unaware that nymphs truly exist?

It doesn’t matter. If those nasty nymphs have some key that gives them power, I need to take it before they use it to hurt Dad or someone else. What did they want the journal for? It was in the backpack near their feet for Ulsa-knows-how-long so couldn’t they have taken the journal for themselves long ago? If the journal had similar information as the papers Axton had destroyed, why would the nymphs care about the magic of the sea? Were they trying to protect the ocean by eating it or do they plan to use the journal somehow? For all I know a tree can’t digest paper. I mean, paper is made of trees, so that would be a bit ironic. I catch myself mid-smile, like a lunatic, and glance over to Axton to make sure he didn’t notice, momentarily forgetting that he’s blind.

He’s pacing, a worn path already tracked within the leaves by his bare feet. I can’t help but notice how adorably his eyebrows are clenched tight. He might even be a little cute when he’s serious, and if there’s anything to be serious about it’s monstrous trees that come to life.

“I’m going back,” I say again and start untying the rope connecting me to Axton. This is what finally grabs his attention.

"What'd you say?" He stops pacing and stares over my shoulder, those eyebrows knit in a line.

"I'm going back. Alone." I tie my end of the rope around Chaos's neck as a leash. "I'd say that I'm sorry to ditch you, but it's not true. You're more than capable of surviving on your own, sight or not, fins or not. Goodbye, Axton, it's been interesting."

"You can't be serious." He reels in the rope, expecting to find me on the other end. When his hand brushes against Chaos, Axton turns around wildly, almost frantically. "Eribelle. Wait. Please, just wait a second."

If I stay silent, he won't know where I am. He'll eventually give up and walk away with Chaos, starting his new path. It's not like we were planning to stay together indefinitely. I have made my decision and taking Axton with me will only slow me down. It's not as if his father is the one the nymphs threatened. He has no reason to put himself in danger.

I hold my breath and wait for him to walk away.

"Eribelle? Come on, I know you didn't leave." He reaches out as if I'd be standing only a foot away. His half smile fades instantly when he only swipes through air.

I don't think I like being the reason for his frown, but there's no point in caring. He'll make his way back to the beach, use his Sea Witch powers, and summon a tail back. Axton's whole life is in Nerida. Here, he is literally a fish out of water. I almost laugh out loud at my own joke but cover my mouth with one hand.

"Eri?" Axton lifts his nose and sniffs the air. His smile returns. He takes a step toward me.

I don't dare move.

He steps again. His body is closer. His chest is square with mine. His stupidly perfect face is angled right at me. If I move back, he'll hear the leaves under my feet and know I'm still here, that I didn't give up on him, but if I stay still, if I let him approach me any further, there's a chance he'll wrap his arms around my waist. Once that happens, I may not want him to let go. Not because of his muscles, or because I'm desperate for contact with anyone in this traumatic experience, but because he made me a paintbrush, and brought me ketchup, and held me the entire time we slept on the beach when his arm probably fell asleep after an hour.

The final gap between us disappears but his hands don't envelop me. I'd define this look of his as a predatory glare, even though it's focused above my head instead of at my eye line. He must think I'm taller. His hands hover near mine. We don't touch but electricity still flows between our fingertips. It's as if my hands long to interlock with his. No. No, no, no. Not happening.

Axton's energy is animalistic. A bear-like vibe rolls off of him in waves that is all-consuming.

"Eri," he leans down near my ear, "your scent carries in the wind." Then he growls. "And if you think you're facing them without me, then…" His jaw ticks. "Tell me what to say to convince you that staying together is your safest option."

My hand, of its own accord, reaches out and almost grazes that angled jawline that has all his stress knotted tight, but there's no point. This is our time to separate. If I turn and run, he will follow, but not successfully without his sight. Eventually, I'll outmaneuver him. He'd still be connected to Chaos and the rope between them would get twisted in the trees and he'd have to stop to untangle her.

I could run.

I could leave.

Instead, I take his hand. The moment we touch, he releases a heavy sigh. I flip his hand palm up and lay the stolen dagger in it. There's no point in me carrying a weapon when I have a trained warrior at my side.

"What exactly is my particular scent, soldier? Is it s'mores by a campfire?"

He grins. "What are s'mores?"

"Oh, Ulsa Below, first you don't know what ketchup is, and now s'mores? This is an outrage!"

Axton holds out his other hand and this time I take it. Neither of us comment on the silent truce. For now, we choose to stay together, through whatever danger awaits. I try to convince myself that it's not because of his earlier pleading to drag me to the Below. Though, I still need to know why he was so adamant about taking me down there.

Mid-stride, I look up at him. It's worth it to see the curiosity in his smirk. "If you want to convince me to drag you around, then I need to know why you wanted to take me Below."

His smirk shifts and if I look closely, I'm pretty sure he's chewing the inside of his lip.

"It'd be a big help to me and my future."

"That's not very detailed."

"You catch on quickly."

Giving up, I march on, avoiding branches that block our way. With our hands entwined, Axton seems to anticipate my movements and no longer stumbles on the brambles and weeds. From my simple guidance, he walks assured, ready to take on a sea of invaders. My breath hitches when Axton glances down at me and I swear we make eye contact. His expression implies gratitude for not abandoning him.

"So, how is this going to work?" He squeezes my hand. "Should I chop down a tree and make you a spear?"

"I believe I'm more capable of chopping."

"Aye, but me dagger says otherwise."

I stop and stare at him. Obscene laughter bursts out of my body uncontrollably. "Did you just try to be a pirate?"

He pulls me along; maybe he's following his nose to the

nymph's lair, and though I can barely believe I'm doing it, I follow him.

"So, mister merman, tell me more about this cruel crown your grandma cursed you with." I glance up at the gem reflecting sunlight.

Axton takes a deep breath. "Grams has granted five bargains in her reign as Sea Witch. Each time, a trade is made. I had to give up something I care about and treasure deeply for what I wanted most in that moment."

"And what you wanted was to arrive naked on my beach?"

His nose scrunches up and he shakes his head. "Anyways, the four others who were given a crown like this all lived decades ago. I'm guessing the only reason Grams helped me is because she raised me. She had sworn off ever completing another bargain."

"Why?"

"All four of the others…well, they didn't ever regain what they lost."

"How do you know if it was so long ago?"

"They're famous," he itches his nose, "because they all died."

"All of them!?" I slap his shoulder. "Why would you risk making a bargain if it's never been successful, you idiot?"

His smile stretches across his cheeks. "Don't tell me you care about what happens to me, Angelfish."

"I don't."

"That's what I thought." He trips on an overgrown root but his shoulder catches his fall against a tree trunk.

I brush off some fallen bark that attached itself to his sweaty forearms. He freezes for a moment, then shakes his head again. "I risked it because I needed a quick solution to my problem and I trust Grams…with my life." He pauses. "Besides, I still have almost two weeks to gain my sight back."

"What do you need to do before time runs out?"

He drops my hand and rubs the stubble along his chin. "Honestly, I'm not exactly sure. You'd think she'd want me to succeed, but Grams was quite confusing. First of all, I never asked for legs or to breathe oxygen, so I have no idea how that happened. And she said to get my sight back that you… never mind."

"Me? What about me?" I rewrap Chaos' end of the rope around Axton's waist.

"It's not important," he says.

"Hey! Stop walking so fast and talk to me."

He keeps trudging along, and his cheeks flush a slight pink.

"What does regaining your sight have to do with me?"

"Can you just forget it, Eri? We should probably be quieter so the nymphs don't hear us."

Birds tweet above and a swish of wings would sound like relaxing background noise to paint the gorgeous scene bubbling around us, but I'm no longer fooled about the innocence of this island. Maybe he's right and the nymphs have ears and eyes as spies following us along the trail, but if that's true then they already know we're returning and will be at an advantage anyway. This may be my only time to get more answers.

"Don't tell me that within only a few days of being a human man that you're like all other males?"

That stops him in his tracks. "What does that mean?"

"So many men assume that by keeping information from me, that they're protecting me in some way. Or maybe it's just your ego wanting to keep control of the situation. That makes sense too. Or…it could be—"

"I'm *not* like human males." Axton bites his lip, then raises his head to the sky as if praying to some goddess of the clouds. "Ulsa-ulmightly! Fine. Grams said that to gain my sight back, I need to see you, truly see you. Yes, I know that doesn't make any sense. Oh, and apparently I need to lose myself to being lost. I haven't figured out that riddle yet."

While I ponder this, we weave around more trees. Chaos leads the way, sniffing every other flower like her life depends on it. None of the terrain looks familiar and yet, it all looks the same. I have no idea what direction we're headed or if the nymphs' lair is close by or not. In fact, coming back was a stupid idea when I have no clue how to find the key they mentioned or how to steal it, but if I don't do something, no one else will.

At least I don't have to do this alone. Against all odds, I'm glad Axton stayed. He's the only person I've met other than Sampson who doesn't feel fake. All my life I've been seen as a tool for others to get their way, a means to an end, a pawn. All it took for someone to take me seriously was to take away their eyesight, but how is he supposed to see me without his sight? Why would his Grams play tricks with him? I want to help, but I'm unsure how.

"So why did the other four merfolk die?"

Axton points to the crown holding his bargain. "The gem inside is created from magic of the sea. The same magic that formed the trident centuries ago."

"The trident isn't real," I say.

"The trident contains mild wielding power, and it's not consistent either. Sometimes it controls the mind or spirit of the other people or things, however, other times it allows the one in possession to take over other's minds."

I half-laugh, unsure whether to believe this new fable. "The gem in this crown has a smaller piece of that same power. All the other four who ever used it touched the gem at the wrong time or for too long, and it stopped their heart." He gulps. "That's why I've told you not to touch it."

"So, when you used the gem to cut through that

enchanted rope, you didn't know if it would take over your mind or give you the control?"

Axton faces forward again. His lack of response is an answer in itself. He had risked his sanity for me, hours after meeting me, without any indication that his idea would pay off. Why? What kind of person is that self-sacrificing? He had already saved me from the wretched storm, and when he showed up naked and unconscious on the beach, that's when all the mermen had disappeared. So, I'm assuming he was to thank for that coincidence. This so-called enemy is continually going out of his way to help me. There must be some ulterior motive behind his choices.

I scan his features, looking for any indication that he's lying. For the first time, I question Axton's purpose here. No one has this good of a soul. He may have been tricking me this entire time. But why? What would I have that he needs? I doubt he's sticking with me to regain his eyesight because I may not even be the human his Grams referred to. There must be some other motive that he's acting so saintly.

What is something that I have uniquely that someone who works for the sea queen would want? Painting skills? No, I doubt they even have paint underwater. Access to Dad? He's rich, sure, but it's not like he's a politician or someone who trades with the merfolk.

Axton's fingers brush against mine as we walk side by side. I ignore the tingling sensation that ripples up my skin and makes my heart beat faster.

Think, Eribelle! Why am I different? The color blue. My eyes are blue, the only human known to have blue eyes in Coendriel. I gasp and stop still as a statue.

"What?" Axton stops too. "What is it? Did we make it back?" He lowers his voice and his fist clenches around the dagger. "Are they close by?"

Anger surges in my veins. How dare he! All of this has

been a charade, from the very first moment we met. A merfolk must have spotted me and the queen must want me for some experiment or something. Or maybe she thinks I have some magic of my own that I've stolen from the sea and it shows itself through my eye color. It's not like I haven't wondered about all of these things myself as I grew up. In grade school, all my classmates had brown or amber or green eyes. I was always the odd one out. Instead of shunning me, they put me on a pedestal. My whole life I've never been viewed as Eribelle, but rather as the girl who is different, the girl with blue eyes. Then as I aged, I became the beauty who could help Dad gain more clients and the girl who could attract attention at a ball for Trey. I've never been seen for me.

Seen.

Fuckin' asshole.

I turn to Axton and slap him across his face.

"Ow!" he yells so loud that Chaos comes running toward us. His hand rubs his cheek. "What the actual fuck?"

"How did you know my story?"

He puts up both hands in surrender. "What story?"

"Did the queen put you up to this or…" I pause. "Maybe it wasn't the queen at all, maybe it's all Ulsa's idea. I bet she's not even your damn grandmother, though, is she?" I storm off, pulling Axton behind me. "I can't believe I fell for it so easily."

"Slow down. What in the Abyss are you talking about?"

I whirl around and shove his chest slightly. "And *YOU*! You're probably not even a soldier but a mastermind liar! I mean, it makes sense with all the lies you've spun!"

"Hold up, did you eat a toxic berry by accident?"

I fake a laugh. "How would you know about berries? You're from the damned sea, Axton! If that's even your real name!"

He rubs his forehead with one hand and lowers himself to the forest floor. "We're not going anywhere until you explain."

I start to untie the knotted rope around my waist, but before I can, he has me reeled in. With a quick yank, Axton tugs me down so I flop next to him in a pile of long, itchy grass.

"Explain. Now." He's facing me, but still not looking at me.

I have to give him credit for doing his homework. The man has clearly spent time researching my past to understand what would impact me so drastically. Of course I'd fall for a sob story of needing to feel seen by someone.

"Eribelle, I can be very patient when I choose to be."

I cross my arms and squeeze my eyes shut, not allowing the hot tears pooling behind my eyes to fall. It's not like he'd be able to see them, but I still have no intention of empowering him right now.

"Just tell me one thing," I practically snarl. "If the lightning hadn't ripped our boat in two, were you planning on abducting me from the yacht that night?"

"What are you talking about?" Axton mumbles something under his breath that sounds like a string of curse words.

I bury my head in my hands, in disbelief that I've gotten myself into such a mess by being so naive. I have little to no real information, I'm stranded on an island with a true enemy, and no way to get home. At this point, I don't even need to go straight to Ozaron. Home sounds better. The comfort of my studio awaits me with all my easels lined up against the bay window. I long for the familiar creaks in the hardwood floors when I snuck out to bars. And Dad may have been right in wanting to protect me. He may have gone about it the wrong way, but what if he knew that merfolk were interested in my eye color?

A sudden realization feels like it has ripped the oxygen from my lungs. My brother, Ben, also had blue eyes. And he was taken by the sea. Maybe it wasn't an accident. Maybe merfolk captured him and now I've fallen into the same trap.

"Fuck this!" I grab Axton's dagger and slice through the rope near my waist.

Without another word, I change directions and run toward where I assume the beach is. Forget stupid nymphs and this world of fairy tales. Forget magical gems and secret keys and symbols. And especially forget lying bastard mermen. I'm done with this disaster.

Brooks has been searching for me so maybe by the time I make it back to the shore, their boat will already be within sight. Axton yells my name behind me, but as expected, he lags behind and I quickly increase the distance between us. Hopefully the nymphs devour him and his despicable soul. How could someone act so genuine yet be full of such darkness? I should've picked up on his schemes from the very beginning, but he had played me for a fool.

Never again.

CHAPTER 14

Axton

Hours of awkwardness between Eribelle and I have been followed by more hours of uncomfortably strained tension. Last night I finally emerged from the terrible jungle, alone and furious. It still took me longer than it should've to follow Eribelle's scent. I'm no longer as bothered at being buried in this tomb of forever darkness, but more so stuck on why Eribelle is giving me the silent treatment and how long she will refuse to talk to me. Something isn't adding up. Yesterday, we were holding hands, exchanging stories, and finally working together cohesively. The next thing I knew, she was using words as whips that stung harshly. I'm so damned confused.

After she fell asleep last night, I still cuddled her close to keep her warm. Her soft skin against mine was like an addictive drug, but the moment she awoke, Eribelle stormed off as if I had accused her of being the world's worst painter. Now, she hasn't spoken to me all day. Sometimes I call out to her to make sure she hasn't disappeared into the jungle and her only response is throwing a stick in the water to confirm she's nearby. Why the Abyss is she pissed at *me*? I'm the one who has the right to be angry.

At least those tree nymphs didn't chase us—yet. Chaos drops her head in my lap and I question the dog's sense of smell since I must reek by now. Holding out my last granola bar, I let her chomp the remaining bite. Wet slobber smears the side of my hand so I wipe it on her fur, then nudge the pup away so she knows her job is to comfort Eribelle, not me. At least they should have five more bars left between them if I've counted correctly. Not that I care if Eribelle's stomach starts to pinch. I truly don't.

She deserves some payback for her choices. Eribelle had been foolish to wander off without me after I warned her of the dangers. Not to mention we haven't had the chance to argue about her taking that journal and keeping it a secret. Obviously, she doesn't care about my kind. If the nymphs give that information to the wrong human, the treaty won't last much longer. If anyone is trying steal Grams' powers, our queen will declare war, and I'll need to be there to support my people—which means I need my vision back.

Plus, if Eribelle's cousin arrives on their ship, it'll eliminate all chances I have to use her to clear my name. Too many lives in Nerida are counting on my protection. It's time to contact Grams and persuade her to change our deal. I shouldn't have even waited this long.

My feet sink into the sand and cold water flows to my ankles, then away again, up to my ankles, then away. I've never considered water to be this frigid. It sends shivers up my spine in contrast to the overbearing suns.

I stop and listen for Eribelle's footsteps nearby but only hear the lapping of the waves. Good. My fingertips trace the magical crown and find the symbol on the side. I push it down with one finger, ignoring the surge of power fighting against me. My chest clamps tight and I dig my heels into the ground. A wall of wind tries to force me back

I whisper Grams' name, "Ulsa, I'm calling to address our deal."

Sounds from the sea echo from inside the gem and I long for home. Dolphins sing to one another, and the tune of a whale call makes my heart flutter with nostalgia. Glassware clinks together and I recognize the scent of Grams' cottage. I suck in a breath and reach out my hand, ready to touch her bottles of potions, but only feel air.

"You're not truly here, Grandson, put your hand down." Her tone is stern like my days as a child. "Why do you call me so soon? This is your one and only chance to communicate with me."

"I asked for a way to prove my innocence, not to be stranded on an island. And I never asked for these legs, or to breathe air, so this negotiation isn't a fair trade. If you can add extra stipulations, then so can I."

"*If* I had given you legs, then you'd owe me a humble *'thank you'* for hiding you from the hundreds of merfolk hunting you, but, grandson, I did no such thing."

Is Grams finally losing her mind after all these years?

"What do you mean? I've been *walking* on a beach, Grams. I have *feet*!"

"You're finally accepting your power. Your sweet mother found hers in her teens, but there's nothing wrong with being almost thirty when you accept it."

"That's not what's happening. Listen, I need a way to clear

my name and be reinstated in the Queen's good graces. Can we make a different trade?"

"Oh, you're not happy?" Grams' voice is spiked with malice. "Let me guess. I bet you want to be the hero to warn Queen Rayna that some bullies are out to dismantle us. Newsflash, my dear Axton, humans have always been trying to stop us. That doesn't mean you needed to destroy the researchers' findings."

"Wait…you know about that?"

"Of course I know. You underestimate me, little one, but you also underestimate the power of a father who lost his child. The woman you have partnered with happens to have a very powerful father on land. He is making every effort to blame merfolk on his misfortune and complete his revenge."

"Eribelle ran away from home. I don't think she's very close with her father."

"She isn't the one Finley Erickson is fighting for."

"I don't understand."

"You will in time." She pauses. "You're looking for the wrong answers. Your magic is trying to tell you something, Axton. Quit fighting it and listen. Why do you think you grew legs? I may not have given you exactly what you expected, but your magic will always give you what you need."

I pause, considering. Maybe my magic can also give Eribelle the ability to breathe water. Grams has given that gift to someone before, maybe I can too.

Grams sighs. "Axton, you already paid the price for our bargain: your sight. Whatever you did to grow legs is your own doing."

I clench my teeth tightly. "This isn't a game."

"If you want your sight back, the human needs to believe that you see who she really is, fully understand her value besides her beauty."

"I already do," I growl, "It's not my responsibility if she has a confidence complex."

"It sounds like she's getting under your skin. Have you kissed the girl, yet?"

"Kissed her!?" This time I yell into the salty ocean air. "Eri hates me! She hates mermen and all of our kind. Are you crazy?"

The memory of waking with my hand on Eri's hip sends a surge of energy racking through my body. In that moment, all I had wanted was to brush my lips against her collarbone and trail down her back, regardless of how much she currently despises me.

"She wants to separate once her cousin drops us off." My fists ball tightly. "So, if you're set on this bargain, you're dooming me to a life of blindness."

"It's not in my control." Her voice is starting to fade away.

"Grams, I need to take her Below. Why won't you help me?"

"The only priority is not letting a human touch the gem of your headpiece. Now, listen to me…take the girl on a proper date when you get ashore."

"This is ridiculous. I need to—"

Something cuts off the feed, making the sounds all jumbled.

"Oh, dear! No, no, no, this can't be," Grams pauses, "Axton, you need to hurry. My neeks just told me that Lena has gone missing."

My knees buckle and the world turns upside down. The dreamy illusion of Grams' cottage disappears, and I'm surrounded by torturous darkness again. Ulsa broke our connection.

"Axton? Who are you talking to?" Eribelle asks from behind.

I shove my fingers into my temple. Grams must be

mistaken. Lena can't be missing. She's the most bad-ass mermaid I know, plus no one would dare mess with the queen's niece.

"Brooks will be here soon." Eribelle is oblivious to the torment striking my brain like lightning as she continues. "How do you want me to introduce you to the crew?"

"I'm not going with you," I snap so fiercely that I hear her step back. "I need to save my best friend. Lena is missing."

When I start to stomp toward our packs, water splashes my knees. I long to dive into the sea, gulp in the water, and forget the last few days ever happened. Saving Eribelle was the stupidest choice I've ever made.

"What are you mumbling?" Eri splashes after me, her words lined with sharp edges.

I spin around and she rams straight into my chest. I don't even try to catch her as she tumbles sideways.

"What is *wrong* with you?" Irritation ignites her words like fire.

"After a day of ignoring me, you want questions answered? Well, guess what, it's too late. You messed up. I'm not going aboard your cousin's ship, and nothing you have to say will change that."

"But I had come to tell you that my ex, Trey is on the ship…and Brooks said Trey captured a mermaid," she whispers, "in a net."

All the times I've given humans the benefit of the doubt are severed in an instant. I take a giant step back from her and hold out a hand like a shield against this woman—my enemy. Chaos starts to bark crazily by our ankles.

"What"—I focus on not snapping something in half—"What does the mermaid look like?"

His face is so torn, I feel a sudden urge to comfort him, regardless of our relationship being rock so far, so I say, "I don't know, but if it's Lena, we can rescue her."

"Mermaids can't breathe oxygen for more than a minute without a spell." I wish I could grip my spear and shove it into the captain of that ship. "If the mermaid is strung in the air, she's dead."

"Look!" She says as a breeze flits by my face. "Oh, you can't see. Sorry, it's their ship! It's out there." The sound of a zipper sliding over its jagged teeth is followed by Eribelle rummaging through her pack. "I'm using the binoculars, Axton." She grabs my hand and holds it tight. "It's okay, the mermaid is underwater on the side of the boat…in the net."

"So, they're dragging her! Send him a message to slow the fuck down, and that he'll be getting an additional passenger."

She ignores me, so I twist her wrist to gain her full attention.

"Ow!" Eribelle hisses in response. "Axton, that hurts!"

"Listen. I don't care what you're pissed at me for or why you've been ignoring me all day. This is what's going to happen. I'm boarding that ship before you, releasing the mermaid, and killing your boyfriend. Do you understand?"

"He's *not* my boyfriend." She slips out of my grasp and I immediately hate myself for touching her so forcefully. "Trey is my *ex*, and we didn't end on good terms."

I face the sea and start counting to one hundred. One. Two. Three. Slow. As. Fuck. If the ship arrives before I finish, I'm going to let Trey feel my wrath for hours until he bleeds to death. Once Lena is safe, I'll figure out the next step to clear my name. For a little bit longer, I still need Eri to work with me. The image of *'Wanted: Felon'* signs plastered in the Below flash through my mind. I can't tell her that the entire RMG thinks I'm a murderer. She'll never view me the same way again. If I'm not a soldier, I don't have anything to offer Eribelle—not that I want to. At the most inconvenient time, Ma's life motto rings back to me from so long ago: *'The only way to lose yourself is to be afraid of getting lost.'*

"Eribelle…I'm sorry I hurt your wrist."

"Whatever. You made yourself perfectly clear. Once we get to land, I never want to see you again."

"Can you at least tell them I'm from Ozaron and crashed in an aero-tran and survived with only my dog until you arrived? They can't know I'm a merman, do you understand?"

"But you're wearing *that* crown. It looks so similar to the queen's guard."

"Lie to them."

"Of course you know all about lying," she spits out, but I have no idea what she's referring to.

"Just say I'm an honorary merman for helping them years ago and this crown was a gift."

She grumbles something incoherent and from the way her voice fades, I know she's moving away. Ever since I left the Below, everything has been out of my control. I can't remember the last time I've felt so lost.

Memories flood me like a tidal wave. Time with Mom and Dad, then I spent my teen years with Grams, trying to make sense of their deaths. Maybe I was lost then and didn't even know it. After I turned eighteen, I belonged to the Guard for years, finding my purpose. Have I always been this lost without knowing it? What is the right path? It's as if everything has been stripped away from me and I'm hollowed out.

I hear an engine approaching. Before we step foot on that boat Eri needs to know what she's dealing with.

"Eribelle, listen," I say, wishing I could see her eyes, "I'm wanted. For murder."

"Excuse me!? This is something you should've told me when we first met. Like, hey, I happened to kill someone recently."

"No," I shake my head. "I'm wanted for *your* murder. My

people think I killed you and my title was taken away. The only way to get my job back, my whole life back is to prove that I'm innocent. That's why I need you to come to the Below and tell your story to our queen."

"How do you expect me to help you when I never want to see you again?"

"I was hoping my magic would kick in and perform a mind-altering miracle."

She groans. "And what do I get if I help you?"

"What do you want?" I ask.

"If you don't remember what I look like then who told you about my eyes?"

"What are you talking about? Do you have three eyes?"

"Ugh, I have no way of knowing if you're telling the truth."

I take a deep breath and lean forward. "Let's break this down. Please. What exactly are you worried about? Tell me what's going on in your head."

I feel her squirm, sigh, sigh again. I wait. She needs to explain it all and clear the air. My response will probably impact her next choice. Whether she chooses to believe me or not is out of my control.

"You're too nice," she says.

"And that's a problem."

"Yes. You have to have some ulterior motive. No one would help me this much otherwise. And the *only* thing I have that others don't, the *only* reason you'd pick me is because of my eye color. I'm not different from other women in any way. Which means you've been lying to me this whole time. Who is it that cares about my eyes? Ulsa or the queen or someone else entirely?"

"Eribelle, it's not—"

"Please. I don't have any magic so you don't need to take me Below. It was clever to try and convince me to volunteer so I thought I was helping you, but we both know that's a sham. Just send a message to whoever wants me and tell them I'm no one special."

I'm in disbelief that she thinks I'm abducting her. How did things get turned around so drastically? I understand we've both been in survival mode for the last few days, but I had truly thought we were making progress as a team. This is one giant step backward.

I guess her fears aren't outrageous when I haven't been completely forthcoming with her, but she's also hidden information from me. Our kind have always been enemies. It's not as if a few tender moments on a deserted island can change centuries of history. Treaty or not, her kind hate merfolk, so she has her whole life of stories being passed down from whoever raised her—stories about monsters of the sea who seduce humans into the depths.

Is there any chance Eribelle found the royal's secret? If so, it changes all my plans. Mysterious keys, ancient symbols, gaining my position back would all come secondary to making sure she never tells another soul about what happened years ago on that beach.

Eribelle may not trust me, but now I'm wondering what other secrets she's hiding from me.

CHAPTER 15

Eribelle

I still hate him, but the confusion in Axton's expression breaks me a bit. He opens his mouth, about to say something, then closes it again.

The yacht floats closer and a silhouette of someone that contrasts against the suns throws an anchor overboard.

"I'm never going Below with you," I start, "but if you tell me what the nymph needs the key for, then I'll free the mermaid Trey captured."

"No. I'm responsible for my kind," he growls, "I need you to help me clear my name. I swear. If you know of a way to do that without having to go Below with me, then fine." His tone is layered with subtext.

Axton doesn't need to know that I can kill two birds with one stone. Once we land, I'll tell Dad to talk to one of his millionaire clients who have sway with the merfolk community. Someone must be able to pass along a message for Axton. In the meantime, I'll be able to figure out what the other symbols mean in the explorers' journal.

"I know a way," I say, gathering confidence.

"How?"

"My father." I wave to Brooks in the distance, who is lowering a rowboat.

"Why? What does your father do for his job?" Axton puts both his hands on his hips and faces the ocean, gold light glistening in his blond hair.

"He sells boats." I gather our items and tap my thigh for Chaos to follow. "Expensive boats to the most connected people in Coendriel. Don't worry, I'll take care of it."

Axton rubs his stubbled jaw. "I can't help but worry. My entire future is in your hands."

"As is mine."

"It might be helpful if we try to trust each other."

We walk side by side toward Brooks' boat.

Just before Brooks arrives, Axton turns to me, but I already know what he's going to say, so I clear his worries with a quick mumble. "Don't worry, I won't tell them who you really are."

"Brooks!" I run toward my cousin. They pull me into a warm hug.

I slide down their front and land back in the water noticing the dark circles under my cousin's eyes that resemble bruised blueberries.

"Holy shit, nice crown, dude. Did you steal that from an RMG?" Brooks holds their hand out to Axton.

"He's blind, Brooks." I lower my cousin's arms.

They scan Axton up and down, then eye me and mouths, *'He's huge!'*

I mouth back, *'I know,'* and roll my eyes.

Brooks glances between Axton and me and cocks their head to the side. They mouths silently, *'Did you two...?'*

I shake my head frantically and chew the inside of my lip. My gaze lasers onto theirs, full of warning. My cousin smiles silently, but I swear to the goddesses that if Brooks even considers asking that question out loud, I'll push them overboard faster than a pelican dives for fish.

"I can hear your silence," Axton mumbles.

"Uh, they were just pointing to your crown," I lie. "Brooks, since you're wondering, merfolk gave that to Axton as a gift for his help. You wouldn't believe it, but he's been stuck on this island with only his dog. I promised him we'd take them to the harbor."

"Alright then, well, what I really need to know is how did you manage to *not* eat your dog all that time?"

Axton forces a fake half chuckle and says, "Chaos wouldn't taste good without some ketchup."

My heart spasms in my chest from our inside joke and I glance up at his stern face, but no hint of our previous connection lingers in Axton's hardened features. I curse myself silently for wishing he'd smirk.

"Can you carry Chaos from the beach? She's scared of water."

"How convenient," Brooks says.

Water splashes as they pass, and then Axton fumbles for the side of the little boat that'll bring us to the yacht anchored nearby. I guide his hand to the edge and even though I have the intention to help him inside, we both topple in. We scramble to sit on opposite ends and I wish I could get the satisfaction of glaring at him, but he can't see any expression I make. My cousin rows us toward the yacht, and I try not to cower under their heavy scrutiny.

"Why did you leave home?" Brooks, the closest thing I have to a sibling, looks at me with such sadness it shatters my heart.

"There's an art conference in Ozaron." I don't want to say more because I can only think of Sampson.

"I could've brought you," Brooks says.

I clutch the backpack to my chest. "No, you would've listened to Dad. He didn't want me to leave, and everyone always takes his side."

Brooks stops rowing. "You didn't even try to ask me."

I throw my backpack at them and Brooks doesn't even dodge it. Or blink. Or move an inch. It smacks them straight in the chest and falls to their feet.

"I...I thought you'd side with Dad," I mumble.

"It's in the past." Axton's voice cuts through the salty breeze like a knife. "What's done is done. Can we hurry up?"

"Well, speaking of your dad, he's very relieved you're okay." Brooks slides the rowboat next to the base of the yacht's ladder. "I can't say he's thrilled about losing his best yacht though."

Suddenly, it feels like my essence slinks away from my body. Of course Dad would be upset about his precious boat. Next to me, Axton's hand graces the small of my back, but it's gone almost before I can fully register it. It's harder to hate him. With watery eyes, I focus on the rocking sensation of the waves.

"Tell your uncle I'll pay for the loss of his precious toy," Axton snaps with bared fangs.

I nudge his side hard. He takes the hint and clamps his mouth shut, but not soon enough. Brooks' eyes widen as they stare at Axton's sharp teeth and asks, "Where did you say you're from again?"

I fumble with the bottom rung of the ladder and rush out an explanation. "Axton was a marketing expert from a small town outside Ozaron. Before his aero-tran crash, he traveled the globe with a team that represented cross-over consumers. The company's focus was on selling items that were functional both Above and Below. Anything that only humans could use or only merfolk could use, they wouldn't market, only products that worked for both cultures."

"Wow, that was a mouthful. Maybe she's *not* a pretty face." The voice comes from the top of the ladder.

Fuckin' Trey.

"Is that *him*?" Axton snarls.

"Yeah," I whisper, "you need to play nice."

"But he has a mermaid trapped!" Axton's fists curl so tight, I'm worried he'll snap his finger in half.

"Hey, calm down," I whisper as my fingers slip on the wet ladder but I manage to climb onto the deck.

"You two would probably give up anything for a good steak right about now, huh?" Trey asks.

"She doesn't like steak," Axton replies quietly.

I stare at him. He remembered. For once, a man had paid attention and tucked my preferences in his pocket like a piece of treasure.

I stand and smack straight into Trey's chest.

He glowers down at me, a filthy smirk snaking up his oily cheeks. "Miss me?"

Goddess, I despise him. I ram my knee into Trey's groin and he collapses to the ship's floor. His ridiculous top hat falls and rolls away. I snatch a dagger from Trey's belt and sprint across the deck. The netting that harnesses the mermaid swings and rattles against the sleek curves of the yacht. I slash. Grunt. Slit.

"Hey!" Trey yells. "Stop it! She's *my* catch!"

My muscles burn. I hack. Saw. I finally sever the last fray

and the net drops with a splash. A mermaid with long, vibrant purple hair swims away and disappears into the depths. My shoulders finally relax and I let out a heavy breath that stings my chest. When I turn, I run straight into another hard chest—Axton. An electric current churns through my belly and for a second I forget why I'm furious with him.

He rolls his lips, pauses, then says, "You freed her."

"Yes."

"What did she look like?"

"Long, violet hair, young, tan skin—"

"It wasn't Lena." He pivots and storms away, speaking over his shoulder, "I'm going to find a way to get clean. Do you have shondels up here?"

"What are shondels?"

"Nevermind, don't set a destination yet." He staggers off with his hands outstretched in front of him, swaying when the boat rocks under his unsteady feet.

Trey finally stands, cupping his groin. "Who the Abyss is *that* guy?" He reaches for his broken hat, like a moron.

"Axton…um…" Brooks pauses and meets my eye. "What's his last name?"

Axton had told me that merfolk don't have last names, so I make one up and say, "Axton Wells."

"I'll look him up." Trey's grin slithers up again. "In the meantime, you should know that he's about to walk in on your Partner in the shower."

"Partner?" I ask, just as I remember Jordan's non-proposal. Chaos scampers after me, almost knocking me over as I rush down the stairs. "Axton, wait!" I run down the little hallway, but I'm too late. Voices roar back and forth like two men brawling.

"What the fuck, man?" Jordan's deep voice blasts off the claustrophobic corridor.

A loud thump thunders against a wall. Bodies smashing. Shit, shit, shit. I dart faster. Axton yells something I can't understand and another loud boom knocks into a wall.

"Hey!" I turn the corner, out of breath, ready to jump between them. "He's blind, Jordan!"

My heart stops briefly. They're both butt-ass naked. Unbelievable. Axton has Jordan's stomach pinned against the sink, with his forehead against the cracked mirror. Both of Jordan's wrists are restrained behind his back by only one of Axton's massive hands.

"Apologize!" Axton roars at Jordan.

"Sorry, man, I didn't know you're blind."

"No!" Axton squeezes Jordan's wrists tighter. "Apologize to Eribelle for what you just said about her to me. Now! You disrespectful son of a..."

Axton twists Jordan's shoulders and a high shriek bounces off the small bathroom walls.

"Okay, okay! I'm sorry."

I don't even know what Jordan said, but apparently, it was bad enough to offend Axton. I stand there frozen, unsure where to move next.

"Good." Axton releases him. "You done showering?"

"Sure, man, whatever." Jordan grabs a towel and bows his head to me. "I'll catch up with you later, Sugar Doll. I'm glad we found you."

Unable to hold myself back, I close the bathroom door and head straight to Axton. My fingers hover over his arm where a small piece of glass from the broken mirror sticks out.

"Axton, don't move, I need to—"

"Just yank it."

Without warning, I pull. Blood seeps out. He applies pressure with a towel and sits on the edge of the bath.

"So, you're engaged?" Axton's defeated posture creates a heaviness in my body. "You could've mentioned that."

I back into the sink. "No, I had nothing to do with that. My dad…no, I'm not engaged."

"That guy seems to think you are, and he has detailed plans for your honeymoon."

Seriously? What would possibly make Jordan say something like that to a stranger?

"Well, he's wrong. I'm not focusing on men for at least five years. First, I need a new place, new job, new connections, then maybe one day I would be open to…"

One of his eyebrows rises like the arch of a bridge, then as if he understands my silence, adds in. "I need to put pressure on this a minute still. Why don't you shower first?"

"But—"

"Eri, I can't see your body."

I bite my lip and focus on the painting of a lighthouse that's hung on the wall, realizing this is the second time Axton has been nude in front of me. "Fine, but don't think about joining me in here."

"Wouldn't dream of it," he growls, obviously still sour, or maybe just in pain.

When my ratty clothes fall to the floor in a puddle of fabric, I suck in a deep breath. We're both naked. Alone. Every ounce of energy goes into not accidentally touching him as I step into the tub.

The stream of the scalding water melts my bones gloriously. I crane my neck back and take in the tile shapes of the ceiling, watching the steam rise. Eventually, coconut soap, my favorite, covers the top of my head to the tip of my toes. Dirty water vanishes down the drain and it takes my anger with it. There's a chance I'll stay here forever and let them bury me in this tub.

A deep voice clears his throat. Axton. Right, I'm not

alone.

My eyes snap open at the sound of his questioning voice. "Eri? Did you love Trey?"

I pause my scalp massage and let more suds run down my back. "I thought I did." Not wanting to elaborate, I shift the conversation to him. "Who was your last relationship?"

"Zilia." His voice softens and I lean closer to hear him over the rushing water. "She wanted someone less focused on his career."

"How long were you two together?" I hate that my stomach burns at the thought of him kissing her, holding her, moving atop her.

"Two years. When we broke up, she moved away from Nerida, which is rare. I'll probably never see her again."

"You miss her."

"No, I miss Lena a thousand times more than I ever missed her."

I turn the faucet and let the droplets form a plinking rhythm into the tub. Axton offers me a towel between the wall and curtain and I smile.

"Thank you."

Something I can't detect flashes in his eyes but disappears in an instant. "So, why does your dad want you to marry Jordan?"

"Business connections." I dry my breasts first, then move down my body slowly.

"He doesn't care about your happiness?"

I sigh. "Of course, he cares, but my dad thinks he knows the best way to make me happy. He's never fully understood me. The only people who got me was my brother and Sampson, and they both—"

The shower curtain flies open and Axton stands there. I squeal and cover myself.

"I want to be someone who understands you," he admits

softly.

No words make their way out of my throat.

"I'm sorry about Sampson and all the grief you must be feeling. You were right before, that I should've tried to save him. I only went after you because I thought…I remember knowing you were beautiful when dancing on that boat, but even if I never learn my lesson…" His jaw twitches. "…I'll never regret that decision, because it means you're here, safe—even if you hate me."

"I don't hate…" I long to reach out and touch his chest. I fiddle with my towel and become hyper-aware of our bare bodies. He can never find out how fast he makes my pulse race. I clutch my dripping hair and drain the water so it splatters against the tub. Right as I'm straddling both sides of the tub, Axton slowly bangs his forehead against the wall.

"Hey, stop that. You'll break your crown. What are you doing?"

"Ugh, I feel like such a jerk. I'm so sorry, Eri. I never should've grabbed your wrist earlier or snapped at you."

"We both made mistakes," I say quietly. "You're also right. We have no chance if we don't try to trust each other. I guess over time, we'll figure each other out."

A spark flickers between torture and hunger in his blue eyes. Excruciating seconds tick by as I battle my desire to kiss him with every part of me.

"I bet"—a smirk lightens his face—"your smile reaches your eyes, doesn't it? I can picture it now."

"You're blind, Axton."

"There's more than one way to see, Angelfish."

A pounding comes from the other side of the door and I jump so fast, my foot slips. My towel drops, and I collide straight into Axton's bare chest. Again. Boobs straight against pecs. Axton's eyes widen and I push off him, scrambling for my towel again.

"Th-that didn't happen." I wrap the fabric around my chest. "D-didn't happen."

"Hurry up. I gotta piss!" Trey hollers.

"Go in the ocean!" Axton yells back.

I don't even hold in a laugh and the pounding suddenly stops.

"Holy Abyss!" Trey's shock registers through the door. "She's in there with *you*? You know she fucked my best friend too? Yeah, he still has pictures of you on his Taj."

Axton mimes a puppet with one hand, mocking Trey's outburst. Wow, he doesn't care about my past, even lies. I laugh but cover my mouth to silence myself.

"It's your turn to shower." With shoulders pulled back, I open the door and approach Trey, whose face is blaring red.

Looking directly into his dirty brown eyes, I leave the bathroom door open behind me and whisper in his ear. "His dagger is twice as big as yours."

Trey's veins bulge in his neck, but he still can't help but glance at Axton's body in the doorway on full display.

As I march past him to find clothes, Trey tugs my wrist and hisses, "That piece of shit won't live to see tomorrow's sunsrise."

I pull away. "If you even think about *touching* Axton—"

Trey sneers, "You'll what?"

What would Trey be afraid of? Anything out of his control. I immediately think of the last page of spells in my backpack.

"I happen to know a magical spell that would send you running," I say.

"Bullshit."

"Fine, test me and see what happen, but if I were you, I'd watch your back."

I begin to wonder why I'm so determined to protect the merman.

CHAPTER 16

Axton

Nightmares plagued me all last night. Swirling vortexes in the sky had sucked me into the Abyss for eternity. I might be losing my mind. My first days of blindness had been a battle between overwhelming confusion and raw adrenaline. Every day since I've been slipping further from rational thought. It's impossible to live in a world of darkness after swimming amid the beauty of the reefs every day. I can't do this anymore.

I stand at the bow of the yacht, gripping the railing, completely helpless. Wind tussles my hair, shorter on one side after I chopped a chunk to make Eribelle that paintbrush. If only I had the chance to see her face when I gave it to her. So far, my inkling that Eri knows the secret we keep in the castle has been squashed by an intense need to protect her. Yes, I may be a terrible soldier to not investigate further to determine how big of a threat she is, but it's a necessity at this point. Eri can't stay among these terrible men. Her cousin isn't half bad, but the other two are rotten at their core. And I still have no way of giving her gills, so the only option seems to be to help her travel to Ozaron like she had originally planned. My worries must be cast aside.

Chaos sways on unsteady paws next to me and pushes her body weight against my leg for support. The poor dog was not made for the sea.

"Want a drink?" Jordan speaks to my right, drenched in heavy cologne. Since our bathroom incident yesterday, he hasn't spoken a word to me until now.

"No." My knuckles clutch the railing tighter. Seagulls call above as we speed along and mist sprays my cheeks. "Where's Eribelle?"

"She's taking a nap." A long pause makes me wonder if Jordan had slipped away, but then he speaks again, "You're kind of…intense…aren't ya?" After he slurps his drink, I can feel his penetrating glare.

Maybe Hat-Boy isn't the guy I need to worry about. Every gut instinct is screaming at me to punch Jordan in the face, but Eribelle has sworn he's harmless. If that's true, why did he make this trip with her cousin and ex? The group dynamic doesn't make any sense.

"Aspen, can I be frank?" he asks. The sound of his slurping on his beer is like a stingray to the ear canal. Without a response from me, he barrels on. "Mister Erickson and I already have everything planned out. You're probably a…great guy, but a career in marketing simply won't give Eribelle what she wants. She's a woman who deserves the finer things in life."

"Well, the woman I know used a rusted fork to comb her hair when we were on that island and didn't complain."

His hand clamps my shoulder. "Anyone would break like that to survive."

I shrug his hand off me. "You're wasting your breath, Justin. She and I are just friends, but take my advice, she doesn't want to marry you."

Turning on my heels, I walk to Eri's cabin. There's no time for naps when Lena's life is still on the line. I'm probably moving further and further away from my best friend at each passing moment.

Chaos rushes ahead, but when I pass the cockpit, Brooks calls out and snaps their fingers at me. "Yoohoo, Axton, come here for a minute."

Seriously? Snapping? All these morons need to take a sensitivity class for the vision impaired. If I don't get off this damn yacht soon, I'll jump overboard.

"Axton!" they shout. "Did you hear me?"

"What do you want?" My heartbeat quickens and my blood boils.

"Give me the scoop on you and my little cuz. Are you into her?" They pat something soft, maybe a cushion or pillow. "What did you do to Eribelle on that island?"

"Excuse me?"

"The way she looks at you…it's not normal for her."

Somehow, the pounding against my ribs intensifies. "I wouldn't know, remember? I can't see." I gesture to my eyes.

Brooks pats my arm like I'm a dolphin under their control. At least I'm wearing clothes this time, even if the borrowed shirt is too small to button closed in the front.

"You don't want to know how she looks at you?" Brooks asks.

"I'm not sure why it matters."

Lies. But there's no point in acting like I care if she seems attracted to me. We have no possible future together. After we figure out this mess and I drop her off at Ozaron's coast, I'll never see her again.

"Guilt," her cousin says, making me hold my breath. "She feels guilty. So whatever happened between you two, you need to leave it in the past. She has shame painted all over her face when you're around."

That was the last thing I expected Brooks to say. Slowly, I nod. "There's nothing for you to worry about."

"That's a relief. I wouldn't want to make things awkward, since she'll be going away for a while."

Just as I'm about to move over the threshold of the doorframe, I stop. "What do you mean?"

"There's been a crazy increase in the amount of humans captured off the beaches. Uncle Finley is upset that Eribelle was so reckless during this dangerous time, so when we get back to the harbor, Jordan plans to take her to a secluded cottage far inland."

My grip could crack the edge of the doorframe. "Does she know about this?"

Brooks sighs. "Listen, Ax, can I call you Ax? My cousin is a sweetheart, and I'm on her side, but my uncle is powerful. I love her with all my heart, but occasionally I'm secretly grateful that my uncle has made some choices for her benefit."

"I see."

They laugh. "Oh, good joke, man, because you're blind. I get it. So, how did you lose your sight, anyways?"

"Um, I need to take a piss."

"Wait, one sec. I wanted to ask, because you used to represent merfolk, do you have any connections to them still?"

My arm hairs raise on end.

"I heard Jordan and Trey chatting last night. They think we should start fighting back against the sea folk."

I need off.

Off this boat. Off. This. Boat.

"Whoa, you don't look too good. What's wrong?" Brooks asks.

I need to play along—for now. I steady myself against the wall and fight against the piercing stabs in my temples. "Yeah, I'm colleagues with about five mermen. Are you asking me to lure them somewhere?"

"No! Dude, I was trying to warn you," Brooks whispers but their voice has a crisp edge of urgency. "If you have contacts Below you need to get them a message to stay away from the surface. All of them. Something big is going to happen. I can feel it."

"So, you don't agree with Jordan and Hat-Boy, then?"

"Is that Trey's new name? Sure, if I could throw Trey to the sharks, I would, but Jordan is a good guy. I think he's just afraid of the merfolk." The boat rocks and jolts from waves and I bump into the wall. "Alright, well I won't keep your bladder any longer."

I walk away aimlessly. A hollow sensation rips out my soul and yanks my spirit straight through my throat. It's all too much, but maybe I can break it down into small tasks. If I complete one piece of the puzzle at a time, everything will be okay. I swallow, trying to rid the tightness of my chest.

"Are you going to knock?" Eribelle's voice projects through a wall and I startle. "I can see your shadow under the door."

The door swings open and her hand wraps around my wrist. Eri tugs me inside and I stumble over the corner of a rug. With the unexpected momentum, I fall into her and we both land flat on something soft. I feel around. A blanket. A pillow. I have her pinned to her bed.

What if…?

What if I kissed her? Would she kiss me back? What does her face look like right now?

Slowly, I brush my thumb over her jawline. A strand of hair sticks to her lips, so I tuck it behind her ear. I'd give up all my hearing and taste and smell to know what her face looks like right now.

"I need to confess something." Eri scoots out from under me. "I feel so guilty."

My heart stops. Guilt and shame. Was Brooks right?

"I know you told me not to, but I kept your dagger. I know I'm stupid because you said that gang hunted you because of the tracker. You told me to leave it behind. I should've listened."

"No, it's okay, this is actually brilliant." I sit on her bed, making sure there's space between us.

"It is?"

"Lena also has access to it. Once we switch the tracker back on, if she's safe, she'll come to me."

"You mean *this* switch?" When our skin touches, an energy pulses through my veins. "This one here?"

"Yes, can you turn it on?"

"I already did this morning. I'm sorry, I should've asked first."

My heart sinks. If Lena has had my location for hours and hasn't reached me, she's probably caged somewhere.

"You seem angry." Her soft voice gives me goosebumps.

"No, Eri." I sigh. "But tell me, is that why you've been feeling guilty?"

"Yeah, ever since we boarded yesterday. It's why I avoided you during breakfast."

What Brooks said makes sense now. Relief swarms through me that she doesn't regret our time together, but that she stole the dagger without telling me. I proceed with caution, not certain I want to know the answer. If Eri does know about the Queen's secret, I have to warn the RMGs.

"Is there anything else you're keeping from me?" I ask. "Now would be a great time to bring it up."

Chaos jumps on the bed between us and her nose tickles my knee.

Eribelle pauses for only a moment, then answers. "No."

Then why does she pull her hand off my leg?

"Can I ask you something? And I'll promise to trust your answer," she asks.

Her hair smells like sunshine on a summer day. I go rigid, terrified by the realization that I never want to let go. It doesn't take sight to know how close her lips are to mine. I barely allow myself to breathe.

"Ask me anything," I say.

Please, goddess, let her ask to kiss me. What does her tongue taste like? Will she run her hand up my chest? Does she like to grab hair? I want to feel her moan into my mouth and press against me for more.

I hold my breath in anticipation of the question on the tip of her tongue.

"Why did you choose to be a guard over learning your magic?" she asks.

CHAPTER 17

Eribelle

I don't think Axton heard me so I ask again, "Why did you choose to be a guard if you have magic?"

Hands outstretched, Axton paws at the air until he reaches the chair next to me. He scoots it closer and sits, so our knees are almost touching. Does he know how close we are? Can he hear my heart thumping wildly? Does he also feel that electric spark flowing through the room? There must be a fine line between hatred and—whatever this feeling is.

"I need to protect people, Eri. I failed at keeping my parents safe. After their deaths, I vowed that I'd make it up to them by keeping merfolk safe. It's an honorable job."

He and I aren't too different. We were both so young when we each lost someone so close.

"It wasn't your fault, Axton. You were only a kid. No one expects someone so young to—"

"I could've done something to save my parents. Anything. But in that moment, I froze. For just those few seconds of hesitation, when fear gripped me with its sharp claws, I didn't know what to do. That's why plans are necessary. We all need rules and procedures to follow because that way we can prevent situations like that in the future. If there's a protocol for how to handle a crisis, then fewer people will die."

Unsure what to say, I move closer. "Why don't you use magic to protect others?"

"Our magic is dark and complicated." His long sigh almost tells me everything I need to know. "It's not my path. Someone out there will be Ulsa's apprentice, but it's not me." He gets comfortable and settles into the cushion. "I guess it's my turn since we're asking questions. Where do you wish you were right now?"

"Somewhere I could paint the ocean. You?"

I'd never try to touch up the small imperfections of the smile that rises on his face as he says, "In bed."

"Oh."

"No, not like that." Axton laughs. "If I'm not working, I like to keep to myself." He licks his lips again. Why did he have to do it again? What would they feel like to kiss? Not that I want to.

In desperate need of a distraction, I swipe up a pen and paper from the nightstand and start doodling. After a few marks and swirls, it resembles the nasty tree nymph that threatened us. I bet nymphs live forever. If I hadn't been so terrified, I could've asked a dozen questions.

"Okay, since we're swapping tidbits, I've got a good one. If I could stay one age forever, I'd choose either ten because I'd have my brother forever or whatever age I'll be when I die."

"Really? Why?"

"Well, let's say I'm seventy-one when I die. If I stay that age, then I'll already know everything I'll ever learn but never have to die."

Axton props his elbows on his knees and leans even closer. "You don't think you'll have any regrets when you're seventy-one?"

"Naw, and even if I do, then I'd have eternity to process them."

He nods slowly, but a tightness stays on his forehead. "What if you're left all alone when you're seventy-one and all those you've loved have already left you?"

"That's what puppies are for!"

I move toward him, able to spot the intricate pattern of shapes in his blue eyes. Goddess, I wish he could see me. Right now, it's like he's staring right through me, like I'm a ghost and this isn't even real. He's not choosing to take this trip because he enjoys my company. Axton is forced to work with me.

"Your turn." I start, "What age would *you* stay forever?"

"Thirty." He leans forward, a sparkle in his eyes.

"Next year?"

"Yeah."

I pause. "Why?"

"Wait and see."

My heart rate triples and every part of me longs to touch him, but a loud thumping pounds to my left.

"Oh my goddess!" I jump up, making the chair legs screech. "There's a mermaid at the window, she's waving!"

Axton rises fast and shields me behind him. "What does she look like?"

A striking mermaid with dark brown skin and long black braids swims outside. Her fangs sparkle like diamonds when she smiles and waves, but when Axton doesn't return the gesture her frown proves to be as devastating as her grin. I try to move around him, but Axton's strong arm holds me back.

"What are you doing?" I dodge around him and rush to the window. I place my hand on the glass, but the mermaid's eyes flicker between Axton and me, appearing to reassess the situation.

"What does she look like?" Axton asks.

I'd paint that quick smile first, the only part of her speckled in warmth. The rest of her is carved of sharp edges and corners. "Um, she has teacup-pink flowers twisted into her braid and the seashells on her top are a mosaic of dosinias and scallops.

"It's Lena." He starts to pace, his head dropped in both hands.

I glance between the two friends, wondering why Axton isn't acting overjoyed that she's safe. If it were Sampson, I'd be over the moon right now. Lena's lips move, but I can't hear anything through the glass.

I gesture to Lena through the window, pointing to my eyes, then at Axton, back to my eyes, then to Axton.

"He's blind." I cover my hand over my eyes.

Her lips form, '*What?*' as she continues to match the boat's pace through the waters.

Groaning, I march to Axton and drag him to the window.

"Hey," he mumbles but doesn't resist.

I yank his face low to the window, then cover his eyes and make a dramatic sad face.

Understanding shocks Lena's face. She holds up one finger as a gesture to wait, and then she disappears.

"We're here!" Brooks yells from the cockpit. "Coendriel is straight ahead."

"No, we can't be this close to land. Lena can't be in the shallows." He kneels by the window and points frantically to no one while exaggerating his words. "Go, leave me. Go."

"Um, she left already," I say.

"Are you sure?"

"Lena isn't at the window anymore."

Axton rubs his chin and rises to his feet. His energy makes me nervous, but I can't help myself and wrap one hand halfway around his bicep. Every part of me wants to ease the tension coiled in his body.

"Hey, it's okay, she's safe. What's wrong?"

"Nothing. Let's grab our stuff so we can talk to your father right away. I don't want this to take longer than it has to." When Axton backs away, the bits of hope of a friendship between us that had started to form split and scatter along the floor. It's confusing. Just when I expect that our relationship is blossoming, things seem to fall apart again without explanation. Having such a roller coaster uncertainty isn't something I'm used to, regardless of how much potential for passion could be weaved in between the ups and down.

In a daze, I walk to the room and gather the few things I don't want to leave behind: the last paper of ancient symbols, the paintbrush Axton created, and of course, Chaos.

"Come on, girl." Her head pops off her paws at the same time as her tail wags. "Maybe you can chase his grumpiness away."

The boat jerks into a sand bank and Chaos rams into my shin. A slow beat of a drum thrums, then a sinful chord from a bass guitar hums from outside.

"What's that?" Axton calls from down the hall.

"I don't know."

Quickly, I stuff my feet into a pair of boots that Brooks had kindly brought along. The fact that Sampson designed them specifically for me isn't something I need to linger on right now. The drumming intensifies, both in speed and volume, and then music joins along. Why the Abyss does it sound like there's a band playing on the docks? I rush after Chaos and Axton up the stairway. Sunlight kisses my skin and I shade my eyes with my hands. An explosion of cheers erupts from a crowd, but all I can see are rays of sun.

"And thanks to Jordan Idros, my daughter has been saved from the wretched merfolk!" My father's voice booms from a microphone. "Thanks to this strong man right here!"

No, merfolk hadn't attacked me. Why is Dad saying that?

Axton joins my side, with an intense energy that could rival a shark. His height blocks the sun so I can see better. Mountain tops dipped in gold tower behind our white limestone mansion. Our estate is the first thing sailors view when docking, set on the edge of a sharp cliff-face, limiting land entry to the main gate unless someone scales straight down the cliffside.

A mass of citizens are huddled on the beach, bubbled by fluttering masts, black as night, behind them. Brooks and Trey stand by my father's side while Jordan, Axton, and I stay on the pier. Chaos barks at a balloon, chasing after it and banners flutter in the breeze, all custom-made with '*Congrats*' scrawled in cursive.

I don't understand. If Dad was searching for me, how was there time to plan a party, invite all these people, order the drinks over on that table, and hire a band? Dad always means the best, but something doesn't add up. I find myself wanting to hide—with Axton. At the moment, he's the only thing that feels safe.

Behind my back, Axton's fingertips skim the inside of my wrist. The thundering in my chest accelerates faster than the drumming of the musician. Is this entangled web of thrilled sensations what passion feels like? The incessant need to be by his side, to argue over who has the quicker wit, and an endless longing to hold his hand? No, I can't have feelings for him; it's too soon, too fast, too impossible. Déjà vu wracks my body. The last time I was here was for Dad's auction festival, with a similar setup. Now that I'm back, the harbor looks almost identical, but nothing here is the same.

"And as if it wasn't enough for Jordan to rescue my daughter, he gave me an even greater gift!" Dad says.

I plead silently for my father to make eye contact. If I rush to the stage, maybe I can stop him in time, but there are too many people between us. Instead, Jordan drops to one knee next to me. "Jordan has offered a lifetime with my Eribelle! My friends, meet the newest engaged couple of Erickson Harbor!"

Immediately, Jordan pushes an emerald ring on my finger, right next to my mother's band. He starts to say something, but I can't hear him over the applause and roar of the crowd. Words don't form. Thoughts cease to exist and my body is frozen. My mouth hangs open as Jordan stands and raises our linked hands into the air.

"She's speechless!" My father smiles from afar, finally catching my eye.

Axton clears his throat and I turn. His deep blue eyes swirl with an emotion I can't describe.

Someone in the crowd gasps and points. "That man is wearing a crown of the guard!"

Soft murmurs and whispers pass from ear to ear behind shielded hands. Before I can answer, the band starts to play louder for the few people who have started dancing.

Jordan tugs me away, leaving my merman standing on the

docks alone and blind. After weaving through bodies, we somehow end up in front of my father. When I meet his excited gaze, confusion washes over me. Dad moves in for a hug but I step back.

"How could you?" I spit out. "I don't want to be engaged!"

Dad wraps me in a hug anyway, ignoring me completely. "Daughter, explain that man and why he is wearing a guard's crown."

"That's the first thing you say to me?" I swivel, scanning over the heads of the dancers to find Axton. No blond bun sticks high above the group. My heart beats faster. What if he's lost? "Brooks, do you see Axton anywhere?"

The wrinkles of my father's forehead form deep crevices.

"Do you see him?" I even ask Jordan, who pulls in his lips tight.

I have to get out of here, away from these men who think they know what's best. None of them understand what I need.

"Eribelle, smile for the camera." A heavy hand pushes me into Jordan's chest and a bright light blinds me until I see spots.

Heart racing, I lurch away, consumed by the loud music. Chaos skips at my heels and almost trips me as I get turned around in a flurry of confusion. Suddenly, I smack straight into a wall—no a man. Axton. Thank all the goddesses. I bury my face in his chest and his hand cradles the back of my hair softly.

"Who are *you*?" Dad glares with disgust at Axton's towering form.

"This is Axton Wells," I start, "he's a marketing expert from Ozaron and the merfolk gave him the headpiece as an honorary gift for helping them. He's blind, so—"

Dad's posture loosens and he chuckles. "Oh, this makes

sense. You came to chat business." Then he tilts his head. "Wait, why is his arm around you, Eribelle?"

Axton tightens his grip but otherwise stays as still as a statue, silent, with a fierce look of murder in his eyes. I realize he's not going to answer for me.

"Because I want…Axton and I became…friends." I quickly pull the emerald ring off my finger.

Even though my body shakes wildly, it doesn't matter what Dad says or does next because I am finally standing up against him and I'm not backing down.

Shock barely settles on his face before Dad pushes it away and disguises himself with his familiar mask again. He glances at our joined hips, then slaps his knee with another laugh. "I get it. You can stop the act now, boy. It's surprising that you tagged along with her on those waters for so long when you can't even see her beauty. You must really want a meeting with me."

His words are like whiplash. Of course, Dad assumes I don't deserve true affection from a man other than for my looks. How could I think otherwise? I might have staggered if Axton wasn't holding me as tightly as he is.

A growl vibrates through Axton's chest and up his throat. Instead of letting the hot tears fall from behind my lids, I don't give Dad the satisfaction. This encounter needs to end.

"Dad, have you ever met a tree nymph?" I ask quickly.

"What, sweetie?" He looks off at the crowd. "That's the craziest thing you've ever asked me."

"So, you don't know Viera and Drei?"

"Oh, those two? Yeah, I met, um, waitresses with those names at an investor event last year," Dad says, without meeting my eye.

"Well, your harmless friends mentioned that they found the *key*."

One of Dad's eyebrows reaches the suns. "I…um…don't

know what you're talking about. The key, though? They found it?"

I don't deserve these blatant lies. It's my turn to call the shots. Dad is obviously linked to the nymphs in some way, but that doesn't mean I need to get caught up in this mess. It's not my responsibility to help him out of whatever issues he created.

"If you want me to marry Jordan, then listen to me very carefully. Within the next hour, you will contact whoever you know to get a message to Queen Rayna that I need to meet with her on the docks tomorrow."

Dad starts to protest but I put one finger to his lips and continue, "Do it. You clearly have your ways. If you make that meeting happen, you have my word that I'll marry Jordan. Is this understood?"

He nods and for a moment I try to decipher the foreign expression on his face. Could it be pride? I shouldn't care. This place and these people are no longer my home. After tomorrow's meeting, I'll be one step closer to freedom because there's no chance I'll ever marry Jordan.

Done with this nonsense, I scan the area for Chaos and see her wrapped up by four little kids in a huddle, satisfied and safe. I pull Axton away from the crowd. "Will you come with me somewhere?"

The corner of Axton's lip quirks up. "Lead the way, and thank you, Eri. I bet that was hard for you."

I huff, acting like his gratitude doesn't affect me whatsoever. "Do you need a stick or rope to hold onto again?"

This time he smiles for real. "Are you asking permission to hold my hand, Angelfish?"

"That isn't what I said."

"I'd be honored if you'd like to hold my hand. In fact, it's not the worst hand I've held."

"Axton, you little deviant! You've held another hand? How scandalous!"

I zig-zag him through a pack of hipsters all hypnotized by their Tajs. Roses speckle the vines that swoop and hang like cursive letters from the rooftops. Half the college girls and one boy glance up and scan Axton from top to bottom as we pass. A shot of pure jealousy floods through me. Does he know how many people gawk at him as he walks these streets? Doubtful, since he's never walked any street until now.

"Well, no other hands I've held have been as dry as yours," he teases me, "that's for sure."

"Wow, what a compliment."

"I'll get you some pendouler for your birthday."

"I'll just pretend I know what that means." I laugh. "But you don't know my birthday."

"I could ask someone about your birthday. I have quite a group to pick from." Axton trips on a curb when I forget to tell him to step onto the sidewalk. "Should I start with asking your ex, the unhinged guy who wants to kill me in my sleep?"

"Actually I wouldn't mind if he becomes a missing person."

"Noted." Axton squeezes my hand. "But why should I pick Trey when I can interrogate your Partner about his plans for your birthday and then steal all his ideas."

"Believe me, I won't like anything my *non-Partner* picks."

"Okay, well that leaves me with Mr. Finley Erickson, the oblivious father who might not even remember your birthday."

"Wow, you're good at this. Last year Dad *did* forget it."

Shadows swallow a string of roses on the stone buildings as we duck into an alleyway.

"Oh wait, let me guess," Axton pants while hiking up the

next hill, struggling with his words. "Your dad probably paid Sampson to buy you a dress last year."

"No, that would mean Dad knew Sampson was my best friend." I sigh from the painful reminder.

He squeezes my hand hard and pulls me closer to his side in silent understanding.

Warmth flows through me at the gesture, small but significant. "Last year, Dad had Brooks pick out a birthday card and put some money in there."

"Hmm, and did the card have a dancing seahorse on the front, dressed for a tea party? Your dad definitely sees you as a tea party girl."

The music of my ridiculous Commitment party fades into a buzz as I lead Axton through the busy shopping center. Chocolate-dipped pretzels are displayed near a liquid dessert fountain outside a bakery. A cart full of sugar-glazed cinnamon rolls whispers my name as we saunter by and sandwiches made from divine cheeses from the deli next door practically wave hello. Across the court, a street performer plucks on a banjo while children chase each other. As they run, a flock of ravens flies and settles on a roof.

"Your city is intriguing. That song is so upbeat and the children's laughter and birds chirping are all so…"

"Magical?"

"Exactly."

"I used to think the same thing. Now, I just want to leave."

We walk by a sign covering the side of a brick building:

Register here for next year's competition

BEWARE THE MERFOLK

Discounted pearls at 256 Jade Avenue

Elite landscape carpenter for hire

Since I'll be leaving this town for good, I want to visit my favorite place once more and share it with Axton. We need to weave through town before the sunset market begins. Erickson is famous for its steep, narrow hills and cracked, winding paths meant for walkers and bikers. Stone bridges curve in front of apartment complexes and disappear behind offices. The unique mix of modern architecture with the old draws tourists here from all surrounding islands. Only Sampson and I know of the secret spot I lead Axton toward —but Sampson won't ever visit it again. Another sudden sharpness clenches in my chest.

With a blind man as my responsibility, I have to be the eyes for two. With each step, the suns set on Erickson Harbor behind us and we go downhill again. Nestled in a valley, my favorite spot hides under a weeping willow. Hopefully, Axton will still like it without being able to see the beauty.

"Oh, Eri, my boots…they're sinking."

"Yeah, maybe we should've taken off our shoes. Move slowly. I wish you could see it. In this swampy area, crocodiles don't differentiate between types of meat, human or not, but don't worry, they're all asleep." I suck in the flowery scent. "Oh, and over there are hundreds of firefly lights flickering. You may want to keep your hands up to swipe the drooping branches of the willow out of the way while I guide you through."

"I feel like I can see it all," Axton says softly. "You just painted the scene for me."

I stare at him, and it feels like something drastic just shifted in the universe.

"Are those bullfrogs croaking?"

He's right. Percussions, strings, and wind instruments are mimicked by the lagoon's plant life, like a song of dusk plays around us.

"Okay, let's keep moving. Go a little left, no more left."

His boot splashes into a puddle and he laughs. "This is a literal challenge of trust, Angelfish."

I nudge his boot over a bit onto a boulder. "There's a rock there, yup, okay, now balance."

"Don't tell me we're going cliff diving." His smile tells an epic story, plotted with a heartbreak at the end.

"Okay, now sit here."

"Are you going to push me over an edge?" Axton's hand gropes for something sturdy, but his body is at ease—trusting me. "Is this payback for not getting you the right ketchup flavor?"

I snort and laugh, a semi-painful combination.

Swampy water surrounds our boulder like we're stuck on a mini island again, but this time, instead of feeling trapped, I welcome the sensation of having Axton all to myself. Ahead, flamingos stand on one leg like sculptures. I'd paint their long legs first in long, clean lines.

Lily pads spot the terrain and reeds shoot up. The navy shade that teeters between evening and night lingers in the air. I suck in the scent of the willow and memories flash back from childhood with my brother.

"My brother was the one who first showed me this place."

With one hand, Axton slowly brings my head to his shoulder, offering himself as a place to rest, a place for comfort, to feel safe.

"I'm glad he did. It's beautiful," he says and I watch his face light with curiosity.

"How can you tell this place is beautiful when I haven't described it to you yet?"

"You don't have to see to know when something's special, Eri."

I examine him again, for the hundredth time. Each hour spent with this man gives me more pieces to a complicated puzzle, but I want to invest the time needed to solve him. I need to know him from the inside out. A strange compulsion to ignore everything that has ever made me doubt him overwhelms me. My worries fade away and the desire to investigate what makes Axton tick overrides everything else. I wonder what it'd be like to live in the sea with him.

"Axton?"

"Yes, Angelfish?"

"If I were blind, do you think I'd see you the same way?"

"That's easy. Close your eyes, but be careful that you don't bump into my headpiece."

I do as he says. Darkness takes over but the crickets still chirp and an owl hoots far off.

"What do you see?" he lays one hand on mine.

"Nothing." I bite my lip. "Axton, I…"

He takes my hand and brings it to his chest. Under the thin button-up shirt, sprayed damp from mist, his hard chest protects a wildly beating heart. A tingle sizzles all over my body, but I don't dare move. What does his lower stomach feel like? My pulse races, making me lightheaded.

"It's okay, Eri, tell me."

Eyes closed, I shift closer, grazing my other hand behind his neck, making Axton suck in a breath. Little wisps of his thick hair that didn't reach his bun tickle my wrist.

Slowly, I straddle him, desperate to open my eyes to read his reaction, but instead, clench them shut tighter. I'm pretty sure he's not breathing. Axton's hands barely touch my waist.

I lean forward, and whisper into his ear, "If you're not a liar, hypocrite, and overall villain, then I see a man who respects women."

I can hear his strained swallow and it makes my heart cartwheel. Is he enjoying this as much as I am? My lips brush the outer rim of his ear, and I whisper again, "If you aren't my arch nemesis, then I see a man with outrageous self-control and the urge to protect those in need."

His hands tighten on my waist.

"If you've told me anything true, then I see a loyal man who swears to defend." I kiss the sexy scruff on the side of his cheek.

Axton's sudden breath blows onto my neck. "Eri…I…" His voice is low, so low.

"Quiet, I'm not done yet."

A soft rumble vibrates from his throat and he shifts slightly, teasing me with his hardness buried under too many layers. Even though my arms tremble slightly, I let my mouth slowly trail his jaw and land at his square chin. "I see a man who sacrifices his comfort for a stranger, even if it's all for show."

Fighting against every urge to open my eyes and check his expression, I hover my lips over his. His hands on my waist move to my lower back. If I kiss him, it'll change everything. He'll no longer be the man who survived an island adventure with me, but the man who accepted a part of my heart and tucked it away. For now, he's here and mine. I need to take advantage of this time.

Before I can decide what to do, Axton commands, "Don't you dare open your eyes, Eri."

Gently, he presses his lips to mine. They're softer than I imagined but he kisses firmly, in charge. Even though I straddle him, he could flip me under him in one motion which sends heat rushing between my thighs. The connection between us outdoes any other I've experienced. A desperate craving for him starts deep in my belly and lowers to a place I shouldn't be thinking about. His tongue darts out and plays with mine. How is this feeling possible? I want to try all his types of kisses, even if it takes me a lifetime.

He pulls me in tighter, closer, as if we're one body and a

need to touch him everywhere overcomes me. My inner thighs tingle, which is when I notice his fingertips grazing my skin. I ache for him to do more, touch more, feel more, kiss more.

"Oh," I moan into his mouth, "Axton—"

Saying his name only intensifies his response. Like a caged animal, he grunts loudly and cups the back of my head. The other hand drops to my ass like he's about to do…'the *move*.' The move I used to giggle about as a teenager.

In one swoop, Axton lifts me, flips me on my back, placing me below him—in the most pristine view—if only I was allowed to open my eyes.

"Axton, please, can I look at you?"

"Beauty isn't always about"—he kisses my shoulder—"what you can see"—he kisses to my neck and lowers the strap of my tank top to fall over my shoulder.

"Please. I want to see you," I whisper.

He groans into my skin, pinning me with his body weight. "If you must…"

I push his chest up and devour the sight of him on top of me. No painting would be this divine. Soft light from early moonbeams glows on his skin and every muscle seems flexed. Half of his messy hair has fallen from his bun and frames his face. As if he knows how much I want to memorize this view, Axton slowly opens his eyes. The blues that have the power to sink ships and create typhoons within my heart glitter with challenge.

I separate my legs further and a hunger grips his famished gaze. A slow smile builds on his face as if he knows how much I'm burning for him. Axton's hands caress my skin where my shirt meets my shorts. He dares me to follow his rhythmic fingers that form circles around my belly button. I arch my back and that fierceness in his eyes looks ready to snap in half. I want to tear off his shirt. Touch him. Possess him. His mouth becomes my master, brushing strokes I never knew existed.

"Axton…"

"Wait," his voice shifts, "I can guess what you're about to say, but give me two more minutes."

"Axton…"

CHAPTER 18

Axton

Eribelle tastes exactly how I imagined. Like coconut punch. The velvety softness of her skin under my palm couldn't be smoother. My pulse is on overdrive as we kiss again. And again. Fuck, she's intoxicating. It's like her tongue is seduction herself tied into a knot of silk. How have I waited this long to kiss her? Hopefully, this won't become a fleeting memory, piled with a stack of others. I want to savor every second I have with Eri and store it in a time capsule.

"Axton..." The reluctant tone in her voice feels like a wrecking ball to my chest. I know she's about to put this on pause.

It takes every ounce of strength to pull away from her. Goddess, I wish I could see her face right now. Are her lips swollen? Is there a pink flush to her cheeks? Are her pupils dilated? I need to capture these little details to know if that kiss meant as much to her as it did to me.

Sounds of the lagoon swarm the evening air as frogs croak in harmony with a soft hum of fireflies. The rustling of the weeping willow branches sing a devastating farewell tune. Why do all good things need to end? All I want is to get lost so deep in her soul that nothing else matters. Slowly, Eribelle scoots out from underneath me.

"Shit, I'm sorry, Eri, I shouldn't have—"

"Please don't apologize. That'll make it worse."

Worse? Great, she already views this as a negative experience.

"That kiss was," her voice lowers, "better than good. If you were human then we could try whatever this is, but I won't attach myself to someone who is leaving." Her voice softens. "I know how badly you want to return to the sea."

My head drops. Of course, she's right. We belong in two separate worlds. There's not much else to say. Sitting next to me on the boulder, her finger slides back and forth over my wrist. Does she understand that even the simplicity of that touch demolishes me?

I need her to stop massaging my damn wrist if I have any chance at controlling my body. Flipping her hand over, I lace her fingers with mine. They feel so small and delicate. These precious five fingers hold her skill of painting and this beautiful woman trusts me to protect them. I want to kiss the tip of each of her ten fingers, but I let out a sigh instead.

Eribelle's entire journey began with a dream to start a new life. I may not gain my sight back, or my tail, or ever see the depths of the sea again, but I can help Eri accomplish her dream.

"Hey, Angelfish. I'm changing our deal. Even if the Queen refuses to meet us, you did your part, so I'll still help you travel to Ozaron, no matter what tomorrow brings."

I feel her bury her head in her hands. "Ugh, he'll find me anyways. Dad will track me no matter where I go and drag me back home."

Unsure of what to say to that, I caress her wrist in slow circles, hoping she's wrong. We sit together as the lagoon's sounds overtake the atmosphere again. At some point, Eri rests her head on my shoulder. This woman will be the end of me. All I want to do is kiss her again, but she's not on the same page. This was a mistake because now I'll compare every kiss of my future to hers, and none will measure up.

Distant crashing water snaps me back into the moment.

"What's that sound?" I ask.

"An owl?"

"No, far away, water is rushing into water."

"Oh, *that*, Mister Axton, would be a waterfall." Her voice perks up.

"What is its purpose?"

"Um, well, when water starts from a high mountain or cliff, it streams down and sometimes barrels over the edge, landing in a pond or lake."

"Sounds like something I'd like to see…or I guess, experience." I clear my throat. "So your brother brought you here? Tell me about him."

She stays silent, and I'd wait years next to Eri's side until she's ready to speak.

"My brother was a romantic, like me, always dreaming of fantastical ideas." There's a whimsical tone to her voice that I try to savor. "Instead of painting like me, he wanted to be an architect. I remember all the notebooks spread on the floor of his room, covered in his sketches of different designs. There was this one he was so proud of—a building in the shape of a bubble, with the entire exterior made of glass. From the inside, viewers would look through clear floor-to-ceiling windows but because of the tint of the material, people on the outside would see a reflective blue."

My whole body freezes after hearing that description.

"What's wrong? Did a bug bite you?" she asks.

"No, it's nothing," I say wearily, tired of lying to her.

Except it is something. We have a similar building in Nerida. It was finished three years ago.

"My brother was eight years older than me. So, we didn't play much together, and my memories of him are already fleeting since he died when I was so young." A loud sigh rushes out of her. "But we joked around a lot. Actually, I always gave him a hard time for coming home late. I'm pretty sure he had a secret girlfriend or boyfriend he would meet at night. I wonder if I met them at his funeral without knowing it. Ben was one of those guys who would've loved with all his heart."

The palm supporting my weight gives away and I collapse to the side, almost rolling off the boulder.

"Whoa! You okay?"

I'm at a loss for words. I shake my head to clear the scrambled thoughts. "I think I misheard you. What was his name?"

"Ben."

"Fuck." I stand fast, feeling Eribelle slip on the boulder below me.

"What is it? You're scaring me, Axton. Your eyes are bulging."

"I need to move…need to walk…this can't be right." I step off the boulder and my boot immediately sinks into the mud pit of the swamp.

"Axton! Wait!"

I stumble forward, but with each step, I sink further until

my feet are completely stuck. The marsh tightens its hold on me and I can't pull my leg out.

"Tell me what's going on. Right. Now," Eribelle says to my left, hopefully safe on a boulder.

"His name is Ben? Are you sure?"

"Yes, I know my brother's name. Why?"

"You're not going to…there's no way to…I'm not sure how…"

"Just say it, Axton!"

My feet smoosh around in the mud. "About a decade ago, Her Royal Princess, Gia, became enamored with a nineteen-year-old boy. Against the queen's direct commands, she took him Below and convinced the Sea Witch to grant him the ability to live underwater for the remainder of his life. Permanently. As a head guard, I'm one of a handful of people that know of his existence. We've had to keep him hidden since Gia broke the treaty with the humans and if they ever found out, there'd be major repercussions. And his name happens to be—Ben."

A sharp slap stings my cheek and my neck twists to the side.

"That's not funny." Eribelle's voice trembles. "How could you make a joke about that?" She grows quieter as if walking away. "That's cruel."

"Come back, I'm not lying. Maybe it's a different Ben, but I can tell you what he looks like."

Only the whistles of the wind through the reeds respond. Did she leave me here? Maybe it's a good thing to process this revelation alone. Later, I can track her scent and we can figure out a plan for what to do next. Unless she never believes my story. I shouldn't have shouted it out without thinking first. Of course, she wouldn't believe me. That news would be equivalent to someone telling me my parents are still alive. She had said goodbye to her brother long ago and moved on. If I'm wrong then I've only dug up false hope.

"What does he look like?" Her unexpected whisper makes me jump.

"Well, he'd be twenty-nine now, not nineteen, so different from what you remember, but this Ben has thick, auburn hair, he's tall, but not as tall as me, so maybe six-foot-one? He wears glasses, is lean and athletic, and was born with one deformed ear."

She gasps and all I want to do is hug her when she whispers, "It's called microtia."

The sounds of her cries are too much to bear so I use all my strength to pop one foot at a time out of the mud and trudge over to her. Following her sniffles, I stop at her side. She's curled in a ball on the solid bank. Her arms are wrapped around her knees and I wish I could scoop her into my arms and remove her pain with a single touch.

"Is it him?" She rocks back and forth until I put one arm around her small frame, and pull her into my chest. "Can it be him? Is Ben alive? It's not possible, right? Ten years is so long. He could've gotten in touch with me? Or he would've escaped by now? Or…" She pushes my chest, but I tighten my hold, letting her punch me again and again. "How could you tell me this? What if it's not him? What if he's being tortured this whole time? What if he's trapped? What am I supposed to do now?"

Finally, her punches soften and her arms drop. She leans further into me and wetness coats the front of my shirt. I smooth her hair and kiss the top of her head.

"We'll figure it out together, but first, you need to sleep, Angelfish. It's getting late. Let's get you home."

Even though I probably shouldn't, I scoop her into my arms and she doesn't resist. It's like a part of her spirit has left her body entirely. I prepare myself for an incoming feminist speech, but surprisingly she curls into my chest. Her body is light in my arms as I start the long, slow walk. Left foot, right foot. Eribelle quietly gives me directions as we weave through the now quiet town. I had expected a human city to reek of trash after witnessing all the pollution and litter they dump into our sea, but the only thing I can smell is unfamiliar, enticing aromas.

So far, the human's destructive tendencies haven't been proven true—except for Trey. What did Eribelle ever see in that guy? Not to mention her outrageous Commitment plans. She and Jordan have nothing in common. The man is vapid, unaware of anything under the surface level. She'd be miserable having to talk to a boring wall of a man like him for the rest of her life.

If I'm stuck with these legs forever, would Eribelle consider dating me? I can't offer money, power, or connections like she's used to—or like her father wants—but I'd prioritize her safety and happiness above all others. Someone with such a vivid imagination deserves a canvas as large as the sea itself to paint her masterpieces. I shake my head, cursing myself for such selfish ideas when Eri is in shock from the news about her brother. Goddess, this is all such a mess. My mind feels like mush.

After a while, my body slows from exhaustion. She becomes heavier with each step. The party on the dock must've ended since I can't hear any crowds or music.

Suddenly, a scream pierces the night air, making Eribelle jerk in my arms. I nearly drop her to the street.

"What do you see?" I tense and sniff the air.

"Someone's over there, on the beach." She gasps. "A merman is dragging someone into the ocean!"

She shifts in my arms and accidentally bumps into my headpiece. Eribelle's pained scream scorches my eardrums. Her body starts shaking violently in my arms. I accidentally drop her and she lands with a thump on the pavement. Heart pounding, I crouch and hover over her body, terrified to touch her again.

"Are you okay?" I ask.

Silence.

I gently slide my hand up her side. "Eri?"

She's completely still. Fuck!

"Eribelle? Eribelle! Eribelle, wake up!"

"Hey, you there!" a familiar voice hollers ahead. "Back away from the girl!"

I recognize Jordan's voice and wave. "It's me…Axton. She needs help!"

Quick footsteps thump over and fabric sounds swoosh against each other. "What did you do to her?" Jordan's voice is spiked with fear.

"Nothing…I…"

"I need to get her to a healer." His voice already sounds farther away.

"Wait, I can't see to follow."

"Stay away from her," Jordan yells.

"Wait!"

His footsteps soften until I can't track which way he went fast enough. With my arms held straight ahead, I can only move so fast without bumping into the corners of buildings.

"Jordan?" I shout. "Jordan! Fuck!"

Why did she have to touch my headpiece? A strange sensation throbs from the gem. Why had Grams connected me to something so dangerous?

I sniff the air and try to track their scent. Nothing will stop me from finding Eri and making sure she is okay.

CHAPTER 19

Eribelle

I awake on a chaise in the middle of our foyer, the very same bed I used to scuff the hardwood floors with as a child. Someone changed me into my favorite outfit, a blue crop top with a flowy blue skirt made of the same flexible material. Sampson used to say that the outfit had been made of waves itself the way it curved and curled.

Above, tiny dust particles float in the bright light streaming in from the suns. I glance around, still in a sleepy daze. A new marble statue sits by the majestic fountain, no doubt on display for one of Dad's business partners. When I tilt my head to the side, the angle of the statue resembles Axton, or maybe he's infested my mind. The phantom sensation of his lips on me makes my toes curl. Wait, where's Axton?

I scan Dad's house, around the circular, open room that serves as our family's foyer for visitors. How did I get back home?

Brooks sits in a reading chair by one of the ten-foot-tall stained glass windows and flips to the next page. "Good morning, sunshine. Your hair looks like the love child of a crazed cat and a porcupine."

"Where's Axton?"

Brooks shrugs with dark circles under their eyes. "The man probably has work to do, deals to take care of."

I shudder at the thought of Axton wandering blindly through the streets. "He hasn't been here at all?" When I move to place my bare feet on the tile, they rub against Chaos' fur instead.

"Nope, did you expect him to?"

The last thing I remember is being carried in his arms. He wouldn't simply leave me. I trust Axton and no one else knows he's a merman with no experience on land or navigating my world. Did something happen to him? I can still feel the echo of his mouth on mine. If I act too concerned about his whereabouts, Brooks might involve Dad, which is the last thing I want. So, for now, I need to calmly gather myself and figure out how to find him. The last thing I remember is a merman dragging someone into the waters. Is that how they took Ben long ago? What if what Axton said about Ben is true? He might be my only link to returning my brother home.

The giant clock hanging like a chandelier from the middle of the room shows ten in the morning. Strange orbs of light hover near the ceiling and they slowly ping-pong off one another in a tantalizing dance. Those decorations weren't there last week. When I fixate on the swirling lights inside of them, a zap of sweet adrenaline tugs at my core as if a thin thread is pulling under my belly button.

I squint, wondering how they work. "Did Dad hire someone to redecorate?"

My cousin follows my gaze up. "Redecorate? What are you talking about? Did you hit your head last night?"

A strong pulse of energy shoots through my veins, reminding me of when I had touched Axton's crown.

I sit up fast. "I need to find Axton. Now."

"Sorry, Cuz, Uncle Fin wants me to make sure you rest until he's done with his meeting in an hour."

I rush across the sparkling floor and snatch the book from their hand. "This is important."

"Because you want to redecorate?" Brooks' annoying smirk rises on one cheek.

I slap their shoulder with the book.

"Ouch!" Brooks bolts upward. "Why are you so bitchy today? I stayed up all night to make sure you didn't have a concussion, and this is my payback?"

"We don't have time for this. Something weird happened last night."

"I know." They sigh, serious for once "A merman took Trey from the beach last night." Brooks eyes me and crosses their arms. "That's what your father is in a meeting about."

"Who is Dad meeting?"

"It's not my place to tell." Brooks avoids looking at me and swipes for the book.

Hiding it behind my back, I dodge their attempt. "Who is Dad meeting with?"

Brooks glances at the twenty-foot wooden door that leads outside.

I raise the book above my head. "Brooks! I'll knock you out right now if you don't tell—"

"Fine. He's meeting with Queen Rayna, at the docks, but no one else knows..."

This mansion itself steals the very breath from my lungs as I search for any reason why my dad would steal my meeting. "What? The Queen?"

"Eribelle, don't worry about it, it doesn't concern you and—"

"Shut up! Ben might be alive."

Their eyes double in size. "Who told you? How did you find out?"

The book falls from my hand and lands on the floor with such a loud thump that Chaos jumps to her feet. Her bark echoes off the fountain and statue.

"Excuse me? You KNEW?" I punch their chest again and again until Brooks' back flattens against the wall. "How long have you known!?"

They sigh. "About a month. Uncle Finley was given intel that merfolk took your brother long ago. He's been trying to figure out a negotiation, but then you ran away and destroyed his plans. Now that we have proof that a merman is responsible for dragging Trey off the beach, the treaty is officially broken, but you can't tell anyone yet. We don't want a war to break out until we're ready."

The orbs of light shimmer and it feels like a shock of new energy rumbles through my blood. Maybe I *did* suffer a concussion last night. I start to pace, rubbing my temples as Chaos follows in my footsteps. Something doesn't add up. Last night, Axton said only a few people knew of Ben's existence. That means someone important, who had sworn to protect the crown, betrayed the marine queen's decree.

"Who told Dad about Ben?" I ask.

"He learned about it anonymously, on a video sent to his Taj."

I move back and forth between the statue to the wall,

statue to wall. "So, it might not have even been a merfolk who told him."

Brooks stops my pacing by placing both hands on my shoulders. "Hey, Cuz, you know I've been rooting for the merfolk and our kind to mingle ever since I was little, but how could any human possibly know that Ben has been trapped in their underwater castle?"

"Why then, after a *decade,* would merfolk suddenly want to admit that they have Ben as a prisoner?"

Brooks rubs their dark brown stubble, and again, I notice the dark bags under their eyes. How many other secrets has my family kept from me?

"I need to find Axton. He can help me free Ben."

Brooks jumps in front of me. The wildness of their eyes doesn't match the tiredness shown in their body. It's quickly apparent that they weren't watching over me to make sure I showed no symptoms of a concussion but to keep me caged in here. I expected more from my cousin, but of course, my father would arrange such an order to protect his *possessions*. Except I'm not a fuckin' object.

The entry doors groan open in their old age and Jordan marches in. "Oh good, you're finally awake." He nods at my cousin and lowers his voice. "Brooks, you're needed on the docks."

Brooks rushes out the door and slams it. From the exterior, a lock clicks in place. Caged. My muscles clench tight as Jordan approaches with a Taj99 in hand.

"I have something I need to show you," Jordan says.

Chest heaving, I'm still trying to process the last conversation. If Queen Rayna is with Dad then she probably never received my request to talk. There are so many spinning plates, I'm not sure which to focus on.

Jordan's dominant stance overwhelms the room but I

refuse to step back. Chaos barks at my ankles and bares her fangs at him.

"Whoa, easy, mutt."

An electric pulse zips from orb to orb above and its vigor intensifies, as if calling out to me. Unable to ignore them, I count over a dozen. The closer they get, the more awed I am by the thin blue light spiraling inside their bubbles.

"What are you looking at?" Jordan's deep voice commands my attention.

When I meet his eyes, it's obvious how much depth they're missing, how little they resemble Axton's.

"Eribelle, look at this. We don't have much time." Jordan holds out the Taj99. "Look, this picture is what I need to show you."

A digital sketch of only Axton's face, depicting his blond bun, matching scruff, square chin, and bright blue eyes stares back at me. The top reads: *'Wanted Felon'* with the reward amount for handing him in to authorities. My heart rams against my ribs. This can't be happening. How did Jordan find out?

"The man you met on that island is lying to you," Jordan says.

"No, he's not."

Jordan forces my hand into his. "Don't worry, doll, I'll keep you safe. The entire town is already out hunting for him. This Axton, if that's even his real name, won't last long in the streets. Now, I need you to tell me everything you learned about him to give us an advantage."

"No...Jordan he—"

"He tricked you, Eribelle. The man is a criminal, a con artist, and a murderer!"

"But..."

"Fine, then maybe you'll believe this."

A blurry image projects on the wall from Jordan's Taj, almost as if the camera has water droplets on the lens.

Gray swarms the scene. Rain in a storm. Lightning streaks split the night sky in the video and severs a yacht in half. A body goes flying overboard. Sampson. A merman swims into view and from the symbol tattooed on his broad back, I know that it's Axton.

Axton ignores Sampson's sinking body and moves toward my half of the yacht. His tail swishes in the water and he cradles a body in his arms. It looks like Axton starts to slam my head on the side of the boat, but I realize he's trying to unwrap my hair from the ladder.

"He's a merman, Eribelle. A merman on land!" Anger creates deep crevices in Jordan's brow.

A knot of rage coils tight in my gut. "Where did you get that video?"

Jordan's jaw drops. "Wuh…I…it was sent to me, along with the wanted poster."

I poke his chest hard and Chaos reinforces my attack with a snarl. "Why would a merfolk send *you*, of all people, a video of a fellow merman committing a crime against their common enemy? It doesn't make any sense."

He swallows, making the bump in his throat rise and fall hard. "Listen, Eribelle, that man isn't human. He belongs in the sea. They're all dangerous and he knows the witch who controls them all. When we catch him, we can force him to give us access to her magic."

"Shut up!" I scream. "*You* filmed that video!" So much rage soars through me that I don't risk moving. "*You* set Axton up! *You* were there during that storm. *You* saw Sampson sink when Axton saved me and you did NOTHING!" I scream louder. "*You* let my best friend die! Why? to frame an innocent merman?"

"He's not innocent," Jordan growls. "None of them are.

Mermen have been grabbing humans off the beach. You saw what happened last night to Trey."

I pause, wondering why merfolk would want to take humans anyway. Axton swore they are a peaceful species unless threatened first. What if the mermen who had trapped me in the enchanted rope are the ones who are taking humans. They said Dad hired them for a job. What if it's all been a setup? It occurs to me that Dad might be staging the entire situation. Why? To start a war—because they took Ben first.

"Honey, why don't we just—"

Chaos lunges. Her teeth grab hold of the hem of Jordan's pants and she tears at the fabric. He kicks her hard, across the room and her side strikes the side of the fountain.

"Chaos!" I run over, drop to her side, and hover both hands over her body.

She doesn't even try to stand.

"You monster! What did you do?!"

The orbs lower until they're above my head. Panic and terror clash together in a flurry in my heart. Then one orb drops itself into my palm. It's somehow both bowling-ball heavy and feather-light at the same time. A dark swirl of shadow moves to the center of the ball with wisps of blue coiling around it. The looping reminds me of a painting of a long deadly snake.

Something from deep in my gut tells me to carefully touch Chaos. Images of the tree nymphs come into focus, as well as a dozen other creatures I had always assumed to be mythical. They circle Chaos and me, chanting a beautiful, ancient language. I understand the foreign words as if they've been a part of me since birth and with each word they sing, calmness blankets me and the symbols I've been studying. Suddenly, their harmonious song zaps away to silence. Chaos jumps to her feet and licks my face, completely healed.

"Wh-what the fuck was that?"

"I…I don't know." Instead of fear, pure awe rushes through me, like the first time I ever visited the art museum downtown. "The orbs were calling to me."

"What orbs?"

"Right here." I gesture around me, the floating bubbles of light that have formed a wall around us. "All of these."

"There's nothing there. That hideous merman cursed your damn mind." With a look of terror on his face, Jordan side-steps toward the giant door, keeping his eyes on me the whole time. "Your father will hear about this."

I'm done with this conversation. Quickly, I grab his Taj that had flown across the floor and shove it in my pocket. He runs out, leaving me with Chaos and the healing magical orbs that vibrate around me with raw power. I lean closer and squint into the flowing ripples of blue streams in the orb. At the center is the same symbol as in Axton's gem. Maybe when I touched his headpiece last night, some of his witch powers transferred over to me. I need to find Axton.

I leap to open the door and almost dislocate my shoulder from tugging it. "Damn it! Jordan! Unlock the door!"

The hallway toward the rest of Dad's house looks clear, but it would take me in the wrong direction. I'd have to dash through long corridors and avoid his guards and security team.

The suns' rays slant through the old windows, but it gives me an idea. I grasp one of my freaky orbs and chuck it at the window. It breaks in an explosion of color. I have to hurry.

"Yes!" I jump like a schoolgirl as the breeze blows in and whips my hair.

When I realize I'm barefoot, I glance at the rest of my outfit for the first time. I'm not wearing the same clothes as last night. If Jordan changed me while I was unconscious, I'm going to throw an orb at his skull the next time we meet. At least I'm wearing something light-weight.

"Okay, Chaos, wait here." I tiptoe around the sharp edges, barely allowing myself to breathe.

Outside, I hit the ground, and grass tickles my feet. Using a long stick, I break the remaining glass and call to Chaos. Thankfully, she hops through without injury and bounds to me. Side by side we dart into the rose garden that surrounds Dad's mansion.

Cotton-ball clouds morph into ice cream scoops in the sky over the docks, right where Dad is presumably meeting the Queen. I can't believe he hijacked my meeting.

If the stories about Queen Rayna are true, Dad's entitled attitude, manipulative attempts and controlling demeanor won't work on her. I'll need to time my entrance perfectly, swoop in and explain to the queen that Axton is innocent. Then, all charges against him should be cleared. Axton will be free to continue with his dream job in a future he has always wanted. After we convince the Queen to free Ben, it'll give Axton his powers back so all will be fixed.

Sprinting toward the beach, my orbs enchant the courtyard to life. The ivy hugging the stone benches waves to me like a familiar neighbor. I don't have time to gape, so I keep jogging. Juniper trees dip, as if bowing to me as I race past and faces appear on them like the nymphs. My heart flutters as I move faster, speeding next to Chaos toward the docks. Hyacinths draping from the gondola smile and point in the direction of my merman. Somehow, I already know where Axton is, as if my heart is magnetized to his energy.

At the bottom of the hill, the waves crash into white foam and I can feel Axton's presence. Of course, he'd be in the water. Boats drift in the distance, but I zero in on the docks by Dad's yachts. Dad stands, tall, and straight with both hands on his hips, staring down into the water. A mermaid with a deadly crown frowns at him. I continue to scan the area for the golden streaks of hair that will catch my eye when the suns reflect off Axton's blond bun. There...I see him.

A few yards behind the queen, Axton wades in the water, hiding behind a rowboat. Relief floods me at the relief of finding him safe.

When a flick of silver also reflects from the suns, I follow it to the sharp spear tip poking out of the water. Axton made a weapon. Shit. Slowly, he stalks closer to the docks. I glance between him, my father, and the queen. Would he truly kill my father? My heart races but not for the reason I expect. For the first time, it's crystal clear what I'm meant to do.

CHAPTER 20

Axton

Fish tickle my ankles, a gentle reminder that I'm forced to wade in the sea without a tail. I know Queen Rayna is nearby from her unmistakable voice, but I can't see a damn thing. She shouldn't breach the surface. Rayna is mid-conversation with someone when I finally wade within earshot, but I can't place the deep baritone voice. His whispers become covered each time the tide rushes in. Maybe the one with her is a new guard.

"You shouldn't have ever taken him to begin with!" The male's voice is hard around the edges, but he still keeps it as quiet as possible.

"He came voluntarily," my Queen hisses, "Ben belongs with Gia and he doesn't want to return to you."

"Lies! My son would never choose merfolk over me! You stole him and if he's not in my home by sundown, war will be upon your queendom by tomorrow."

It all clicks into place, but Finley Erickson has no right to speak to my queen like that. And why is she giving him the chance at all?

"Stop!" From my right, Eribelle's voice projects like a warrior. "Wait!"

I clutch my makeshift spear harder, adrenaline pumping.

"What are you doing here, sweetheart?" Finley's voice hovers between concern and irritation. "Go back home to Jordan. Right now. The beach isn't safe."

"Drop your weapon," Eribelle whispers, followed by the sound of swishing water.

Little splashes hit my bare stomach. My grip on the weapon loosens when Eri's coconut scent surrounds me. Is she moving toward *me* instead of her father? Eri wants *me* to wait? To lower *my* weapon?

Her hand brushes against my side and she whispers, "I have a plan, play along."

"Who are you talking to?" Finley's footsteps sound louder on the wooden pier. "Why are you swimming behind that boat?"

In moments her father will probably find my hiding spot. Finley isn't an idiot. Once he sees my spear in hand, he'll piece together the rest of the puzzle.

"Drop your spear, Axton," Eribelle's whisper becomes more forceful. "Before my dad sees it."

Since Eri has led me through haunted forests, helped heal my pain, and shared dark parts of her soul with me, I can trust her. Eri also knows how important my duty is, so she probably wouldn't craft a plan that will put the queen's safety in jeopardy.

Plus, She's not only an artist of canvas and paint, but a master creator. Her ideas to design a raft with leftover supplies on that beach after her ship sank demonstrated her quick wit. Her genuine grief from losing Sampson proves her loyalty. When given the chance to continually blame me, Eri has chosen forgiveness and the ability to move on. Maybe we could be a good partnership.

I let the spear sink to my feet, even though I spent an hour creating it last night.

Eri quickly plants a soft kiss on my cheek and says, "On the count of three, act like you're under my control."

If only she knew that I already was. Eri has me wrapped around her little finger.

"One," she whispers.

She has been my rock ever since I became a human. Nothing will change that now.

"Two."

Her quick wit might be what we need to get out of this mess.

"Tell me what you need," I whisper, "Whatever idea you have will work, I have faith in you, Angelfish."

I hear her suck in a breath of shock.

Bright sunslight assaults my eyes. "Holy shit! I can see!" I lose my bearings and flop into the water like a seal. The beach flashes before me, complete with floating seaweed at my waist, teetering boats, strange orbs of light hovering midair, and a giant limestone mansion. A woman in a blue outfit with a sweep of smoky red hair. Eribelle? It all disappears as quickly as it came.

"Whoa, what the Abyss?" Eri pulls me and I rub my eyes as she asks, "What happened?"

"My vision! It returned for a second."

"You can see?"

"No. It's gone again." A pounding throbs in my temples but we don't have time for me to elaborate. "Go ahead, I'm ready for your plan."

A splash ripples by the docks.

"Wait, Queen Rayna, come back!" Finley's stern voice rips through the morning air. "Damn it, Eribelle! Your foolishness cost me everything! Now the queen left!" Her father hollers and stomps closer.

"Eri, hurry up, what's your plan?" I ask.

"We can use my—"

Her words are cut off as she screams, then something drags her underwater. Her body pushes against my legs below the surface.

"Fuck!"

I suck in a deep breath and plunge into the water. Why did my vision return only to fuckin' disappear again? I can't follow her if I can't see a damn thing. I stroke faster. Kick harder. Must keep swimming. Lungs on fire. Unable to bear it any longer, I return to the surface and gulp air.

"Axton," Lena's voice whispers, barely louder than the soft laps of the water against my chest, "We're over here."

"Lena? Is that you?" I ask. "Do you see Eribelle?"

"Yes, follow my voice." My hand rams straight into something hard.

"Eribelle Mae!" Finley hollers from somewhere close. "Come out!"

Someone shoves my back against a boat, then covers my lips with one hand. "Sssh."

Coconut lotion. It's her. Is this all a part of Eri's plan? I hold my breath and don't dare move a muscle. Eribelle's chest is pushed against mine and both our hearts beat frantically. I feel her pulse race. If we shift even a little, the sounds might signal our location to her father. Minutes pass and his footsteps eventually fade into the opposite direction. His shouts increase with panic as he heads toward his estate.

Finally, Eri's hand drops from my mouth and a part of me feels colder without her gentle touch.

"Is Lena still here?" I whisper.

"Yes, you moron. I'm not gonna leave you." Lena playfully smacks the side of my head, making some of my hair fall loose over my face. "Seems like you can't stay out of the water, even as a damn human."

"Hilarious, as always. So, what's the plan?"

A long pause heightens the harmony of birds squawking. "I was going to offer to trade you for Ben. Since you're a wanted criminal," Eri says, and I can detect the smile in her voice.

"Wow, ruthless, this one." Lena wraps a wire around my wrist.

"Hold this. I'll lead you to Criggin Cove. There we can figure out the next step," Lena treads water slowly, trying not to splash.

We drift into deeper waters and I have to work harder to talk and tread at the same time.

"I can taste the sexual tension between you two. It's a good thing we got the upgraded suite in this cave," Lena snickers and I realize we've stopped our momentum. "How about I go find a rowboat? While I'm gone you two can...*chat*."

I hear splashes as she dives into the water.

"Eribelle?"

"I'm here," she whispers, "Did you really mean what you said earlier? That you'd support my plan without knowing what it was?"

"Yes, of course. I have faith in you. You've shown more natural survivor skills and common sense than half our guard. I know you have creativity that extends past a paintbrush. I mean, don't get me wrong, one day I'll want a whole gallery of your pieces, but your brilliance doesn't stop on a canvas." I bite the inside of my cheek. "Your spirit *is* the masterwork. When Jordan stole you from me last night, I realized one thing for certain; you've completely enchanted me, Eri. Whether I get my eyesight back or not doesn't matter anymore, you're already the most beautiful soul both Above and Below."

Eribelle's chest collides with mine and her arms wrap around my neck. For a second, we both lower in the water, but I kick harder to support her. Our lips crash together with the strength of a tidal wave. She explores my tongue in a way that's made for fantasies.

"Axton?" Eribelle whispers in my ear.

"Yes, Angelfish?" I open my eyes and shock paralyzes me again.

I can see.

I can see her entire face.

I blink. Blink again. This time my sight stays. I'm locked onto Eribelle's bright blue eyes and the radiant vibrancy of her gaze steals my breath. Swallowing the swirl of emotions cascading into my chest, I tuck a long soaked strand of auburn hair behind her ears.

"You can see me, can't you?" Her eyebrows raise in the most adorable way and I wish I could memorize each tiny change of her expressions.

I nod and she kisses me again. And again. Through smiles and wandering hands as we stand in the water at a cave's entrance. When Eri pulls away, a few tiny red freckles speckle her cheeks that remind me of Moina's Constellation. Her ruby lips are thick and swollen and almost mine. Maybe not quite yet, but Goddess, I hope she'll let me be hers.

"You see me." She smiles, and teeth whiter than pearls shine with joy.

"Hey there, Angelfish." I lick my lips and pull her closer. "You could've mentioned once that you're not a mermaid."

"Oh, would that have been helpful?" Both her legs wrap around my waist.

Eribelle hangs on me like a little monkey. We kiss until I can no longer breathe. She arches into me, angling her hips, and I take the momentary break to scoop her out of the water and onto the rock slope. Laying her on the smooth surface, I marvel at the light in her eyes, how her smile is soft, and I wonder if she ever smiles at others like that or if it hints at a deeper connection only shared with me.

My heart pounds frantically. I lean over her, letting my hair drip onto her shoulders. If I had more self-control, I'd let the droplet trail down to the ground, but I lick it slowly and taste her salty, coconut-soaked skin.

The need to know everything about her consumes me—her favorite genre to read, where she buys her tea, what haunts her dreams, and what inspires her art.

"You can see me," she whispers again and lays a soft hand on my cheek. "I've been waiting for those wicked eyes to truly look at me, not through me."

I can't help but chuckle. "Wicked? Am I evil now?"

Her cheeks flush. "It's the first thing I thought of you when I found you on that beach, that your wicked blues had the potential to destroy me, but this is the first time you've truly seen me."

"I've been trying to see you, this whole time." I brush my lips over her forehead. "If you ever think I'm not trying anymore, throw some ketchup at my head."

"There's a lot to unpack in that sentence."

Inside the cave, Eri lays on her side on slippery wet stone that projects from the water and trails past the dark corners into the unknown. She pushes me to lay next to her and I grunt as my back meets the stone. Together we stare up.

She's probably focused on the hanging bats, but I'm captivated by the orbs hovering over us.

I squeeze her hand. "Those orbs belong to Grams."

"They do? That makes sense. They're definitely magic of some sort. They healed Chaos." She sits upright fast. "Shit! Chaos is still on the beach somewhere! What if my Dad—"

"Your dad won't hurt an innocent animal," I say, unsure.

She nods and glances at the cave entrance. "Last night, when I touched your headpiece, I think some of the gem's powers transferred to me. I'm not sure what else these balls of light can do yet, but they have the same symbol as your tattoo." Eri scans my face like it's a test.

"It's the symbol of the ocean's powers." I pause and rub my thumb along her wrist. "Do you think I could ever do both? Be a guard and use my magic?"

"Of course, but Axton, you've been fighting to protect others your whole life. When was the last time someone fought for *you*?"

My jaw drops. I can see it in her gaze, Eri wants to fight for me, but eventually, we will go our separate ways. As if reading my thoughts, she leans her head into my chest. I stroke her hair softly. Imagining living a life without her is like a dagger to the chest, but we come from different worlds.

"I still need to go back. I can't run from my people when they're in need, but, I promise, Eri, I'll find you a new home."

"Okay," is all she says.

I rub her arms, trying to erase her shivers.

"The mermen took Trey last night." Her eyebrows work out a silent puzzle and I refrain from letting my smile show. Her '*thinking*' expression might be the best thing I've ever witnessed.

"I have an idea who is taking the humans," she says, "Have you heard of a merman named Striker?"

"No." I hug her closer. "Why do I get the sense you're plotting something dangerous."

"Well, hear me out. Maybe there's a way to clear your name and rescue my brother. We need to try and catch the culprit in the act." Eri tilts her head and I don't have to have experience reading her facial expressions to understand what she means.

Automatically, my hands clench into fists. "No, no, no, no way. I'm not putting you at risk."

"You said you'd support *any* idea I had." Eri rubs her temples. "Plus, I have my superhero orbs to protect me. If we nicely threaten him, he could give us the answers we need."

Goddess, she's absolutely divine. "What do you have in mind?"

CHAPTER 21

Eribelle

The moon shines dimly from outside the cave into the arched entrance. After we spent too much time going back and forth finalizing our plan, Axton won the coin flip determining when we'd make our move. Tomorrow. I argued to lure the mermen sooner but he made me promise to wait and try to figure out some of the orb's protective powers. So far, we haven't learned much from them except for putting some accidental holes into the cave walls.

Next to me, Axton's eyes remain trained on me. I've been trying to ignore how long his dick has been hard between us.

It shouldn't be possible to feel weightless and grounded at the same time.

"I want to stare at you every moment," he confesses, "and memorize every expression."

"That sounds painful."

The darkness of this cave at night drastically contrasts with the brightness of Axton's eyes. I can't believe he can finally see me. Each deep gaze sends my heart into another frenzy. Glittering blue swirls from the magical hovering orbs shine the only light.

Lying on the smooth stone slope, the cold surface is a relief against the humid night air. Maybe he's right. We deserve a night of calm before the possibility of all Abyss breaking loose. For a few hours, I don't want to think about nymphs or orbs or wanted posters or evil gangs or lost brothers or controlling fathers.

I want to get lost…with Axton.

"If you could live anywhere, what place would you choose?" Axton asks, his thoughts paralleling my need for escape. Still angled on his side with his head supported by one hand, he traces the line of my jaw.

Despite the intensity of his gaze, I can't make myself look away. "Does this have to be a place that people can visit?"

He smiles in a way that melts my heart when he purrs, "No, my Angelfish."

"Then I choose your mind."

"Interesting." His devious smirk returns. "If I could get lost anywhere, it'd be in your eyes."

My heart pounds harder as his finger drops from my jaw and moves to my collarbone. I already know where his thoughts are, but acknowledging them would change everything. What if our plan doesn't go well tomorrow? What if the mermen don't show up to fall into our trap? What if I can't free Ben? What if the queen doesn't believe

Axton's innocence? What if she does and I never see him again?

Axton smooths out the creases from my frown with his tender lips. His tongue asks the pivotal question, and my answer is to lean further into him. His lips paint lyrics of a love song and his tongue strokes hopes of a future together. My moan slips into his mouth and it's all the encouragement he needs.

"Goddess, Eri." He groans between kisses. "You…are going to destroy me."

He moves, positioning himself fully atop me and asks, "Is this okay?"

"Yes," I barely whisper. I can't help but be in awe of how his skin glows under the faint light of the orbs, but I need to see more of him. All of him. I pull at his shirt and tug it over his head. The quick motion makes the rest of his long hair fall from where it was tied together. Now those blond locks frame his face, dangling in the air between us. My hands explore his hard chest, sending my heart into a frantic overload, unsure how to cope. The sleek contours and curves of his body is art in its highest form. I could spend hours charting the exact spots to touch that make his body shiver.

"I want you. Everywhere. Now," I whisper against his skin.

His eyes change from raw hunger to uncertainty. "I haven't done *this*…as a human."

My hands drift lower, outlining the defined rectangles on his stomach. "It's okay if you're nervous."

He bites his lip. "It's not that, I haven't practiced with this…anatomy…to know if I'll hurt you."

I kiss away his worry. "I'll let you know."

"Promise?" he whispers, as his hands move under my shirt, touching me like I'm precious, cherished.

"Yes, and…ooooh." I gasp and arch my back.

"Yes?"

"I forgot…oooh…what I was going to say."

When Axton grins my entire world implodes and explodes—at the same time. Nothing makes sense as everything I've ever wanted falls perfectly into its place. Axton slips his hands under the hem of my shirt and pulls it over my head. Gently, he lays the fabric between my skin and the rock. Scrapes against my back will be well worth the pleasure I crave from his lips, body, cock. I need it all. Now. Before I know it, I feel a large hand between my thighs, slowly, so slowly coasting upward.

"Holy Goddess, Eri." He stops and locks his gaze on my eyes. "This wetness…is that normal?"

I blow an out-of-control breath and nod, realizing that sex as a merman must really be different. The creatures of the sea are already surrounded by water so maybe he hadn't experienced this part of how turned on a woman can get from his touch.

"Fuck, Eri. What if I like this better as a human?" His eyes ravish me and I already feel naked under him.

I gulp and move my hands to the hem of his shorts. "Why don't we find out?"

My hand dips under the fabric of his shorts and there are no surprises underneath. I've already seen the mast that he carries and my heart rate spikes in excitement.

"Take these off." I pull at his clothing.

He kicks off his shorts and springs himself free. The anticipation of feeling him push into me soon is more than I can handle, but, as it's his first time on land; he needs reassurance. I'm not going to show any nervousness that might scare him off. My fingers mirror what he's doing to my own body, by running along his inner thigh. His cock twitches and his blue eyes go wild.

Quickly, I tug off my shorts and panties, yanking them over my heels.

"Eri…" All his muscles tense so fiercely that I might not be able to contain myself another second.

What would he do if I guided him into me right now? Damn it, no. He needs to go slow, and someone to support this first-time experience. Though, my senses scream in ecstasy as his fingers circle my heat. All I can think of is the desire for him to dive in already. Damn it. I need him to possess every inch of me. Damn it all.

My legs flex. I want to coax him closer. This time when my eyes shift from the location of his hand to his face, there's no denying this man knows exactly what he's doing to me. He may be a human virgin, but the experience and confidence of his motions ignite lava in my core. Fine. I can play along with this madness.

My fingers skim the side of his erection, and it flicks up slightly. Those ravenous blues pin me in place.

"Try that again, Angelfish, and I'll eat you alive," he growls.

Holy shit. I hadn't predicted this side of him—more dominant—more everything. This version of Axton definitely doesn't need any directional tips. It's time to challenge the man made of both Above and Below. I graze my finger teasingly slow along the underside of his length again.

The beastly snarl that explodes from him makes all my hairs stand on end. With a dare in his gaze, Axton pushes a finger inside me. I yelp in pleasure, my voice echoing against the cave walls as I squeeze my eyes shut.

"Look at me," he growls low as he adds another expert finger.

I follow his command. In fact, I'd follow him into the depths and back with fingers like these. The marine ocean waves reflect in his irises as if the sea lives in his soul. There's no way I'll ever get enough of this, of him. Each caress of his fingers inside me inspires a new painting idea. Colors blast into euphoric blends and patterns behind my lids. I need to touch him. Desperate. Panting, I reach, but because of the angle he has me pinned, I can't get a hold of him again, so I wiggle playfully.

"Mmm. Trying to escape me?" His beautiful lips meet my stomach and drop lower. Lower. Lower. His tongue licks my clit like no man should know how to do.

"Fuuuuuck!" My hands find his hair. I'm helpless against his skills.

With his fingers and tongue dancing in sync, I almost reach the point of orgasm, but then he tortures me again and again. He keeps me on the brink. I'm about to go over the edge, and my entire body shakes. He slows and smiles against my skin, subtly creating friction at the softest part of me.

"Damn you, Axton!" I grip his hair harder. "Stop that!"

His fingers cease the hypnotic circles. "You want me to stop?"

"I want..." I undulate my hips against his hand in a wave. "Give me…" I moan as his fingers slowly stir again. "I want you inside me."

He licks his scrumptious lips with a predatory gleam. "I think I already am, Eri."

"All of you." The tightest tension in my core make my toes curl. "Please."

His fingers retreat, leaving me empty, soaking wet, and wanting. That tiny flicker of doubt flashes across his features again, but he disguises it by asking, "Please, what?"

"Please…make love to me."

Axton freezes, then scans my face up and down, one, two, three times. "Love?"

I nod. There's no point in asking him to fuck me. It's not

what I want. Our connection is already too real to mask it or build a wall around my heart.

"Love? Yeah, I can do that," he whispers.

His lips part and those sinful eyes turn soft. No words are needed as he shows endearment with each touch. Devotion ripples between us as his palm slowly cups my breast and my nipples harden, wanting his mouth. This man can never be close enough to my skin. The inches separating us feel like a never ending canyon.

"Are you ready?" he asks, the cherished passion in his gaze makes my heart gallop.

I let my knees drop open and spread my legs wider. "Yes."

The tip of his cock presses at my opening. Waiting. This is it. What I need. All I want. Locked onto his vicious blue eyes again, I nod, and he slowly pushes into me. I suck in a breath and my nails dig into his shoulders.

Inch by inch he carefully drives deeper, testing the limits of what I can handle. The way he fills me is out of this world, indescribable. Not breaking eye contact, Axton makes the most animalistic sound I've ever heard.

"Ah, Eri! Oh. My. Goddess." His eyes almost roll in the back of his head, and I dig my nails into him again.

I can barely breathe as he holds himself in one position, planted fully inside me. I've never felt anything this amazing. Is it because of his angle? His girth? The fact that he's stretching me out? Is it his length? I can't even…

"You gotta quit making that sound," he whispers into my skin, "or I'm not gonna be able to please you for long."

Axton kisses my lips softly as he starts to thrust. There's no chance in Abyss this can be real. I curve into him, matching his slow pace. My hands grasp his flexed biceps and I use every bit of effort to maintain focus on his gaze. Each time he sinks into me, he buries a separate vow.

Thrust.

A vow to protect me.

Thrust.

An oath to make me laugh every day.

Thrust.

A promise to be honest.

Slower thrust.

A swear to hold my hand on walks.

Deeper thrust.

A pledge to buy me ketchup.

Over the next blissful hour, the moans we both make would wake an entire village if we were closer to land, but the only things that can hear us are the walls in this cave. The light from the orbs above shimmer against the sweat glistening on his forehead. My legs become tired and I wish I had something more sturdy to hold onto so he could properly demolish me.

"Eri…this is"—he pants—"so much…better than…I just can't last much longer."

"It's okay…"

Thrust

"You've lasted…"

Thrust

"…a long time…"

Thrust

"…going this slow. Now, fuck me! Now!"

Harder thrust. Again and again, pounding into me. All I see are stars.

"Come, Axton. come."

"Ohhhhh." Axton roars and rams into me with such ferocity that I think I might snap in two. His face screws into knots and the way his veins pop from his arms shoots a rush of paradise straight to my center. The sheer level of carnal masculinity he exudes shatters me completely.

Out of control, I clamp around him and scream out. We

climax at the same time as he jerks above me. Panting, sweating, I soak in the waves of euphoria and try to memorize the sensation of him inside me and the way his eyes swallow me whole.

He pulls out slowly, then collapses next to me on the stone. Axton laces his fingers through mine, then kisses the back of my knuckles. Silent for minutes or an hour, I'm unsure. Hand in hand, we both stare at the orbs, which have witnessed everything.

"You think there's any spy cameras in those things?" Axton's joke falls flat when he coughs, unable to catch his breath.

I roll into his embrace and kiss his slight beard. "Probably, and broadcasted for everyone to see." I change the pitch of my voice to mimic a news reporter. "What a scandal: a common girl from Coendriel seduces a merman spy in the midst of an upcoming war."

"Naw." He scoots me closer to his chest. "The headlines would be: poor unfortunate merman saved by the good graces of his one true love."

I angle my head and meet his eyes as I whisper, "So that *was* lovemaking?"

"Uh, oh." He smiles adorably. "Did I do *love* wrong? Am I a heartless human?"

I smack his chest. "You know what I mean."

"My stubborn, gorgeous Angelfish." He sighs. "Even though your toenails are all painted different colors, and you have an obsession with the most intriguing food, and you think blankets are the world's greatest invention, I do think I may in fact, love you."

His words undo me, but I have to hold it together. I squeeze his hand tenderly and bury myself into his chiseled chest as far as possible, then whisper, "Shucks, we may have a problem then."

"Indeed."

Axton will return to the Below soon and our people might go to war. I wish I had time to take him to my favorite art museum, build a doghouse together for Chaos, and kiss him openly in front of everyone, but it's an impossible future. These few moments in his arms will be all we have. For now, nestled close, I breathe in his scent and dream of an alternate reality.

Soon, he's snoring, and even though I'd love to talk to him until the suns rise again, the man deserves a moment of rest from all that hard work. Maybe I'll wake him later with my tongue. My belly flutters at the thought.

Just as my eyelids slip into darkness, a rumbling stirs from deep within the cave and I brace myself for falling rocks, but none crash. In fact, the water stills, as if time has suspended. No more soft waves lap into our space from the grotto's opening. A dark presence lurks like a panther crouched and ready to strike. I hold my breath, willing myself not to check over my shoulder.

Axton's grip suddenly tightens and he pulls me closer. "Eri. Don't. Move."

For the first time, I notice stalactites above us stabbing the air like icicles ready to impale. Heart racing, I clamp my teeth together. What's behind me?

CHAPTER 22

Axton

A cave nymph steps out from the dark wall. Two legs protrude first, sleek with moss, followed by a long sturdy torso. I scramble into my shorts and pull Eribelle to her feet. She flings her clothes on too, terror lining her eyes. There's no possible way I'll let anything hurt the woman I love.

Love…

Shit. Fuckin' shit. I do. I love this woman. But I'm not human. We have absolutely no possibility of a future together.

Heart pounding, I glance at the grotto's exit, where all the orbs hover, as if trying to guide us to a quick escape, but the water rises unnaturally, forming a wall where we'd slip out. If we tried to dive through it, how long could Eri hold her breath?

I try to shield her from the cave nymph, but she steps toward it, the creature now completely formed into a human-shaped rock. Over seven feet tall, the rough edges that form shoulders and a hard jawline would intimidate the best of guards. Unfortunately, I have no weapon.

"Eribelle! Stay back."

The cave nymph tilts its head and steps toward her, creating a crack in the ground. A spray of water shoots from Below. If the creature forms an earthquake in here, we'll drown within minutes. Pulse racing, I lunge to tug her to safety.

"Wait, Axton, look." She points to the heart of the cave nymph, where a symbol is etched into the stone, matching the one tattooed on my back.

"There's no time. That thing can kill us with one swing of an arm."

She ignores me and steps forward again, hand outreached. Her fingers hover over the nymph's chest and suddenly the orbs of light shoot over to her. They shine on the symbol, making the ancient shape glow.

"Why are you here?" Eribelle searches for answers in the hollow eyes of the nymph.

It shifts loudly. Pebbles tremble underfoot and echo from down the tunnel, then it roars unnaturally, "Nerida's Sea Nymph needs your help."

"Who's the Sea Nymph?" Eribelle asks, but I already know the answer. Some call my Grams Ulsa, some call her the Sea Witch, or the devil Below, but others know her as a Sea Nymph.

"What does Grams need?" I step between Eri and the giant rock statue.

"Nerida's Sea Nymph needs your help. Use the orbs she gifted to you to save the children's fate."

"What children?" My fists ball tight. "Where is my grandma?" I press the gem of my headpiece to call out to Grams, but there's no response on the other side. Sweat starts to pool and slip down my neck. I shove my finger at the gem again and again. "Grams? Answer me!"

Wide-eyed, Eribelle stops my frantic movements. "Breathe, Axton. We'll figure it out." She turns back to the nymph. "Which children need to be saved?"

"Nerida's Sea Nymph needs your help. Touch the gem to the power source to stop it all." It steps back into the cave wall, laboriously.

"No, wait!" I claw at the stone, but the nymph has already merged back into the cave wall.

We need to leave. Why couldn't the nymph have been more clear? What children? Merkids are the only thing that makes sense, but...realization strikes like a lightning bolt.

"The annual ritual!" I kick at the pebbles and yell, "It's in two days. How could I have been so stupid!"

"Hey, hey, it's okay. Axton, look at me." Eribelle takes my cheeks between both her hands. "It's okay. We've got this." Her tone is confident despite the trembling she tries to hide.

"I completely forgot the date. What if something happened to Grams? If they don't receive their maturing potion to drink, they will never develop into males or females. There's always been a Sea Nymph to complete the rite of passage. If Grams isn't there, another Sea Nymph would have to complete the ceremonies."

Eribelle glances over my shoulder and nods. "Okay, it's okay. All we have to do is change our plan. We need to split up. I'll get answers we need and you find your grandma." She sounds like she's trying to convince herself as much as me. "We can do this, it's alright, breathe."

Her plan has a major flaw though. There's no chance I'm leaving Eri's side. I gaze into her bright eyes, which seem almost identical to the swirls inside the floating orbs. "I'm not leaving you."

Eribelle takes my hand, but she's trembling. "But what about your grandma?"

"She has overtaken enemies for centuries. She can manage things on her own for a few more minutes." I focus on Eri's gaze, still full of uncertainty, but here to support me.

"Let's use the orbs to get out of here," she says nervously.

"I don't know how to use these."

"I might know." She drops to the ground and crawls, scrambling fast. "Look for something sharp."

"Why?"

She grabs something and holds it up. "Got it! I need to tattoo the magical symbol on my skin."

When the light of the orbs reflects off the object in her hand it's a sharp point of a stone. Before I can stop her, Eribelle digs the point into her thigh, drawing a thin line that flows crimson.

"Fuck, that hurts." She flaps her hands and cranes her head to the ceiling. "I can't do it to myself, Axton. You need to."

I back away. "No. I refuse to hurt you."

She holds the rock out to me. "It'll work! There are directions written and translated for controlling the magic."

I freeze and stare at her. "How do you know that?"

"Um, I kept one of the papers we found on the island."

My heart sinks. "You lied to me."

"I'm sorry, Axton, but we don't have time to hash it out right now. Please." She gestures with the rock again.

Hurt rushes through me like an overflowing river. What else has she lied about?

"Fine." Muscles flaring with Goddess-knows-what-emotion, I crouch as she braces herself and turns away from witnessing. Blood trickles down her thigh from the previous cut.

My job is to protect. How am I supposed to cause her pain? I made love to this woman and now I have to injure her. Fear attacks me like a swarm of killer sharks. I hover the sharp edge over her leg, unwilling to make the first slice. I'm furious that she's putting me in this position.

"Do it, Axton," her voice is soft, trusting. "It'll work."

If only Lena showed up with the rowboat like she was supposed to, this wouldn't be happening. Sucking in a deep breath, I jab the edge into her leg until it breaks the skin. Eribelle hisses and I want to stop, but it'll only prolong the process. I pretend it's a dagger's blade and quickly cut the rest of the symbol into her thigh. She cringes and her shoulders hunch in. Eri's skin is covered with red blotches and her hands are balled tightly at her sides. Finally, it's done.

The reality of what I've done hits me with the weight of a submarine. A human isn't supposed to have access to ancient magic. I don't want Eribelle to carry the burden of any dangerous responsibilities. Plus, what if the magic doesn't accept her? She's not a nymph, a royal, or a mermaid. There's nothing in her blood that shows she's strong enough to handle the power. Regret immediately floods my thoughts and I wish I could erase the scratches.

Eribelle stands, tears falling from her cheeks and she whispers, "Thank you."

At a loss for words, I stare at her. She's sacrificial. Courageous. Mine—liar and all.

Eri claps her hands, trying to summon the orbs to her. Nothing happens.

"It was a nice try, Eri, but I don't think this is the way."

Eri waves her hands toward the orbs, again, attempting to control them. That thick red hair bounces like flames with each of her movements and I'll never forget how it surrounded her head like a halo when I was thrusting into her. A shiver crawls up my spine and my dick hardens again. Damn it. Even when the world is crashing down around us, I want her again so desperately.

She mimes as if she's pulling the orbs to her with an invisible rope. Her eyes turn from sapphire to pure determination and her tenacious ruby lips pucker, sending my body into a frenzy. Even her scent radiates conviction. This woman will conquer those orbs or she might take down this cave into a crumbling mess while trying.

Her freckles scrunch into a knot on her cheeks. Internally, I try to wield my own unfamiliar magic to support her, but have had no practice or training yet.

Suddenly, the orbs fly to us and attach like a magnet to form a flat surface.

"Whoa, did you see that? I'm a certified bad-ass witch!" She lifts herself onto the orbs, sitting atop like it's a sturdy plank. "Come on!"

"Those things won't hold my weight."

"Get your fine ass up here, soldier." She points to the empty spot next to her. "I'm cold and need your body heat." A smirk tugs at her lips.

Somehow, I manage to pull myself onto the magical plank as if I'm doing a pull-up.

The plank of orbs zooms forward, carrying us out of the cave. We fly over the water so fast I can't see any fish. In another world, I'd be whooping and hollering with joy as we defy physics by gliding faster than an albatross.

But my girl lied to me. I asked her to destroy the papers for a good reason. What else has she kept a secret? And what if we fail? The merkids need protection. Ben needs to be freed. And lastly, we need to live through this night so I can have a fight with Eri about her hiding things from me. Our makeup sex will definitely be worth the harsh accusations roaring in my mind.

Moonbeams reflect off the surface of the water and for a carefree moment I savor the feeling of Eribelle's arms wrapped around my waist as we soar faster and faster toward our possible doom.

CHAPTER 23

Eribelle

I stand vulnerable on an empty beach, hoping the merman takes our bait—me. The first moments of dawn still hides below the horizon, wary of our new plan. I resist glancing over to where Axton is hidden by the bottom of a boat, where he's ready to swim out. He's trained not to make a sound, but my orbs circulating behind a palm tree have a wild mind of their own. They better listen.

I wring my hands together. The eerie quiet gives me chills since there are usually a few fishermen packing their canoes. This used to be my favorite time of day, but right now, while I am offering myself as prey, it only gives me shivers. Soft, frigid water laps at my toes, and the gentle waves bring seaweed to my ankles. I glance down at my favorite blue outfit. Phantom touches from Axton's hands still linger on my calves, my thighs, my everywhere. There's no time to think of the upcoming heartbreak. I sigh as the first rays peek above the skyline, grasping my attention.

"Hello again, little dove."

I jump and turn to the left. The merman I had met on the island, Striker, treads the water a few yards ahead, with his tail flicking and splashing. His leathery skin resembles even more of a raisin compared to the last time he threatened me and he still wears the mask covering most of his face. I won't let my fear show.

He lays on his back and floats, with both hands behind his neck as support. "You know it's not safe these days for a maiden like you to be wandering the beach alone. I don't think your daddy would be too thrilled to hear you are breaking the harbor's new rules."

I sense my orbs wanting to attack Striker but I try to stay calm to keep them under control. "Take off your mask so I can curse the man who steals my people."

All I need is to distract Striker for a few more minutes while Axton sneaks closer.

Striker's laugh mixes with a cough like he's choking on a piece of crab. "You already know the intimate details of the face who is to blame, and it's not mine, but don't you worry, little dove, most of the humans that have been taken are still alive."

"Like Ben?" I shouldn't have said his name, but the way Striker is moving closer makes me want to throw him off his game.

He freezes for a beat, then acts as if I hadn't given up the princess's secret. "Is that a boyfriend of yours? I heard you were intended for Jordan Idros."

Striker's too close, almost at arms' length. I take a step back and glance around for Axton. Where is he?

"Why do you want to take humans?" I say with a shaky voice, focusing on keeping the orbs under my command.

"Give me one good reason why I should tell my secrets to you?" He spits out the last two words like poison.

"Probably because I'm too stupid and worthless to be considered a threat." I roll my eyes. "So I'm not smart enough to do anything with your information anyway."

"I'm not like humans, dove, I don't underestimate a strong woman. The ocean herself is female." Striker drops both his hands underwater and suddenly, a dozen other mermen swim into the shallows. No, no, no, no. This wasn't supposed to happen. Axton can't defeat them all at once.

Their heads pop above the surface, many with dirty hair. One shows off missing teeth with his nasty grin as he shows the same enchanted rope that trapped me back on the island. I retreat further until sand sticks to my ankles. Our plan is damned.

"Axton!" I yell and frantically scan the boats. "Axton!"

"You mean *this* felon?" Jordan appears on the docks, dragging something heavy behind him on the wood.

I gasp at the sight of Axton grunting and fighting against the enchanted rope that's being used as a net. His skin is already covered with sickly red welts all over his body. From experience, I know how much that rope burns.

"Let him go, Jordan!" I try to dart to the pier, but Axton screams something in another language and thrusts one hand out.

I run straight into a solid wall of fog. A couple of my magical orbs of light soar toward me from the other side but bang against the barrier, unable to join me on this side.

"You're working with these mermen?" I snap at Jordan.

He chuckles quietly. "No, dollface. I despise all the

creatures of the sea. They scare away our customers from buying more boats. Our economy is suffering because of these demons taking over our harbor."

"The seas don't belong to *you* or anyone with legs." Striker's hiss is sharp as knives.

In horror, I watch helplessly as another merman tugs up a different net and winks at me. Lena writhes inside, blindfolded. She mumbles something but I can't understand a word. The merman shoves her face back under so she can breathe the water.

"Noooo!" Axton screams on the other side of the mist and tries to rip at his netting but hollers in pain when his fingers touch the rope. "Lena!"

"Help!" I glance at my father's mansion atop the hill. With the suns slowly rising, at least one fisherman should be close by. "Stop!" Tears threaten to fall as I glare at Striker. "Lena is *your* kind, a merfolk. What are you doing?"

"She has helped *you*, a *human*. She's a disgrace to our species, and we need to make a trade. Lena is the queen's niece, so the humans know her worth."

"A trade?" I stumble. "What are you talking about?"

"Before, taking the humans was to piss off land-dwellers so they'd be the first to attack. We had to trick our queen too. She'd eventually come to see the need to protect her queendom, and order the entire RMG to attack the harbor." Striker drops down and sucks in a mouthful of water, then continues. "But no matter how many we snatched, humans were too weak to make the first move. So, we had to bring someone we trusted into it, little Axton here."

I glance at him. My man. He's part of the RMG, so could he be in on this? I had lied to him, so would it be so crazy that he lied to me too?

"But now, Axton's plan has gone to shit," Striker continues. "The humans stole Ulsa last night. We need her for the survival of our kind. Nerida's annual ritual is too important to fuck up. So, to get Ulsa back, we're handing over all the humans we've taken in the last month and Lena." Striker points behind me. "We're doing this for *her*."

An elderly, pale woman with unruly white hair is wrapped tightly in a rope, guided by my father, who stands on the dunes behind her. He starts yelling, "Get away from the shore, Eribelle! Don't let those creatures touch you!"

"Dad, what are you doing?" I glance back and forth between my father and his prisoner. "Who is that?"

Dad's eyes turn catacomb cold. "Ulsa."

But she has legs, like Axton.

Dad continues, "This witch is responsible for tearing our family apart. So I took what matters most to her, her powers." He holds up his wrist, where the same ancient symbol has been scorched into his skin, the same as on my thigh, the same as on Axton's back.

"Shit," I mumble under my breath.

"How...how did you...this isn't right." I stutter.

"Of course, it is. This witch needs to pay. All the merfolk need to pay!" Dad yells. "Their worthless queen wouldn't see reason, so I had to resort to working with the nymphs. Thank you, baby girl, for passing along the message from Drei and Viera. Their key led me safely to Ulsa's cottage Below. All the tree nymphs wanted in exchange was a soul. I'm sorry to say you won't have the opportunity to make up with Trey. May he rest in peace." Dad winks, oblivious to how revolted I feel.

"You sent Trey to his grave?" I'm suddenly very aware of how large my father stands over Ulsa.

"Of course not, sweetie. My hands are clean. Those tree nymphs on the other hand are monstrous things."

I try to fit the details into place like a puzzle, one piece at a time. Dad had tried to negotiate for Ben's freedom. The

Queen said no. So, he worked with nymphs to make a bargain. They took too long to give him a clear answer, so Dad hired the mermen gang to create havoc. Then the nymphs eventually gave Dad some key that led to Ulsa. I shake my head. This belongs in a fairy tale.

Dad steps forward, but I move away. "By the way, thank you, daughter, for your help with all this. You brought back the last step I needed. The paper had a specific spell translated. I'm not sure how you knew what I was looking for, but I'm so glad I can finally count on you."

From the other side of the foggy shield, Axton's furious thrashes within his net settle down. He looks back and forth between me and my father, confused. "Eri…? Tell me you didn't help him."

"No, I swear I didn't give my dad anything. I didn't know any of this."

Axton's brows furrow and he nods slightly, but I can still detect hesitation in his betrayed gaze. Shit, shit, shit. How am I supposed to fix this?

"We have your trade, Finley," Striker cuts into our conversation. "Give us back Ulsa, and you can do whatever you wish with Lena."

"I also want Ben. Then I'll give you this *criminal* too." Dad points to Axton, still being controlled by Jordan.

I can't move. Can't think. This is all wrong. Axton can't go Below right now. What if he can't summon his powers to breathe water? What if they execute him for treason? I never got a chance to plead his case, to explain how he had saved me. I'd never see him again.

"Wait! Take me instead." I raise my hand.

"No, Eribelle!" Both Axton and my father yell at the same time.

Striker checks the rising suns, then quickly paces in the waters, swimming back and forth. "You have nothing to offer me, girl. At least with Axton, I'll receive my royal reward from the queen."

"I have magic." The orbs crack through Axton's foggy shield and hover above my head. At first, I'm not sure if Striker will be able to see them, but when his eyes lock on the globes, it's obvious he knows their power.

"Eribelle, don't do this." Axton claws at the toxic net binding him.

Heart racing, I ignore my love's pleas and focus on Striker. "I'll teach you how to wield the magic inside these orbs as long as you leave Axton on land and give Ben back to my father."

Striker's eyes widen. "Hmm, I like it…a daughter for a son." He licks his lips. "Which does a father treasure more?"

"Eribelle, stop talking nonsense," Dad says, almost in hysterics, "Come stand by me, child."

Dad's tan skin glitters with the morning light shining bright. The new day awakes, ignorant of the havoc on our beach. Once the mermen gang drag me Below, I'll be trapped forever more. This will be the last time I witness a sunsrise and its beautiful colors streaking the sky like a brush on canvas. Ink, paint, acrylic, chalk, lead, or anything used to draw, write, or create art are impossible to use in the endless waters. To save Axton's life, I'd be giving up my dreams, my passions, my family, my life, and my future.

"I gave you the light, dear one." Ulsa speaks clearly on the beach and nods to me. "Use it wisely."

Ulsa smiles, showing dimples that Axton's genes didn't inherit, but otherwise they have similar cyan eyes. This is the woman who helped raise Axton, who made him into the man he is today.

In the blink of an eye, the junipers and oleanders next to her side bloom larger when she brushes the edges of the plants. "Even those with dark magic can create life and goodness," she says, "We all have a choice."

"Eribelle, do as I say," Dad roars. "Come here!"

"No, I can't let anyone hurt Axton. I love him, Dad."

Dad's face turns red but I can't allow my attention to linger on him any longer. I lock eyes with Axton's terrified expression. His arms hang defeated by his side within the net. When I'm Below, he'll be safe from the bounty. Our love was never meant to last an eternity, but at least this way an entire war will also be prevented. Ben will be returned home. Axton will be safe.

"Eri, please don't," Axton whispers, and I can feel the pain in his soul.

I fight back tears and memorize his features, then take a step toward Striker. "Promise that Axton will go free."

"First, come here to me, dove." Striker holds out his dirt-crusted hands. "A little further…one more step."

"No!" My father screams so loudly that I jump and pivot. "I refuse this trade!"

Light reflects off a sharp blade in his hand.

Ulsa smiles gently at her grandson and says, "Don't fear getting lost, my boy. That's where you'll be found."

In one sweep, Dad slices a deep slash across Ulsa's neck. She collapses by a pile of mollusks in a heap. Dead. Madness erupts.

"Grams!" Axton's raw scream splits my heart in two.

Dad waves and rushes toward me. "Eribelle, come."

I can't believe it. Dad is actually choosing me?

Jordan yanks the heavy net and jogs toward our estate, dragging a screaming Axton behind him.

Striker hauls me into his chest and pulls me underwater. I kick and thrash but his hold is too strong. The orbs follow like a school of fish. We swim lower, where it's darker, and my lungs burn. The water turns colder, freezing. Need air.

I'm going to die. When my vision turns hazy and I almost suck in a giant gulp of water, an orb melds with my tattoo. The symbol glows bright blue, but it's too late, I can't wait any longer. I open my mouth to command the orbs. They may have damned me, but they'll also be my salvation. I refuse to let this by my last breath. They listen.

And I suck in water. Relief floods my veins and sweet liquid glides down my throat. The sensation is so odd, yet I can barely focus as my mind races to catch up. Am I in shock? I can barely process what happened on the beach.

Axton may still be under Jordan's control, but at least he's away from the bounty and those hunting him. I don't even know what happened to Lena. Horror strikes like a drum in my chest. Dad killed the Sea Witch. He killed Ulsa. The scene replays again and again. All I can see is her lifeless body falling to the ground and Axton's distraught face.

"You will be loyal only to me," Striker growls in my ear, "or else I'll hunt down your boyfriend, do you understand?"

I nod, exhaustion washing over me. Too scared to ask where he's taking me, I scan the seas and pretend that the merman's scales aren't pressed against my skin. My eyes droop with fatigue when jellyfish float by. I should be mesmerized. Instead, I can only picture Axton's red marks from that wretched rope. He will escape. He must.

"We're here. Remember, keep your mouth shut. Actually, whenever we're in Our Royal Majesty's presence, you are to stay silent."

I snap my head up and gawk at the giant castle Below. "Majesty? The queen? But you're a criminal. Why would she see *you*?"

"I said no talking." Striker rips off his mask, revealing a RMG royal crown around his forehead, complete with a golden gem in the center.

"You're in the Royal Marine Guard?"

He grips me tighter and I know bruises will form. "I'm not just in the RMG, girl. I'm the *head* guard; your precious Axton's commanding officer."

It takes a moment for it all to register. Axton's dagger had his tracking location. The only people who knew that were Lena and the RMG. Which means RMG members were in the gang. Which also means this merman knows more than most. He knows secrets.

"Where's Ben? Where's my brother? Take me to him!"

He clicks his tongue. "Sorry, dove. Your brother died years ago, courtesy of the princess's jealousy. Now stay silent."

No, I couldn't have given up my freedom for nothing. A thousand questions burst to the forefront of my mind, but we dive closer to the castle, so I have to stay silent. What in the Abyss am I supposed to do now?

CHAPTER 24

Axton

I'm strapped to the outer wall of Finley Erickson's estate, where the waves crash into the limestone wall and hit my waist. The damned enchanted rope scorches my skin each time I shift from this painful hanging position. With my wrists tied above my head, there's no point in trying to break free of these binds, so I simply await my inevitable death. Stone scratches against my back and water slowly rises. An hour ago, it only sloshed at my knees, but soon, at high tide, it'll hit my mouth—and drown me.

It's almost laughable. I'll be the first merman to die from too much water. It's better this way, to be gone from the world before knowing about any of the pain they cause

Eribelle. Plus, Grams is waiting for me in the Abyss, to cross over together. The scene from the beach replays again and again in my mind, torturing me. The sharp blade against Grams' throat. One last second of eye contact. Crimson blood spurting out, soaking the sand.

I wince and shake my head. Why didn't Grams use magic to kill them all? I've witnessed her capabilities, and no mere human should be able to capture a Sea Witch. I didn't protect her. From any of them. Paralyzing defeat crashes over me.

I failed. Again.

Both my parents died because I wasn't fast or brave enough. Grams was murdered for those same faults. Eribelle was taken and probably already murdered.

Grams' last words haunt me: *Don't fear getting lost, my boy. That's where you'll be found.* The only way I wanted to get lost was with Eri. Now, she's gone. Tears pool behind my eyes but I don't let one fall. I'm supposed to be strong, a warrior, a fighter, second in command of the RMGs. My entire purpose is to keep people safe, yet the ones who matter the most to me continually leave. Hopelessness presses all around and engulfs me.

I'd rather meet my end than survive without Eri. She had made her last choice, a sacrifice, and I'm making mine—surrender. If only the tide would rise faster, then I could slip away sooner.

"Are you done feeling sorry for yourself?" Lena's voice cracks to my right as she lifts her head above the water.

I had been close to forgetting she was there and don't even look over. Also, tied up, but upside down. Lena will be the last victim of my parade of deficiencies. Once it's low tide, she will suffocate when air is her only option to breathe in.

"Boo hoo. The big bad merman has hit an obstacle. I guess it's time to give up."

Squeezing my eyes shut, I try to block out my friend's voice each time she strains above the water to speak.

"Poor Axton needs someone to hold his hand through his tough time. Poor poor, baby."

I focus on the sounds of the last place I'll ever be. It seems as if I had gotten used to living in pitch darkness. Seagulls squawk overhead and wind whips against my ears. Battering waves crash against the wall and each time it splashes a new section of my skin, I shiver from the abrupt cold.

"My best friend *used* to be someone who never quit. Have you seen him anywhere by the way? I need to beat his ass for feeling sorry for himself."

My leg muscles clench in response to Lena's sarcasm, then cramp from the painful angle I hang from. Ignore her. Ignore her. A bell clangs in the distance, somewhere north, signaling noon. Hopefully, I won't be here anymore the next time it strikes at thirteen o'clock.

"You haven't seen him?" Lena drops Below for another gulp of water then emerges again. "Well, my friend *used* to be a guy who fought for what he loved. I need to find him and relay a message."

When I hear her drop Below, I open my eyes again. There's nothing I can do. I have no tail, no ability to breathe underwater, no energy left to help. There's more than one way to lose oneself. The moment Eri was dragged Below, any clarity for answers disappeared with her. My mind is currently wandering in a messy maze of chaos and the only way out of this disaster is to accept my fate.

"Once, a little fish told me..." Lena struggles each time she's above water but keeps talking. "...that my friend, Axton—that's his name—that he doesn't even know what ketchup is."

"Yes, I do," I whisper.

"Ahhh! He speaks!" Lena quickly dips into the water, then

up again. "Welcome back to life, soldier. Hurry up, let's get out of here."

"No, Lena." I sigh deeply. "Free yourself. It's over for me."

She spits water at my face and it drips down my chin. "You asshole! I need you. Eribelle needs you."

Ignoring her glare, I stare off at a sailboat cruising miles away. They can't see us hanging here on the cliffside of the harbor, but even if they did, rescuing me would be a waste of time. I don't have anything left.

"I'm not going to give you a pep talk, Ax." The edge in her voice gives away how worried she feels. "If I had your spear, I'd gut you with your own weapon right now," she snaps. "You deserve it. Actually, I know who deserves pain...Eribelle..." Lena sucks a breath from Below then joins me again. "I can see her now, scrapes bleeding on her face, bruises on her wrists, scars decorating her legs, nightmares singing to her when she sleeps, harsh words thrown her way, unwanted hands on her body, that merman pressing into her—"

"Shut up!" I scream, making the seagulls nearby fly off. The water level is already at my chest when every muscle writhes against the ropes. "Shut up, Lena! SHUT UP! Don't you think I'd try to escape if I could do any good? And that I'd try to protect and save her and everyone if I had the ability? I can't! I CAN'T!" Panting, I stare down at her liquid brown eyes, the ones I've known since childhood.

"Ulsa knew what she was doing," Lena's voice softens. "It wasn't your fault that she died. Your Grams loved you and she knew it was her time."

Tears burst from my eyes and streak down my cheeks. I can't even use my tied hands to wipe them away, so I let them fall into the rising waters.

Lena disappears below, giving me a moment. With each muscle flaring, I scream and scream and scream and scream into the cursed afternoon air. When my throat turns raw, my entire body feels heavy and sags against the stone wall.

Lena slowly breaches the surface again and pulls against her binds to lay her cheek against the side of my waist. "Ulsa's magic will stay in all of us, as long as we still have *you*. I know it's scary." She continues, "Have faith in your Grams. She always had a plan. You're ready to be Nerida's Sea Nymph, but first, you need to get lost in the magic. Let go of your fear of not being enough to save everyone."

Dumbfounded, I can only stare at the water level hitting my shoulders now.

"I need you, Ax. Not to be a hero, but to be my friend. Trust your magic, Ax. Don't give up."

My mind and my heart go to war, wreaking havoc on my soul. I'm only supposed to be a merman who fights to keep his queen alive. There has never been a plan for me to take over the most important job in all of Nerida. How am I supposed to know how to fill Grams' footsteps without training? I don't even know what that magic feels like.

A lie.

The distant voices of the wretched neeks crawl up my spine.

You've forgotten who you are.

"No, I know who I am," I say tiredly.

Lena looks around fast. "Who are you talking to?"

A strong hold clamps down on my chest and the sights, sounds, and scents of this cliffside vanish. I squeeze my eyes shut and my world spins into another dimension.

My father wore the uniform of the RMG. He smiled down at me. I was only a teenager but already knew I wanted to be like him someday. During negotiations with a leader from Above, something felt very wrong. His essence stunk of rot and manipulation and the sharpness of his eyes was only made of deceit. On instinct, I stretched my palm out to the human, and black liquid, thick as oil shot out at their leader. It strangled his neck like a noose and the other men began hollering and pointing their weapons at my father.

"Son, it's okay. You're safe, but I need you to calm down. Listen to my voice and come back to me."

I locked onto my father's blue eyes as the human kept yelling. Realization struck that I used dark magic. Grams' power must've passed down to me like we always expected. Before I knew it, my father was shielding me.

Then suddenly, the human waved a trident in front of my father's face. The blues of Dad's eyes turned ghostly in an instant.

"Dad?" I shook his arm. "What's wrong?"

"I have no son. Get off me."

His fuzzy image is replaced by the twin neeks, who hiss in front of me, here and now. "Answer the question, young one. In what ways do you truly feel most lost?" one neek snarls.

Father's face morphs into Ma's, then Lena's, then Grams', and finally Eribelle's. Love. The answer is love. I have no control over my love for them or the feelings that make my heart tick. Being in love with a woman is the most disorienting emotion of all, aimlessly wandering without a compass, and terrified of the unknowns that our future holds. I've been holding back in fear, not wanting to relinquish that control.

"Love," I whisper out loud, terrified, but ready to accept my magic.

In that instant, I know I already possess the Sea Nymph's magic. In my veins, I hold the power to cast spells, keep all of Nerida safe, concoct the potions for the maturation ceremony, and assist as a secondary forcefield around the castle.

When I open my eyes to the bright day, the water level slaps against my chin. There's no time left.

"I can do this, Lena."

She only nods from under the surface, her big brown eyes showing full trust in me. I recall the ways Grams had wielded her magic by practicing yoga in her cottage when I watched from the shadows, but her methods never made sense to me. I have to find my own way.

"I need a weapon," I mumble to myself.

Unable to grab anything with my hands tied, I scan the surroundings. Jagged corners of the stone wall could scratch deeply, and one individual piece would be heavy enough to knock someone out, but I can't chop a section out without another tool. For clothes, I only wear shorts and…the belt!

"Lena!" Water splashes into my mouth.

She pops her head up, terror swirling in her gaze due to the water's higher level.

"I have a plan. Use your teeth to loosen my belt."

Her eyes widen. "Ugh, this is gonna be so awkward. Don't tell Nolia about this."

With her teeth, Lena rips, tears, gnaws, bites, and chews my belt until the leather finally comes undone from its clasp. Pain surges in my shoulders as I try to bend my elbows and pull myself higher to suck in more air. When she finally loosens the belt, it drops and sinks so fast that neither of us can catch it without our hands free.

"Damn it!" I yell as she dives down to try and fetch it.

I gasp for breath, harsh water smacking into my nose. When Lena remerges, she shakes her head wildly. "It dropped too far, my ropes won't reach!"

"I need a weapon!" I shout, and Eribelle's face flashes

before my eyes. Why the fuck did I wait so long? I wasted all that precious time.

"You ARE a weapon, Ax."

I crane my neck back and gulp in my last chance of air. The tide rises to my eyes. I am the weapon. Dark deadly power lives in strength, force, and hard assertion, with unrelenting decision-making. I'm all of those things, but what balances my darkness is my counterpart. The cunning woman with creativity, light, imagination, affection, passion, and vitality. Together, with my dark magic and her orbs of light, anything is possible.

The crown on my forehead starts to heat against my skin. My lungs burn for air.

I picture Eribelle's fascination with her dancing orbs and looping blue swirls inside. The awe on her face resembled a master painting. Beauty and love can be weapons too. My muscles strain with such intensity that I feel like I might explode. Bubbles shoot out of my mouth and rise to the surface. Fish scurry away in fear and Lena drops from view. An abrupt shock racks through my core so strongly that I black out for a moment.

"Axton!" Lena yells.

I snap my eyes open and immediately know something is different.

CHAPTER 25

Eribelle

The damaged mirror doesn't show who it's supposed to. The red-haired woman staring back at me with defeated eyes and brows tightened with misery isn't the vision I had planned for myself. Sampson and I had shared one simple dream, to spread our passion for art and start a new life. Instead, only loss has knocked at my door and burst through without welcome. Sampson is gone. My father is a criminal and I'll never see Axton again. The reality of that last thought feels like a bulldozer slamming into my chest.

In the mirror's reflection, the orbs no longer swirl with cyan streams of light, but inky black fog. I can no longer see the intricate pattern of the magical strings twisting and looping endlessly. The orbs huddle together like a nervous group of students on their first day of kindergarten.

Again and again, Striker tries to grab them. He's never quick enough as they swim in tandem out of reach each time he lunges.

"Ah!" Striker growls and swears under his breath for the hundredth time. "Tell them to come to me!"

I ignore him since he has demanded my silence, awaiting when he will lash out at me with violence. Multiple weapons hang from his belt loop, their engravings worn off from where he has gripped them over the years of training.

"You bitch! You have three minutes left to give me the orbs or I'm dragging you to the queen."

Striker makes the enchanted rope on my ankle zap me with a new burn. Pain radiates from my ankle up my leg and I hiss in a ragged breath.

Even if I knew how to master the orbs, which I don't, I wouldn't acquiesce to his request. It doesn't matter anymore if this guard kills me, I simply wish he would do it quickly. What more is there to live for after handing my future over to this monster?

My life is fucked.

I made a mess of everything and didn't think this through. I probably didn't even save Axton. His pained expression when Ulsa dropped to the sand will always haunt me. If only the last memory of him was his crooked smirk that made those devious eyes come alive. I shake away the grief-stricken version of Axton and replace it with how he appeared when locked with my gaze. At least I managed to help him return his eyesight.

I can only hope he has escaped. Otherwise, Dad will use him as leverage. Whether he actually misses me or not, Dad will spend his empire's fortune to prove that he has the situation under his control. He will start a war because of his pride, but I'll probably be a corpse by the time it's over, like Ben. Dad doesn't even know he's fighting for a dead son.

"Two minutes, girl! Give me access to the orbs!" Striker yells.

I sigh and flatten the ridiculous dress that he demanded I wear. It was obviously stolen from a shipwreck, but the vintage fashion proves that the treasure is at least a century old. My cleavage resembles a pirate's wench in this suffocating corset and the heavy skirt parallels the weight on my heart. Everything feels different underwater, including the texture of these clothes. No wonder merfolk don't wear much.

"Blue looks good on you, dove. It makes your eyes look edible." Striker hisses as he swims for another orb.

I cross my arms to cover my cleavage.

He chuckles, a sour nasty sound. "Oh, don't worry about that. I warm the beds of my mates. I don't want any woman."

I lower my arms and glare, wanting to snap back that even if my body won't be touched by him, it doesn't mean I'm safe.

"Time's up," he says before the two minutes are up. Another torturous burn scorches my ankle and I'm surprised I have any skin left there.

"Let's go, dove. The majesties are eager to meet their new servant and the princess wants to use you as her new dress-up doll."

My spirit sinks further. Of course, *that* would be my fate, to become a mannequin for a spoiled brat.

Striker guides me down a daunting hall and I'm still in disbelief that I can breathe down here. Will this magic ever run out? How painful is drowning? Can I command the orbs to kill me?

"Hurry up, dove."

Swimming is awkward and slow going without a tail or fins, so he basically drags me with the rope.

"When you meet the queen, you are to remain silent, do you understand? And anything I say, you will nod your head in agreement."

I swallow the hatred and shove it deep into my belly. Extravagant gold and blue shimmery squares decorate each surface like scales of armor and reflect my face. Just like in the mirror, I despise what I see. My fingers long to claw each scale down and let them shatter to the floor, except gravity is different in the sea, so they probably wouldn't even crack. There's not even a chance to harness my rage into destruction.

We wade into a massive room with glamorous thrones made of coral, but all I can focus on is the decay dripping from the edges of the Delphi roses that are entwined in Princess Gia's long braids. She sits by her mother, miming in the water as if she's conducting a silent orchestra. The deranged expression in her ghostly gaze fills me with dread.

"Sebastian, the tempo must be faster, hurry!" Princess Gia demands to a pile of dead crabs at her feet.

Her mother, the queen, acts as if this is completely typical and gestures to Striker calmly. "You failed to mention the important detail of the human's orbs, my *loyal* guard."

"Yes, they turned black, my queen, but I can fix it."

"Delirious disease drinks disgusting dynamite," Princess Gia chants, giggling, then points to an imaginary musician. "Delirious disease drinks disgusting dynamite."

They both ignore the princess, but I can't manage to look away. She's probably eight years older than me, around thirty. The princess is striking with violet eyes, vibrant blue hair, high cheekbones that shimmer with gold glitter, and long eyelashes meant to seduce anyone with a beating heart. And I'm going to be her puppet. Fabulous.

"The humans broke the peace treaty when they killed our precious Ulsa and captured my niece." As she speaks, the queen ignores her daughter's outrageous movements on the adjacent throne. "We all know by now that the traitor is Axton, so during our upcoming rescue mission to free Lena, he will *not* be saved—"

"But Your Highness, shouldn't we be in charge of what punishment he—"

"Do not interrupt me, soldier. Axton does not deserve to return to our Below. That is the ultimate form of punishment, worse than death itself. Whatever the humans do to him Above is no longer of our concern. As long as he doesn't set tail or fin in this sea again, we will forget his existence."

I gulp, not knowing if this is good or bad news for the man I love.

"You will assemble the RMG, ask for aid from neighboring armies, and prepare for battle against the humans. We need to know how many will fight. Expect the nets on boats to be lined with tree nymph's enchantments." Queen Rayna's challenging purple eyes dive into my soul and after only a few moments of our locked gaze, it seems I have passed one of her tests. She nods and turns toward her daughter. "Gia, darling, you have a new friend to play with. Go on and bring her to your chambers."

"Delirious disease drinks disgusting dynamite." Princess Gia swims to my side, her scales dyed a cotton candy pink. She takes my hand and pulls me in the direction of a back tunnel. My heart drops like an anchor to the ocean floor. Gia truly is deranged.

When the orbs follow above my head, Queen Rayna bolts straight off her throne. "You told me you'd have control of the orbs." She scowls at Striker. "This human cannot be responsible for our people!"

Princess Gia stops our momentum and turns to scan me for the first time as if she's studying my potential. "Is it true?" she whispers to me. "The orbs answer to you?"

Her scrutiny sends shivers up my spine, but I still don't say a word out of fear of more burns on my ankle. I roll in my lips and cower at Queen Rayna's continued reprimands to her head guard, asking, "How has a human mastered our magic?"

Princess Gia glances from me to my orbs again and then winks. "Come on, I have something to show you, friend."

As she tugs me down a bright corridor, I glance out the windows into the sea. Behind us, Queen Rayna yells about a ticking time bomb and how tomorrow will be their end if Striker doesn't sort everything out. Maybe I won't live through the night to witness the devastation myself.

Suddenly, out the window, I see a building in the shape of a bubble, with the entire exterior made of glass, reflecting multiple shades of blue. I clutch my chest and stop in my tracks. It's the same building Ben drew in his architect notebooks a decade ago.

Gia notices my reaction to it and tilts her head. "What's your last name?"

I point at the gorgeous building, jaw dropped, and move to wipe away a tear, forgetting that I can't cry in the water. Bracing myself to receive a burn on my ankle, I speak anyway. "Erickson. Ben was my brother. I'm sorry he cheated on you, but did you really have to execute him?"

"Execute?" Gia giggles. "Dynamite! He still *is* your brother."

"What? I was told he died a few years ago."

She giggles again and pulls me along. "Wrong, friend. My Partner is alive and happy."

"Partner?"

"Oh, yes, you arrived right in time for the ceremony. Our

wedding day is tomorrow. I'm so glad you received your invitation by human mail. We will be sisters!" She twirls in the water. "I loved my Ben the moment I laid eyes on him in that boat so long ago. He looked like a mighty prince with his untidy hair blowing in the wind and that scruffy dog by his side."

Ben never had a dog to my awareness, which only proves that Gia is a bit unhinged.

Instead of leading me to a bedroom as expected, Gia peeks over my shoulder and then lowers to the tunnel floor. I stop caring what wild game she's imagining in her mind and stare at my brother's masterpiece outside. Artwork. My chest seizes in a flurry. During his time down here, he managed to leave a piece of himself and create something beautiful before he died that will stand the test of time.

The pristine arches of the exterior are so smooth it doesn't seem possible to have been created without magic. In awe, I gape at the size of it and immediately wonder what's inside. A little tingle starts deep in my core and travels to every limb, all the way to my fingertips and toes. If Ben transferred his dreams and art to the Below, maybe there's a small chance I could still have a future here. It'd be lonely, without family or a sane friend, or Axton, but I'd have one small thing that would motivate me to trudge along day to day. Art.

The orbs surrounding me seem to flicker with their natural blue for a moment but I probably only imagined it.

Little sparks of inspiration tickle the idea button in my brain. What if?

What if Ulsa gave me these orbs for a reason? What if she deemed me worthy enough to make a difference with her people? With the power of the orbs, I can implement an art program. No species should have to live a life without paint, ink, chalk, or a way to fully express themselves. I don't have to be useless down here but I can find a way to make art possible in the water. It'd be a way to blend two separate cultures—a common ground.

If I can befriend Gia, maybe she can help me sway the queen to change their plan for me. Even if they hate all humans now, I can change their minds and be the bridge that closes the gap between the two species. If this works…even though it's a long shot…there's a small chance…I can eventually find Axton.

Just as a hint of hope wraps around my heart like a ribbon, a loud click comes from below Gia. She hauls open a door to a lower level. What's inside steals my breath away.

CHAPTER 26

Axton

My magic works. Kind of. I breathe in water in deep gulps and the relieving sensation feels like coming home, but when I swish my hips to flick my tail, there's no momentum in the water. Legs. Fuck, I still have legs. Unable to swim well with these long, dangly limbs, at the surface again, bobbing Below and Above. Up and down. Each time my head rises above the water level, I can still breathe in the oxygen as if I'm human.

"Well, there's still some tweaking to do with this magic," I tell Lena. "Can you pull me?"

"It'll take too long," she says.

I breach the surface again and glance around for boats

headed in the direction of Nerida's castle. There's not one, but ten giant sailboats leaving the port simultaneously, all headed in the same direction, with Finley's sails, black as death, proudly fluttering in the wind.

"Shit!" I explain the scene to Lena, not exaggerating about the dozens of giant nets they're prepared to drop.

"We need to warn my aunt!"

For the first time, my duties to protect the queen aren't my priority. "You can, but I need to see if Eribelle is still alive first."

"How? You can't swim and I can't pull you that far. You don't even know where she is."

"Just pull me to one of their ships. I'll climb the side ladder," I point and Lena's gaze follows.

She nods and grabs my wrist. It doesn't matter that water slips right into my mouth because miraculously I can breathe both. Even though Lena struggles to pull me, I relish the water flowing over my skin and her dolphin-esque motions that my body longs to mimic. We barely make it to the side of a ship that's already gaining speed.

My best friend gives me the look I've seen a hundred times and silently we agree to meet after the impending battle. If I were smart, I'd stick by her side because the men on this ship are the ones who chained me to the side of the mansion to drown, but Eribelle might need me. I have to believe she has survived.

Holding her breath, Lena boosts me to the ladder and I grip the slippery rung. I shake water from my hair and droplets fly in all directions as I peek over the edge. When something sniffs my forehead, I gasp and almost fly backward into the sea. Chaos licks my face. I'm so relieved she's safe, but worried about her falling over the side of the boat.

"Go below deck, Chaos," I whisper but she ignores me.

Instead, our pup barks excitedly, alerting the entire crew to my location. I'll be more vulnerable hanging here so before they approach, I jump to the deck quickly.

"Whoa!" Brooks hovers their hand over their weapon. "I thought they put you in the dungeon."

"No," I snarl at Eri's cousin. "Her charming intended *Partner* chained me to the side of the mansion to drown at high tide."

"I did. So, how the fuck did you get here?" Jordan says from across the deck, holding the trident.

The trident.

The legendary weapon.

It's here.

I've only seen it in person once before, as a merteen, right before my father was hypnotized. My entire body goes rigid. How in the Abyss did this man come to possess it?

All my rational plans blow away in the wind. Instinct takes over.

I attack. My fist collides with his nose and Jordan's neck snaps back. He stumbles and trips over one of the nets, dropping the trident.

"Fuck you!" Jordan screams and wipes the blood from his face.

A handful of his comrades point their spears, daggers, and knives at me and form a half-circle. I'm backed against the edge. Jumping overboard wouldn't get me where I need to go fast enough. I should demand they change course to Eribelle's location, but my thoughts rush with rage toward the human race.

"Give me back our trident!" I yell, with both fists raised. Muscles pumping, I lunge for its silver handle. A man blocks me and swings his sword. I leap back. Heart racing, I twist and come behind him. In one single motion, I steal his sword and grip its hilt.

Game. On. Assholes.

Jordan rises from the deck and draws his sword, leaving the trident where it is. He charges. Our swords clang and clash. One. Two. Three times. The suns bear down on us. Sweat drips down my back as our swords collide again and again.

I scoop up the trident.

When the silver touches my skin, a raw magnetic pull of power tugs within my headpiece. Paired with the trident, my gem's magic rejoices in its completion, and I hold the strength of the seas at my fingertips. Energy washes through me like a tidal wave.

I scream at the top of my lungs with fresh force and an abundance that's all-consuming. The afternoon clouds are immediately overcome by shadows, making the skies darken to match my rage. These humans stole our trident decades ago. Queen Rayna never should've signed the treaty with these thieves. No human deserves another chance.

And merfolk Below stole my Eribelle. None of these souls will live another day. Lightning splits the afternoon sky and lights one of the sailboats in this fleet afire. In the distance, men scream and rush around as I grin.

Chaos growls at me and lowers her tail between her legs. My heart skitters with excitement as I point the trident between her eyes. Maybe the dog's skull will be my first trophy. I can envision it now, shelves and shelves of skeletons, for each of my kills. How many hundreds can I take?

I swivel on my heels, basking in the potential of this trident. Jordan and his men gape at me in horror and one crew member cowering in the back points at my crown. Good, they should be fuckin' scared.

"The gem," Jordan gawks stupidly, "it turned gray."

I point the trident at him. A streak of lightning explodes

from it and hits him in the chest. He drops to the deck in an instant.

Dead.

A whisp of his spirit floats into the air. I suck it in, inhaling the man's soul and swallowing it whole. Damn, it feels good. The other men all step back.

"Axton, Son, give me the trident." An assertive voice that sounds both familiar and not, speaks from the helm.

I turn and meet the gaze of Finley Erickson. His brown eyes swirl with fear. Good. They should all suffer by my hand —him the most. This monster imprisoned my Eri her whole life. Now he will know what it's like to feel pain. Gladly, I point the dagger at his chest, ready to impale him with a new bolt. He needs to suffer the same fate as Grams.

"No!" Finley raises both hands and steps in front of the crew, closer to me. "The trident will consume you, boy. It's why your great-grandmother gave it to us humans years ago. The trident and your powers are opposites. If used together they only create destruction. The treaty originated to balance the power."

I pause and scan the skies. Not because I need to hear more of his lies, but to absorb the electric energy from the roaring thunder booming above. For the first time, everything makes sense. I truly am a weapon. All of us nymphs are weapons and we won't be used for others' agendas any longer. Once I find Eri, I'll gather all the Sea Witches together into a coven as we should be. None of us should have to abide by human treaties. It's now clear that Grams was a slave all those years, trapped by rules and used for her powers. Never again. A new era will begin, starting with the demolishing of anyone who stands in my way.

I raise one hand high and make rain hurtle down in a shower of death.

"Axton, you're going to hurt us," Finley comedically tries

again. “Hand the trident over.”

“I’d rather not,” I growl and point the trident at each crew member’s chest. “I can’t man this ship alone. If you want to live, go exactly where I say. You!” I shout at Brooks. “Head due south.”

The men all rush around in the rainfall, except for Finley, whose glare burns a hole between my eyes, below my sacred gem. He looks hungry enough to try and rip the crown from my skin. I’d wipe him out before he ever has the chance. Eri will eventually thank me for it later.

Thunder rumbles and the waves grow, shaking the side of their ship. I breathe in the mayhem and stand at the stern as the ship tosses the men and Chaos around. I suppose the animal can live for another day unless I see those fangs once more.

“Axton, stop this storm! Eribelle wouldn’t want this!” Finley shouts against the wind and blinding rain.

I dart toward him, fingers clutching the staff of the trident so tightly, I might split it in two. I pin Finley between my hip and the gunwale so that we’re almost nose to nose. My chest rises and falls fast, adrenaline pumping.

“My Eri despises you,” I snap. “You’ve never seen who she really is, her strength and creativity, or what she wants. You have NO idea who she is.”

Finley stands straighter and slowly reaches for his back pocket. I allow him to pull out whatever he is trying so desperately to show me. As the men behind us struggle against the storm, Finley’s eyes glisten in earnest. He holds a piece of paper in his hand and rain splatters it. He quickly unfolds it to show a painting done by a young child. The colors and brushstrokes are elementary in nature but still gorgeously intentional. The image depicts a girl with long red, unruly hair standing by the sea. One arm is stretched toward a mansion where a man reaches back to her, but they're too far away to make contact. The girl's other hand extends to the wild ocean, where a mermaid protrudes from the waves—also too far away to touch.

"Eribelle and her brother are the only recorded hybrids that we know of," Finley whispers as the rain smooshes the paint together into an incoherent mess. "Their mother was a mermaid."

Lightning strikes and I see the ferocious truth in Finley's eyes. How is this possible?

"I've carried my daughter's painting in my pocket for two decades to remind myself that she can't be reminded of her origins, of what she is." He crumples the splotted paper and throws it overboard. "Of course, I know she loves art and wanted to leave our harbor. I know she's stronger than I let her believe, but I couldn't lose her too. The sea kept taking my family. Eribelle was all I had left and I'd do it all again to keep her safe by my side." He grabs the trident, above my hand and we both tug hard in a battle of control. "And I'll do anything to return my daughter from the Below."

"Good, so we're in agreement," I growl, the storm egging me on. "We'll find Eribelle and kill whoever stands in our way."

"Yes, but not this way. You're a danger to her under the spell of this weapon." Finley tries to yank the trident from me but I rip it from his hands and march away.

Over my shoulder, I call out to him, "And you won't see your daughter again if you threaten me once more."

We will sail to the border of Nerida and when the annual festival of their ritual begins, it'll give me the ultimate opportunity to take teenage hostages until they hand Eribelle over. I won't leave the royal courtyard without Eri—even if I must murder the entire community who raised me.

Another shock of lightning disturbs the sky, but all I can do is smile and set my sights on the raging ocean.

CHAPTER 27

Eribelle

My older brother stares at me. Ben is here. His face hasn't changed much. Other than the thicker beard, longer hair, and slight wrinkles around his eyes, it's as if I've been brought back in time. Ben squints. Maybe he won't even know it's me since I was eleven the last time we stood next to each other. The moment he recognizes me, he staggers back into a table twisted in coral.

"No! Why is she *here*?" His gaze darts from Princess Gia back to me. "Why are you *here*? It's not safe. Go home!"

"Um, hey bro. Long time no see." I salute him awkwardly, then fiddle with Mom's ring still on my finger.

"You're not supposed to be here," he mumbles and runs a hand through his beard. "Gia, babe, what did you do?"

"She's my maid of honor, sweetie. We need to get her a dress for tomorrow. I think blue would be good, to match her eyes and the—"

"Gia, focus." Ben takes her by both shoulders and grips too tightly. His thumbs dig into her skin, leaving indentations.

I step forward to stop him, shocked that my brother would ever hurt someone when suddenly Gia shakes her head wildly and gasps. She glances between us, confused.

"Well, fuck!" Gia rubs her eyes and slaps her cheeks. "You look just like him. You must be Eribelle? Welcome to Nerida. Anything I've said in the last few minutes…or maybe hours… I won't remember and whatever I told you might not even be true." Gia starts to rush around the coral-filled room filled with treasure chests. She opens multiple that are overflowing with a variety of weapons and backpacks. "There's a powerful trident in the possession of humans that can hypnotize and control minds. It was used on me years ago and even though I'm slowly recovering, my mind hasn't been the same since. Once it took me a week to snap out of the trance."

I nod, mouth agape as I take in her wild movements around their hidden vault. "So, you're not Committing?"

Ben laughs and nods. "We are, but first, we need to escape Nerida. Now that her symptoms are manageable, we're using the ritual tomorrow as a distraction while we slip out and move to another sea." A look of dread washes over his face. "But, Eribelle, how are you here?"

I'm hovering in the water and my muscles cease to function. "Me?! How are *you* here? How are you even alive?"

His brows furrow together. "Alive? What do you mean?" When Ben scans my face, I'm not sure what he sees, but he slowly sinks into a coral chair. "Oh my Goddess…you never got the letter."

My heart races a mile a minute. "Letter?" I can barely breathe.

"Before I left home, I slipped a letter under your door, then said my goodbye to Dad."

Dad knew…this whole time. On top of everything he's done, this betrayal feels like a shark has ripped off every limb and torn me to pieces. Dad lied to me. So many times. All my life. He hid my identity. He fabricated stories. He contained me to his harbor.

"I always expected to come back and visit, Eribelle. I'm so sorry, but there were…complications." He pauses and watches Gia zoom around the room frantically. "Dad should've at least told you that I chose our *other* option—the life Mom wanted us to explore."

"Excuse me?" I swallow and try to stop my hands from shaking. "What other option are you talking about? He said you died in a boating accident…a storm took you under the sea."

He dropped his head in his palms. "Oh, Eribelle. No, no, no. I chose a life as a hybrid."

"Hybrid? What's a hybrid?"

Gia stops collecting items and freezes, watching our exchange.

"You…you don't know?" Ben runs a hand through his thick dark hair. "Dad didn't tell you?"

"Tell me what?"

"Our mother. She was a mermaid."

I fall into the coral chair next to him, unable to process. There's no telling what my expression shows because I can't move. Can't think. Can't talk.

Wide-eyed, Ben seems at a loss for words, then finally

says, "Haven't you ever wondered why you can breathe underwater?"

"I never tried."

Ben slowly reaches for my hand. "And you thought I've been dead this whole time?"

I pull away, words failing me.

He sighs. "I always meant to visit, but Queen Rayna had other plans. When she found her daughter and me spending time together, she knew that no human would understand if we were ever caught. She feared that anyone Above would've considered me taken, meaning the treaty would be broken and then they'd retaliate against her queendom." He stands again, and it hits me how much broader he has become. Yes, he is a different man altogether. "It's why Gia and I need to flee. We finally have our chance for a life together."

"But what about me? I just found you."

"Come with us," Ben says.

"I can't."

"Why not?"

Maybe of anyone on this planet, my brother would understand that I fell in love with a merman-turned-human, but there's no point in telling Ben about any small hope I harbor for seeing Axton again when my purpose for coming Below is to give Axton a chance to survive.

Loud trumpets blast and echo down the castle's tunnel.

"Shit!" Gia grabs three spears and swims over. "It's Lena's horns."

Pulse speeding, I ask Ben, "What do those horns mean?"

"I don't know. In the ten years I've lived here, those ones have never been blown."

Gia swims toward the exit door. "It means an ambush from Above. The treaty is officially void. This is war."

Ben's grip on his weapon tightens until his skin turns

ashen. "No, we lasted ten years. We only need one more day. One." His breath turns ragged. "Why now?"

"It's Dad. He's here for you," I say.

The last place I want to go is anywhere near our father. He deserves the wrath of the ocean and a lifetime behind bars. I snatch the smallest of the swirling orbs and tuck it in my dress, between the fabric and my skin.

Quickly, I try to memorize all of my brother's features. Even if we only had a few minutes together, it's more than I ever expected. He's safe, alive, and in love—and I plan to keep it that way. For my own sanity, I must believe his story. I must trust he had good intentions and planned to visit. Circumstances out of his control caged him. Even if I wish my brother never left home in the first place, I'll always love Ben.

"You two need to leave." I manage to sound strong even though I feel anything but. "There'll be a battle, so the RMG will be too busy to notice you've left."

Ben and Gia exchange a meaningful glance and communicate something silently. "No," they respond in unison. "We won't run from a fight or abandon our merfolk."

Ben closes his eyes and his legs change into a tail. My heart stops beating for a moment. He holds out his hand, ready to pull me along. The three of us dip through a secret door I hadn't noticed into the vast waters. We dive and glide toward the attack.

As Ben pulls me, for a moment, all my worries fade away, as well as the reef, the turtles, dolphins, and suns rays surrounding us. When Ben smiles over his shoulder, everything fits into place, as if this is where I've always meant to belong. It feels more natural here than I expected. I try to accept the idea that our mother was a mermaid. I'm half mermaid. This can be my home too. The orbs following us buzz with energy.

As we curve around sea life and the corner of the castle's exterior, a massive formation of RMG hover in lines. Their matching crowns remind me of Axton, however, their gems aren't the same color as the one in his headpiece. Hopefully, wherever he is, he'll never learn of what takes place today. I'll do whatever I can to keep his comrades alive. None of Axton's people need to die because of my arrogant father.

Ahead, Striker swims by the Queen in the front lines, obviously looking for me and my orbs. I can't sit back and witness pointless deaths. As Queen Rayna gives the soldiers orders, I slink behind Ben and blow him a kiss through the water. I'll probably never see my brother again, but I have to try and stop this. Suns rays grow brighter, and the waters turn warmer as I swim higher. At the surface, I gulp in the air, surprised that I still have the ability.

Waves crash into my head. I turn around and gasp. The sky straight above is cheery and bright, but a thick wall of suffocating gray barrels in, only a few minutes away. Over twenty giant sailboats with sails as black as Dad's heart, head straight for my location, dragging the storm with them. I must stop them all.

The orbs float next to me, my only companions. Instead of the blue strings looping together, a bright white light shimmers, its source of pure magic fuels my veins. Unsure if it'll work, I tread water and grasp the nearest orb. With all my might, I chuck it straight into the sky and say a little prayer to Ulsa that something goes right for once. Lightning strips the air of innocence and hits my orb. A thousand colors burst from its core and explode in every direction like fireworks, from magenta to juniper to parakeet shades. My heart skips at the majestic beauty. If only an alternate dimension existed that'd allow me to paint those deep lace-purple and highlighter-pink blooms leading to the heart of the storm.

The lead ship changes course and charges straight to my explosion—and me. I wave an orb above the surface to guide the boat. The ship has a carved horned siren on the prow. Of course, Dad's would be leading the assault. My muscles clench tight as I search for his red hair behind the helm, but I don't see his silhouette yet. Darkness prowls closer and soft drops of rain flirt against my cheeks.

My arms grow more tired trying to stay at the surface, but I only need to last a few minutes longer until Father arrives. All I need to do is give him a good enough reason to leave the merfolk alone. What would motivate Finley Erickson more than anything? His pride. I could blackmail him with the information that he reproduced with a mermaid. Twice. None of his friends would understand that and he'd be disgraced. But will I resort to destroying his future happiness? To save an entire society Below? Yes, yes, I will.

As the waves grow rougher, I worry about my stamina as Dad's ship closes in and I dodge the bow. I hear a familiar barking and my heart spasms at the possibility of Chaos flying overboard in these crazed waves. The anchor splashes into the water only a few yards from me, then thunder rips through the skies. I jerk my attention to the calloused, large hand that grips the rail.

Wait, that isn't Dad's hand. A figure leans over, with long, wet, blond hair followed by blue eyes. Axton. His gaze flashes threats more dangerous than the howling winds. He glares at me like we've never met, hatred devouring his face. When he shifts, a trident is gripped in his other hand. Before I can gather any thoughts, a ravenous smirk rises on his cheeks and he points the tip straight at my head.

CHAPTER 28

Axton

The precious trident speaks to me. *Take back what is ours. Find the orbs and bring them to me.*

Its raw power roars through my blood. *Hurt. Slaughter. Maim. Murder. Fetch the powers no matter the cost.*

I nod and smile. The magic it calls for, that power we need is visible, within our reach, hovering in orbs near a wretched woman with flaming red hair.

CHAPTER 29

Eribelle

My heart pounds harder in my chest. Why is Axton looking at me like I'm the enemy? Lightning attacks. Bolts shred the sky in white veins, contrasting against the dark clouds. Suddenly, light shoots out from the trident. An orb darts in front of me as a shield. I scream and cower as the bolt crashes into the sphere of power and explodes into a thousand glittery shards. They mix into the rain, so it looks as if gold specs fall into the sea.

"Axton! It's me!" I scream through the wind, but he either can't hear me or doesn't care anymore.

The murderous glare morphs his face into one I can't recognize. My pulse beats frantically. I swim toward the side of the ship, where nets are being lowered into the water. No! I must stop them.

Muscles flaring, I swim to the side, careful not to touch the enchanted rope. The ladder is slippery. I grip each rung as if my life depends on it and haul myself higher. Rain gushes over my face. Panting, I reach the edge and topple onto the deck.

Immediately, the remaining orbs shield my body. I scan the crew. Half are tied in their own netting, including my father and Jordan. Tilting my head, I open my mouth to speak, but a flash of lightning hits the deck near my feet. The wood scorches ablaze and flames spark.

"Shit!" I hop away. The growing fire forms a barrier between my father and me.

Up close, when I finally meet Axton's deadly glare, I gasp. Any words I might speak to dissuade him are stuck in my throat. Why did I think I could handle this?

"Give me the sea's power!" Axton roars in a menacing voice.

My entire body tenses. Why is he acting like this? I meet my father's eyes through the rising flames. "What did you do to him?"

I can't hear, but Dad mouths, "*The trident*" and points.

Gia said a legendary trident had hypnotized her and controlled her mind. Is the same thing happening? Ben snapped her out of her hypnotic state with a rough shake. Will the same thing work if I try?

"Axton! Drop the trident!" I take a trembling step toward him.

If I can't get him to listen, this entire crew might perish. Even though the rainfall is controlling the spread of the fire, it's not enough to completely put out the flames, and the storm has only worsened. Once we're knocked overboard, there's no way we'll be able to survive in these intense waves.

I have a few orbs left, but don't know how to control their power.

Axton's godlike muscles flex. He raises both arms to the sky. True fear coils around my neck like a poisonous snake and tightens its hold. Tears of warning pour from the crying sky. The ship rocks violently. I stagger to my left, then my right.

"Give me the orbs!" Axton screeches.

I grab onto the railing, so I don't get tossed over, but still take slow steps toward my man.

"Don't come closer!" He screams and points the trident at me again.

My chest clamps. I swallow my terror and move forward again. A lightning bolt streaks the air and I squeeze my eyes shut. Another orb jumps, colliding with it, and shatters. I can almost feel the raw power floating around us like dust powder. The wind carries its remnants across the surface of the sea.

If Axton keeps smashing them, I'll run out of protection. Water sloshes against my shins. I might die. There's no way I can stop now. He needs my help, like when he was blind, but now he's lost in a different way, unaware of what's real or who he truly is.

"Axton!" I slip in a puddle and land on my knees in front of him. "Axton, stop this! I love you!"

This time when he points his trident at my heart, it's clear that a piece of him has been broken. He yells something into the wind and lightning zaps out of his weapon again and again. My orbs shield me. They combust and disintegrate one after the other until only a single ball of light hovers between us.

When Axton crouches to my level, there's no recognition or adoration left. He lifts my chin with one cold, wet finger and says, "It doesn't matter how beautiful you might be, I could never love someone as worthless and mundane as a human. You're such a fool. Everything I've ever said to you has been a silly game. How have you not figured it out by now? Are you as stupid as your father claims?"

The pieces left of my heart chip off into fragments and slivers. Not because I believe him—but because, once upon a time, I would have. Axton loves me without a doubt.

I can stop this madness. There's one more hidden orb I tucked away. I swivel fast, kick a sweeping leg behind his ankle, and knock him to the deck. Axton's hard grunt of pain tears a hole in my soul. He lands hard on his back as the trident twirls in the air. It slices through the raindrops as if they were solid marbles. I reach out to grab it, but the trident is too far and lands a few feet away.

"Axton, this isn't you. Come back to me."

He finally stops reaching for the weapon and stares. A burst of electricity explodes from the trident straight at me. I raise an orb to block. A ferocious energy bounces off. It strikes Axton straight in the chest.

It hit him instead.

Axton goes limp, deadly still.

The world stops.

Rain hovers midair.

All-consuming terror severs what's left of my hope.

I can't breathe.

I can't breathe. Goddess, help me breathe. The rain falls again but softens to mild tears. I crawl to Axton's side and hover my hands over his unmoving chest. What do I do? My hands tremble as I shake his shoulder.

"Axton?"

Nothing.

Thunder quiets and only the confusion of the crew remains. Some of them break through the ropes.

"Axton!" I shake harder but his body stays loose, flopping against the deck. "Axton! Wake up!"

A strong hand rests on my back. "He's gone, baby girl," Dad whispers. "He was a monster but you saved us, sweetie."

"No!" Tears well and I brush the sopping hair away from Axton's face. "Come back to me!"

Dad tries to pull me away but I scratch, claw, writhe, and scream until he drops me.

"I love him."

"You can't."

A weight heavier than imaginable bears down on my chest as I whisper, "Just like you couldn't love a mermaid?"

Dad's jaw drops.

I cling to Axton's chest, burying myself in his skin. Not once in my life have I felt such raw pain. Sounds around me disappear and the only thing I can see is the gem of his headpiece, pulsing blue.

Wait. I freeze. Axton once said that the gems are connected to their souls. If it's still full of light, if it hasn't dimmed yet, then he must still be alive. I lean closer and almost touch the stone. The little ancient symbol in its center glows and flickers, like its fighting to stay lit. I scramble to retrieve the last orb.

Desperate, I give it a shake. "Wake him up!"

Dad sighs behind me, but if Dad touches me once more, I'll snap him in half.

Out of options and ideas, I stare at the looping streamers inside my orb. For the first time, the thin swirls inside contort to something entirely different. Two long neeks wrap around each other in loops. Have they always been there?

"Can you hear me?" My hands tremble so intensely, I'm worried the orb will break. "Please, I'll do anything. Keep him alive. Save Axton."

"Dark magic needs a trade, child," they hiss in unison and I startle from the eerie pitch.

"Yes, okay, I'll give anything." I nod and grip the orb harder. "What do you want?"

"What is he worth?"

"Everything! Let him live!" More tears spill onto Axton's chest. "Please!"

The neeks push together so their eyes line side by side, and hiss together, "So be it, child."

A bright light shoots from the orb and wraps around my body. It lifts me in the air and I'm weightless, spinning slowly, out of control.

"No, wait! Don't use the magic on me! Save Axton! Save *him*!" I try to wrestle free of its invisible hold but it's useless.

Magic churns and ripples of light flow out from my limbs, tangling me in an illuminated web. A blow of power bursts into my chest and runs down my torso to my legs. In a heartbeat, my lower half turns into a tail. Choking from shock, I gape at emerald scales as the beams slowly lay me back on the deck. Completely in awe, I reach to stroke the gorgeous scales attached to me. Is this real?

I suddenly clutch my throat. Water. Need water. Gasping to fill my lungs, I panic. The side of the ship is too far away. The crew circles me, all mumbling and pointing. Wheezing, both hands find my neck and I try to speak, but…fuck!

Can't breathe!

Water!

My chest tightens…

And vision blurs…

Water!

Head spins…

Sturdy arms lift me and I force myself to focus enough to meet Dad's eyes. They're rimmed red with regret and apologies. Before I can read more into it, he heaves me overboard with one giant toss. Need water. I soar. Fall. Splash into the blue, and suck in exquisite frigid water.

My senses return with a tsunami impact and I scream, "Axton!" again and again until my throat burns, "Axton! Axton!"

Did it work? Underwater, goosebumps prickle my arms with the sudden sensation that I'm being watched. I swivel around and the entire queen's army is ready for action. Lena, Gia, and Ben all wear stern expressions, positioned in the front lines with spears pointed at the vessels behind me. I'm the only thing that stands between the start of the battle.

Striker is about to give orders, but I cut him off. "Lena? Ben?" I glance between the two, mind racing. "How long can I hold my breath Above?"

Lena shakes her head and Ben starts to move forward, but Gia grabs him by the wrist, keeping him at her side. I don't have time to wait for a clear answer. I swim up, where a few rays of sun have broken through the storm clouds and shine into the blues. Faster.

I break through and a breeze slaps my face. "Axton!" I try to shout but it comes out strangled and unnatural.

Scooping a gulp of water quickly, I yell again, then drag my nails over my cheeks and swear, progressively louder with each passing second. Pushing my limits, I climb the ladder and peek through a hole.

Axton sits, panting, but alive. His eyes are wild and out of control. He notices the trident and tries to roll to it but my father blocks him.

"Dad!" I force but still catch his attention.

"Get in the water, Eribelle!"

But I can't let this battle begin. Too many lives will be lost if anyone touches that trident. How can I destroy it? My lungs burn. I can't fail my kind, merfolk or humans, but if I'm a hybrid, what does this mean? Am I a nymph?

The nymphs all gave mysterious advice: *Touch the gem to the power source to stop it all.*

I freeze, thinking.

Touch the gem to the power source to stop it all.

I need to touch the orb or trident to the gem in Axton's headpiece. A strange gut feeling tells me I'm right. He's so close, yet the distance between us may as well be canyons.

My body is shutting down. I dig deep within and force manic energy to consume my movements. Desperate, I want to wail and beg for help but my lungs deceive me. I strain up to the deck. My fingers grope the wood flooring and I drive my hips back and forth to squirm. The flopping tail hinders fluid movement, but I can't focus on that because the crew is pinning Axton.

"Eribelle!" Ben somehow stands on two legs in front of me and grabs a bucket of water and dumps it on my face. It tastes like fish and grime but gives me the fuel I need. "What are you trying to do?"

"Touch the power source..." I pant. "...to the gem. Touch the trident...to his gem." I point with a wobbly hand to Axton's headpiece.

Shit, what if Ben doesn't know that I meant the orb. Ben bounds across the deck, scoops both the trident and the remaining orb. My brother howls in obvious agony when gripping them.

I can't let him do this alone! It's hurting him! One laborious step at a time, Ben drags them to Axton.

"Move!" He bellows and elbows the crew out of his way.

Ben rams the point of the trident straight into Axton's crowned gem. They both roar in pain. At the same time, sailors are thrown from the impact. Bound by a ball of mixed light and shadowy mist, Ben wrestles against an invisible pressure. He hauls the orb to the gem, but he's not strong enough. The orbs resist. I'm too far away to help. It's too late.

I claw at the deck, wood stuck under my fingertips, but am unable to slither toward the side of the ship. Water. My heart thuds so fast it might rupture my ribs.

Out of time. Suffocating.

I'm going to faint, yet I see our father crouch next to Ben. With their joint strength, they groan loudly. Together, they heave the orb toward the gem. Their tendons nearly tear through their skin. Their mouths spew excruciating shrieks.

It finally brushes against the gem. My father's entire ship detonates in a cracking boom. The deck topples into a slope so steep that I roll off the side and splash straight into the sea. I gasp from the cold of the water.

Bodies crash into the ocean. All unconscious. Men sink fast. Damn it! I grind my teeth and pivot in all directions, searching for Ben and Axton. Wait, Ben can breathe underwater and Gia will help him anyway. I must save Axton.

I poke my head Above where scraps of scattered wood float in the waves.

Axton's blond hair reflects gold from the sunlight. He clutches a plank. No movement comes from his broad back. Then he coughs and relief pours into me. I swim over, but he slips below the surface.

I follow. Gab him. Pull Axton up. Hurry, damn it. Swim faster.

I grab the crown on his head and snap it off.

Nothing happens. His body is slack, heavy, drooping

"Axton!" I scream and shake him. "Wake up!"

Wind howls through the air. I won't be able to hold him much longer. My muscles shake and exhaustion hits me like a tsunami. As new tears streak my cheeks, I kiss him gently on his lips.

Axton's eyes spring open. "Angelfish," he whispers.

That adorable smirk immediately rises on his face and he holds out both arms to me. He's alive. He's okay.

In shock, I scan his body. The headpiece is gone, but more surprisingly, his tail has immediately returned.

"Come here, Eri," his scratchy voice sounds exhausted.

Heart pounding, I swim into Axton's arms, and almost knock him into a piece of the ship.

"Whoa, no need to get frisky."

I laugh, snort, and cry at the same time as I burrow into his chest. He wraps both solid arms around me so tightly that I become oblivious to the rest of the ocean. For a simple moment in time, everything is okay. Axton kisses my forehead and I sob, unsure if I'll ever truly know whether mermaids can cry tears of joy under the sea.

CHAPTER 30

Axton

The events of last week are a blur. I can't count how many times I've apologized to Eri. Maybe once more will erase the festering guilt.

"I'm so sorry." I hover my hand over a healing scratch on her collarbone as I clasp the shell necklace she picked out for the annual ritual.

In front of the mirror, Eri swishes that magnificent tail, eases her back into my bare chest, and meets my eyes in the reflection. "If you apologize one more time, I'll go find that trident and do a stabby stab to you myself."

I grin as she playfully tugs at the rod of my spear I hold in one hand. The other arm I wrap around her waist and force myself not to explore further.

Eribelle turns toward me, batting her long eyelashes as the current rocks our hips together. "It wasn't your fault that it hypnotized you."

"What if I had hurt you?"

"You did."

I groan and back away, but she catches my wrist and pulls me in. "When you didn't understand what ketchup was, I mean, that's *hurtful*."

"Well, since I'm back in the Below, I might not ever learn what ketchup is. Can you live with that?"

Eribelle tilts her head and scrunches her adorable nose. "Let me think on it for a bit." Her thin fingers graze the necklace, one of Grams' favorites. She brushes the largest conch shell in the middle. "You don't think she'll mind me wearing this?"

"She'd threaten me if you didn't." I squeeze her tighter, never able to get enough.

Eri cranes her neck and looks deeply into my eyes. "Do you think Sampson is putting makeup on Ulsa somewhere?"

"No way, Ulsa is teaching him how to mix potions."

"Yeah, he'd probably want to haunt someone." She chuckles and leans her head on my chest. "Are you ready for this? We could've delayed it a few more days.'

"Well, I do wish Chaos was here...for emotional support," I say to her, in denial of my nerves.

"Brooks said we can visit her every week on the beach."

I'm glad my girl takes the bait as a distraction to change the topic. Before yesterday, my answer would be *no, I'll never be ready to replace Grams*, but magic runs through my veins.

As we swim toward the castle, I can't help but bask in the fact that our queendom is safe, for now. With the trident shattered, the humans can no longer create havoc for Nerida, and after Ben, Brooks, and Eri had a long chat this morning, the human fleet returned to Erickson Harbor, nets and all.

Her father, however, had gone missing. At some point during the storm, the man vanished or drowned, and I've yet to know how Eri's processing his disappearance. He's the one who believed wholeheartedly that the merfolk broke the treaty and was so determined to destroy us. Maybe seeing both his children choose a life Below, the life of their mother, forced him into a new outlook. We may never know why Finley aided Ben with ramming the orb into my gem. Was his intention to help or harm? I'm just thankful it worked.

I pass Queen Rayna, who uncharacteristically bows her head to me. I blink, grateful that she has dismissed the accusations against me, and bow further in return.

Next to her, Lena stands as the new head guard who has already imprisoned the traitorous Striker and his followers. The new guards grip their spears and stare off into the deep marine colors, ready to protect the throne. The spear in my own hand no longer serves the same purpose; it's only for show. As the new Sea Nymph of Nerida, I clutch the familiar weapon mainly for comfort.

Dozens of merteens hover on a stage in front of a large, silent audience. These are the last moments before these children choose their identity and future. They all stand straight, shoulders back without any sense of uncertainty. Pride washes over me with extra appreciation for our culture.

I reach the podium, where vials are locked into one of two cases—potions to finalize their sex and transition them through the next steps of maturation. Luckily, Grams had already mixed all the ingredients for today, giving me another year to learn that magic.

At the podium, I brace myself to speak to the crowd.

"Hello. Thank you for joining Nerida's sixteenth falcon year Choosing Ceremony!"

The crowd all wiggles their fingers in the water to applaud.

"I humbly ask for your support in this new role as Nerida's Sea Nymph. Please know that I take it seriously. Ulsa was loved by us all, even though we each had a healthy dose of fear for her too."

A round of chuckles from the front row prompts me to loosen my grip on the spear.

"These merteens know the important choice they're making and we all vow to respect their decision."

"We all vow to respect their decision," they chant in unison, as tradition.

I cast a glance at Eribelle, who nods in encouragement.

"Lastly, please show your appreciation for Eribelle." My voice booms through the microphone over the crowd. "Without her help, bravery, and creative wit, this ceremony might have been a mass funeral today."

Some merfolk drop their heads to honor the deaths we suffered, while others wiggle their fingers and smile in agreement. We still have some work to do as a community to make sure that our relationship with humans remains nontoxic, but Eribelle has already shown interest in serving as our ambassador. A hybrid born from a mermaid but raised on land has more weight to carry in our negotiations. Not all of them agree that she should live here, but we will all work together to find a common solution. Until then, I'll protect her until my dying breath.

"Let's not delay." I snap out of my daydreams and continue, "The first merteen is…Arlo."

A youngin with long wavy brown hair and freckles steps up and points to the safe on my left. I nod, hand over a vial labeled 'female,' and they drink the contents quickly. Under her ceremony robes, her curves start to become slightly more pronounced. The shape of her face shifts slightly and I soak in the wonder from the powers pulsing within the tattoo on my back. Arlo turns toward her comrades, lifts both hands in the air, and hoots with joy. They shout back to her and an enthusiastic round of hollers carries over the crowd.

I smile and offer the next name. "Renley."

They move forward, and make the accepted gesture for selecting neither potion, then return to their spot. The crowd erupts again in cheers and settles quickly.

As I continue with the list, and watch each merteen go through their ritual, my mind wanders across the glorious blues to the distant coast of Ozaron. Eri always planned to start a new life. She'd been trapped at the harbor for over twenty years, awaiting the day when her Dad would finally accept her. I don't want her to feel trapped here either.

"A toast!" Queen Rayna's voice jolts me back to attention. She doesn't need to yell for her voice to vibrate through the waters. The merfolk raise their glasses in unison and say, "To Nerida!"

"To Nerida," I whisper.

Across the stage, Eri winks at me, and I immediately relax.

"...and a better tomorrow!" Queen Rayna finishes her speech and hugs Gia. "Okay, everyone, enjoy the celebration and thank you."

As if reading my mind, Eribelle swims toward me, her red hair pulled back into a thick twisty braid.

"You did great." She plants a kiss on my lips. "You can relax now, no one exploded from the potions."

I wrap her into a hug and ease into her familiar embrace. "We can change you back, you know," I whisper in her ear. "If I turned myself into a human without using Ulsa's powers, I can learn how I did it and turn you into a human again. I wouldn't even have to drop you off at the harbor but at Ozaron instead."

"Are you trying to get rid of me, Mister Axton?"

I pause. "Will you ever regret this life? Being stuck Below?"

"I'm not stuck if I choose you." Eribelle trails her lips down my jaw and tenderly brushes them over my mouth.

"But you didn't choose me." I grip her waist as her hand roves my chest. "The magic forced you into a mermaid form."

"Hmm…" She pecks the tip of my nose and one brow arches. "Hybrids can have secrets too, ya know."

"Secrets? What secrets?" I gulp as her hand strokes down my stomach, my muscles hardening.

"First, why don't you tell me one of yours." A devilish predatory look flashes in her eyes. "You once told me that mermen anatomy is…different."

I can't help but smile. "Ah, that secret. Yes, I can teach you, but my lessons are long."

She pulls me further away from the crowd and my heart flutters with anticipation.

"How long are we talking?" Eri asks.

"Oh, a whale's lesson couldn't compare."

"I see."

"Actually, no, Angelfish, seeing isn't an option. I was blind for so long." I reach for a ribbon that washed away from the ceremony and clings to coral, then wrap it around her eyes. "Now, it's time for you to get lost in your new land."

With the top half of her face covered, my girl is still as radiant as scales in the sunslight. Even if I fake complete control, her sweet smile spurs my every move.

"Give me your hand," I command.

She tries to hide her grin but fails miserably and holds out her hand. Hidden between the trench walls of Nerida, I move her fingers down, down, down, watching her face the whole time. Eri licks her lips, sending my sanity spiraling. When her hand finally reaches my so-called-anatomy, so hard for her, a slight gasp parts her lips.

She wraps her hand around me and whispers, "Now I know what every human Above will be wondering."

I laugh. "You mean, whether it's made of skin or scales?"

"No," she kisses me softly, "Who is the muse of all my future artwork."

EPILOGUE

Eribelle

One year later

I can't contain my excitement. A giant banner, larger than a yacht, flutters high in the breeze, welcoming hundreds of artists from international waters, labeled, *'Ozaron Art Festival.'*

Wading in the shallows, the sand tickles my stomach, just above my tail. Both hands prop my chin, and my elbows sink a little as the tide washes in and out. On my left, Axton scans the beach for threats—the forever guard– but we've had successful peace with the humans for the last year.

Music flows from a live band down the street and the

scent of cinnamon wafts in the salty breeze. My hair whips around, slapping Axton in the face, so I quickly gather it and twist it together into a thick braid.

His shoulders finally loosen as he glances over. "You're nervous."

"Am not." I bite my lip and continue to stare at my booth, only a few feet away where Brooks displayed my artwork for both humans and merfolk to browse.

So far, dozens of bystanders have stopped to study my unique pieces, but no one has made a purchase.

"Maybe they don't know what it is yet," Axton says, "It's… provocative in its own way…" He tilts his head and studies the rare materials I gathered from Below to forge them with tools from Above, a combination of both my lives. "Give it some time."

I let out an overwhelmed anxious little growl of protest and try to focus on the scenery instead of the crowd of shoppers walking through the aisles of tents. In the background, there are two distinct sectors of this city, ancient and modern. On one side, skyscrapers made by the most prestigious architects tower on the cliff sides, challenging the goddesses to send them crashing into the sea. And as if the city is split in half, the hills on the other side undulate like waves. What lies hidden in their valleys I can't tell, but some of the visible old fortresses and castle-like buildings catch my eye. I'll never walk among the rubble, but maybe I could still create a replica with my art someday.

Even if that never happens, my life has been a fairy tale for the past year. Lena isn't the cleanest roommate, but she cooks me breakfast each morning. The art club for the youth has finally started. We already have eleven merteens signed up. Most days I don't even miss my life Above since I'm able to visit Chaos. Plus, I have my brother back now. The only piece missing is Dad, but I don't think I even miss him. I grieve a relationship lost, a possibility of what could have been.

I sigh at the last memory of Dad helping Ben shove the orb into Axton's gem to stop its crazed powers. I may never know why he changed his mind, but am grateful for that moment of support either way. After months of the RMG searching for his body in the depths, we finally had a small funeral for our father and let him go. Not knowing what happened almost feels poetic in a way. It mirrors Mom's disappearance.

Brooks jogs over from my display booth, waving. They purposefully splash Chaos, who outruns my cousin to our spot in the shallows.

"You've sold two pieces so far," Brooks smiles and gestures to the people hovering around my art. "We've got a new family business on our hands."

I shake my head. "Don't you even dare, Brooks. We sold the boat company for a reason."

"I know, I know, but what if I want to live in a place like *that* someday!" They point to the stone mansion on the farthest hill. From here it merely looks like a crumbling dollhouse, covered in ivy.

"Why would you want to live *there*?" I tease. "It's probably haunted."

"Oh, it definitely is." Their eyebrows dance. "And rumors around Ozaron say that a witch lives inside."

"Really? What kind?"

"No one knows."

All curiosity vanishes. "Then it's a myth, Cuz."

"No way, it's real, and maybe I won't have enough to buy it soon, but maybe I can find out who owns it and run a ghost tour."

"Brooks, you don't know anything about…actually, you know what…that sounds cool. Keep me updated."

Chaos licks my face and leans against my propped arm. I'm grateful that Brooks has spent so much time helping Chaos conquer her fear of the water, so now I can pet her again.

"Hey, girl." I soak the top of her head and she shakes her fur out, flinging droplets over Axton's back.

No matter how many times I see his eyes light up, a flurry of energy zips through my veins. When Chaos barks, I jump with guilt for staring at my man's perfect body. There's a red fanny-pack connected to her collar that I didn't see before.

"What's this?" I unzip the little bag as Axton turns toward me. The playful smirk in his blue eyes tells me that my man is up to no good.

"Axton? What did you do?" My heart thumps quickly as I rummage through the contents.

Inside, there's a bag of mushed blueberries, a bag of crushed strawberries, a little apothecary bottle from Axton's cottage, and paper.

"I thought you'd want to take advantage of our day to breathe air and enjoy some time to paint."

A thrill shoots through my core, but I'm too afraid to touch the paper since my wet hand will drench it.

"Don't worry, these have been *magic-ed*." Axton winks at me and I can't help but roll my eyes.

My greedy fingers grab the papers, ready to create a masterpiece by finger paint if I must. Instead of a blank sheet, there are already colors swirled and looped into a familiar scene: Ulsa's cottage. Its vibe no longer drips of shadows and loss. Bright coral and sea flowers bloom around its exterior, like how I've come to know it over the last few months after cleaning the place up.

At the very bottom of the paper, a tiny line is written in cursive. I squint and bring the paper close to my face. "What does that say?"

"What?" Axton snatches it from my hands and narrows his eyes. "Where?"

"Right there." I point to the tiny scrawls in barely legible handwriting and continue, "It says…will you…"

Axton lowers the paper from his face and that charming smirk flirts with me again. "Will you…"

My heart falters. My tail stops swishing. The waves freeze.

"Will you…move in with me?" Axton rolls in his lips and holds his breath.

If I had legs, I'd jump into his arms. Instead, I wiggle in the shallows and curl into his chest. His scent radiates off all the warm memories from the last year together.

"Only if I get more pillows than you."

He laughs from deep within and it blasts across the beach so loudly that patrons stop their browsing to stare. "Deal, Angelfish."

I kiss his chest, his collarbone, his neck. All I ever wanted was to be a part of a world where I was accepted. Not only did that happen but I found love in the process. Axton and I will be okay, no matter what obstacles stand in our way. A vision flashes in my mind of our potential future, our shared life in Ulsa's cottage, with miniature paintbrushes held by tiny hands. Our potential future.

Above Ozaron's flags, fireworks explode into the sunsset, ranging on a spectrum of cerulean to lavender to shamrock shades. Axton rolls on top of me, pinning me in the shallows. Above his messy blond hair colors shoot in all directions. He lifts my chin higher with one finger and lets me drown in his wicked blues. His lips hover over mine and a strong hand wraps behind my neck.

"I love you, Eribelle." He pecks my lips once, making me want more.

"I know you do," I whisper. "I love you too."

"And you can have all my pillows if you want them." His mouth is on mine again and I moan into his mouth.

"Is that a promise?" I slip both hands into his hair, always needing him closer.

"Only if you finally get me real ketchup."

THE END

Check out **"The Phantom Ink."** Set in the stone mansion on the farthest hill in Ozaron that looks like a crumbling dollhouse, covered in ivy, a witch has been hiding for years, trapped under a curse. This is a Beauty and the Beast, gender-reversal retelling. Read how Mora and Brody turn from 'irritated to lovers.'

Names in the Wicked Blue

Axton- second in command of Royal Marine Guard in Nerida
Ben- Eribelle's older brother
Brooks- Eribelle's cousin
Chaos- dog
Drei- forest nymph #1
Eribelle Erickson- heroine, protagonist, painter
Finley Erickson- Eribelle's father
Gia- Princess of Nerida, daughter of Queen Rayna
Hans- Axton's father
Jordan Idros- Eribelle's intended Partner
Lena- Axton's best friend, mermaid
Nolia- Lena's girlfriend
Queen Rayna- leader of Nerida
Sampson- Eribelle's best friend
Striker- mermen gang's leader
Trey- douchebag in a nutshell, Eribelle's ex
Ulsa- Axton's Grams
Viera- forest nymph #2
Wells- Axton's fake last name
Zilia- Axton's ex

ABOUT CASSIE SWINDON

Cassie Swindon loathes wet socks, leaf blower machines, tight hugs, and rickety fans. Things she might murder for: a free massage, cuddles from a kitten, chocolate milkshakes, and long naps. Some of her favorite activities include decorating for the holidays, playing board games, and avoiding phone calls. She has four more ideas for upcoming books so sign up for her newsletter below.

Check out free short stories as prequels to my upcoming works in progress and also sign up for my newsletter here: https://cassieswindon.com/

facebook.com/cassie.swindon.3
twitter.com/CassieSwindon
instagram.com/cassie_swindon_author
bookbub.com/profile/cassie-swindon
amazon.com/stores/author/B091N72414
goodreads.com/cassieswindonauthor
tiktok.com/@cassieswindon

The Phantom Ink

Prequel

Cassie Swindon

MORA'S THORN

A short story
By Cassie Swindon

A Fairy Tale Flip prequel to "The Phantom Ink"

I slam my hands on the counter again, flop my head down onto the cold surface and let out a loud groan. What other ingredients could possibly create this wretched ink? In my apothecary studio, the size of a closet, shadows flicker on the wall until the sole lamp finally burns out. That's fine. I can work without light.

I hover my hand over more options, from strawberries to crushed rubies to red zinnias. So far nothing red has formed the correct mix for the ink of my cursed pen. The last batch was too mushy and this one is too dry. Yesterday's attempt smelled like a sewer so I threw that one out without even testing it.

"Mora?" My roommate and best friend, Feathi, shouts from somewhere down the hall. "Mora? Where in the Abyss are you *this* time?"

I ignore her, lean closer to my shelf of hodgepodge red items and squint. My body sways from exhaustion, but I must keep going. If the pen runs out of ink then my life is over, as well as Feathi's and our other two roommates.

Guided by only moonlight, I accidentally knock over a bottle and it shatters near my foot. Stupidly, I shriek and jump out of the way, only to step on a broken piece of glass.

"Ah! Shit!" I bend, grab my barefoot and feel warm liquid dripping down my heel. "Awesome. As if I didn't already have enough to worry about."

The spiders keeping me company don't respond to my hilarious humor. A simple, *'you're trying your best, Mora,'* from one of my eight legged friends would be more than enough encouragement to keep trying. Silence surrounds me. Not even the usual sounds of wolves howling in the distance break through these walls.

I'm about to hobble over to the antique lounge chair in the shadowy corner, ready to give up for the night, when another idea strikes.

Blood. Blood is red. I can't believe I haven't tried that yet. My heart rate accelerates. Quickly, I grab an empty bottle and hold it until several drops hit the bottom. It's obviously not enough, but if this works, I'll worry about that detail later.

"Now, what should I mix *you* with?" Keeping all my weight on my good foot, I scan the mess again– red geraniums, Cabernet Sauvignon, and ocean perch from the Barrett Sea.

I gag at the thought of fish guts being inside the ink that writes my life story day after day, minute after minute– never ending until the curse is broken. In fact, right now, in the West Wing, the pen is probably scribbling some sarcastic commentary about how my lack of creativity will be my demise.

"Mora!" Feathi yells again, more urgency in her voice this time. "Get your ass out here!"

It's a good thing I haven't disclosed my secret studio in the few months we've been trapped in this mansion. Though, if the ink runs out soon, then no one will ever find my body behind the secret door. It'll be as if I never existed, like my story never mattered.

That sentiment doesn't scare me as much as it should. The one terrifying idea that does rattle my heart is considering a world without Feathi, Yin, and Nax smiling, laughing, and bantering with each other around the chimney. If I die, they die. So, I must live.

I grab the red wine and pour a tiny bit into the bottle with my blood. The two shades swirl together in a syrupy tornado. No, not quite right. The consistency looks too thin, but the color is perfect. Maybe I added too much wine. There's no time for more mistakes.

Bending to reach my heel, I push against the wound.

Blood flows out of my flesh again. This time I collect more. When I add in the wine, I'm careful to pour less. It blends like Yin dances, fluid and graceful. I hold my breath. Once it settles, I don't dare breathe. The potion inside almost resembles the ink I've stared at for countless hours.

Every hair on my arms stands up on their ends. From the moonlight shining through the window, I read the label of the wine, memorizing the name to use in the future. What if this is it? The possibility is almost too much to hope for. If I replicated the ink, then my roommates and I have more time to figure out how to break our curse. We'll finally be able to live in peace again.

With an attempt to glide to the door, I nearly trip over the old. frayed rug. If even a drop of the potion falls out of the bottle, the mixture might change. This door often sticks so I'd have to yank it open, which might make the potion spill over the side. And I can't yell for Feathi to open it for me, because she has no idea where I practice my apothecary.

If I only I still used magic, the door would swing open easily. Risking everything, I tug on the handle, praying to whatever Goddess above that nothing tips out. Step by step, I try to float down the long, dark hallway to the West Wing, but my injury makes me limp. Maybe keeping my sights set on one thing will help me keep my balance and focus. So, I stare at the wall covered in peeled wallpaper of winged fairies. They look like guardians made out of gothic fairy tales.

I shiver from the cold leaking in through the old windows. "Damn it. Please don't spill," I whisper, "and please be the right potion."

The West Wing is still a few minutes' walk away. Alone, I trek below dusty chandeliers, by cracked stained glass windows, and through magnificent double doors from one room to another until finally I reach the library. It's empty, as expected.

The Book– my stupid, rotten Book– hovers over a table, the one that has every moment of my life detailed since the day my sister cursed me. Some days it's hard to keep track of how much time has passed. And I hate to think of how many more pages will be filled until I find a way to end this once and for all.

An owl's hoot outside jolts me back to the task. My hand is shaking, so I gently set the bottle down next to The Book.

A soft creak of hardwood echoes from down the hall and I freeze so Feathi won't hear me. It's not as if I like keeping secrets from my roommates. But they shouldn't have to know the sacrifices I make to try and solve our dilemma. Maybe the creaks and groans I hear are only the house speaking the language of midnight.

The pen continually writes on a page, so I peak over to read the latest addition:

Mora believes she has outsmarted her problem, once and for all, but she'd be mistaken. Her glorious hope will soon be squashed by yet another failure. The witch is a walking wreck. Not only does guilt weigh down her shoulders from past mistakes, but now she also keeps secrets and lies from the three people who have always been there for her, the three people counting on her to save them. Somewhere in the stars, a moon goddess joins me in laughing at Mora, not for her ridiculous cat sweater or bedhead hair, but for her flittering moment of hope. How she could possibly believe she can save her roommates? But Mora has not yet learned the answer. She's clueless–

"Shut up!" All my muscles are tense.

I grab the pen as fast as possible, pluck off the top and pour the contents of my bottle into the small cylinder area where the ink is placed. It immediately bubbles and bursts out of my hand. Crap. The potion I had poured in flows out like a volcano erupting and splatters all over the floor. The enchanted pen launches out of my hand and fixes itself by reconnecting the tip, then continues to scrawl.

See, I was right. Mora knows nothing. She will run out of time. She's no closer to finding the correct ink than she is to figuring out how to get rid of her hideous thorns torturing her.

I glance down at my cat sweater, where holes open from the thorns that protrude from my wrists, forearms, elbows, shoulders. My curse. These thorns will end me.

"There you are!"

I jump and swivel around fast to meet Feathi's bright eyes–well fake eyes, since she's been made of origami.

"Why didn't you answer me? I've been looking everywhere for you," Feathi says as she crosses her paper-arms.

"I, uh, I was reading and got caught up in the story."

She shakes her head, making the blonde paper-hair swish back and forth. "You're a terrible liar, Mora."

"Shouldn't you be asleep?"

"Woah! What's all over the floor?" She's about to crouch down before I stop her.

"Nothing. It's wine. I was having a glass while I read and dropped it. I'll clean up, go back to bed."

"I'll go back to bed the second you stop ordering me around." Feathi doesn't hide her sarcasm.

"I've got it covered."

"Mora, just let me help you." She stoops again, but I pull her up.

"No, I told you I've got it."

Her paper-eyes narrow. "If you don't tell me what's going on right now I'm gonna go wake up Yin and Nax and all three of us will be hounding you until the suns all rise."

I rub my temples with one hand, careful not to scratch my face. "Fine, I'm trying to mix more ink for the pen."

"You mean, the phantom ink that you told us would *magically* replenish itself soon?" Her tone is sharper than the icicles hanging outside the window.

"Exactly. And I don't need you or anyone else bothering me."

She stares me down, not moving an inch, then glances at the near-empty pen. "I'm going to pass over the fact that you've been lying to all of us for months and assume that there's not much time left to refill it?"

"There is no *'we'* Feathi, just *'me'*. It's dangerous. I've already hurt my–"

"I knew I smelled blood. Where are you hurt?"

I groan and slowly cross the injured leg behind the other. "Please, just go to sleep so you're not in my way. This nonsense is only slowing me down."

"I love you too," she stoops down, rips a piece of her paper-dress off and blots the open scratch on the side of my foot. "There, that should act like a bandage for now."

When she stands, I look up at her beautiful face, wishing the curse hadn't destroyed my best friend's life too. She'd be so happy if she weren't trapped here, hiding from society as a non-human. Maybe she and Nax would already be Committed to each other, living in a little cottage a few miles away.

"What ingredients have you tried so far?" Feathi takes my

hands into hers, still as strong as a human's, but no longer formed from flesh and blood.

"Apple peels, tomatoes, peppers, lobsters, ladybugs, chili, cranberries, raspberries, cinnabar, scarlet macaw feathers, beetroot–"

She holds up a hand. "Okay, I got it. What about plants, flowers?"

"We don't have much of a variety during the winter."

"Roses."

"Roses," I repeat.

We make eye contact and both slowly nod. "Roses!" we say in unison.

There's a rush through my veins, like a spark has been ignited inside me, energizing my body from head to toe.

I dash to the library door, deciding there's no time to grab a coat or gloves. Knowing Feathi is behind me, I jog down the dark hallways. Each tap of my feet along the hardwood floors might wake Yin and Nax, but at this point, I can't delay in any way.

Basically stumbling down the grand staircase to the foyer, I try to save time by mentally checking off the locations where winter roses might still grow in our forest. None will be by the cliffside and it's too dangerous to travel closer to the town in the valley. That leaves us only one option, wolf territory.

At the front doors, I shove on my worn boots lined with fur, then use every ounce of strength to pry open one of the massive doors just a bit. The bottom scrapes and screams against the flooring, not used to being opened at all. A gust of wild, crisp wind attacks my face but I won't turn around.

"If the wrong wolf pack wakes up..."

"I know. Which is why I'll go alone."

"No, Mora. I hate when you do this."

I spin around, faster than lightning. "Do what?"

"Decide everything as if you always know what's best." Feathi blocks my path to the front patio. "Have you even considered that I may have a better idea than you?"

"You're staying here. If Yin and Feathi wake up and try to follow, then we'll have even more problems. I need you to stay to explain, just in case."

"You're the most stubborn, annoying, irritating, arrogant witch I know." Feathi places one hand on my shoulder. "Please be careful. You're also the heart of our little family. We won't be okay without you."

I don't have the courage to tell her they'll definitely not be okay without me, because if I die, they die.

Without looking back, I race down the frozen steps. Even in moonlight the stairs shimmer like crystal. One day in the future I may look back on this time and consider myself lucky for ever being able to live in such a gorgeous home, surrounded by a breathtaking scenery as if we're encapsuled in a snow globe winter wonderland.

"Remember, if the wolves charge, climb up!" Feathi yells behind me.

That reminder isn't needed. I'm thoroughly aware of this possibly suicide mission. Or I may get lucky and run into the one friendly wolf pack that lives nearby.

My boots sink into the snow, one heavy foot at a time. Cold stings my face and I continually sniff to keep my nose from running.

"If I die, they die," I whisper again and again, my breath visible in front of my face with each exhale. "If I die, they die. Keep going."

Eventually my ears go numb and I have to keep cracking my fingers within my pocket to keep the blood flowing.

The treeline ahead shifts from white pines to black spruces. I'm here. Any moment the wolves will smell me and alert their pack. I haven't been this far from home since my sister cast her curse. My body gets tense and I check the snow for signs of pawprints. Nothing. Yet there may still be giant beasts hiding behind the trees in the distance.

I need to keep moving. Where are the roses they guard? I creep forward, hyper aware of each crunch of my boot, each sound of my breath. My heart rate sounds like drums beating wildly for the entire woods to hear.

If I die, they die. Keep going.

To my right, a shadow of movement flickers. I snap my attention in that direction. Only trees. And snow. More trees. More snow. And in the distance – red.

I bite my lip to refrain from whooping and march straight toward the winter rose bushes. At least twenty roses are in full bloom, the perfect redness for the ink. This better be what I need or I'm risking my life for nothing.

They're ten more yards away.

I scan the area again, my body trembling.

Seven more yards away.

I can do this.

Four more yards.

Then a growl.

"Fuck!"

I lunge for the bush. Snatch three roses. Shove them in my pocket.

Turn.

Run.

Something large and heavy swipes behind my knees. I collapse into the snow, hands first. The freezing temperature burns my skin. A scream threatens to break free, but I don't want to alert any more creatures.

Heart pounding, I crawl to the base of a tree. All I have to do is reach the trunk.

A sharp claw slices at my calf. I yell in pain. Keep crawling. Almost there.

The beast behind me flips me over straight onto my back and drags me closer. I can't help but stare at the animal over me. Since it's at least five times my weight, I have no chance.

If I die, they die.

So, I fight. I writhe. Kick. Scream. Slash at it where my thorns are the longest. Swipe with the goal to kill. My limbs flail wildly. Huge paws pin down my stomach but I can't give up.

Suddenly, another thorn sprouts from my finger. Then another. I gasp. I know what this means.

Back in the West Wing, Feathi is purposefully attacking The Book. Each time we try to destroy it, more thorns grow on my body, each more deadly than the last. A new third one grows out of my palm, the largest so far.

Just as the wolf lowers its snout over my face, I ram the thorn straight between its yellow eyes. It wails and backs up, staggering. A strange black ooze comes out of the wound. Intriguing color for blood.

I sprint towards home. Out of breath. Chest burning. Terrified to check behind me. Faster. My legs wobble in protest. My face is on fire from the freezing wind. The iron gates finally appear.

I'm almost there.

So close.

A too-close howl pierces the night air.

Feathi appears in the crevice between the two front doors. "Hurry, Mora!" She waves me closer, then her eyes settle on something behind me. "Hurry!"

I push through the broken gate. Slip up the icy stairs. Fall into her embrace. We stumble onto the floor inside. Feathi heaves the door shut, then slides onto the floor next to me.

Both panting, she lays her paper-hand over mine. But I pull away. Because there's wet snow all over my clothes and skin. I won't risk her deteriorating.

"Did you…" she pants. "…Get any?"

Unable to breathe, I pull out the three broken roses from my pocket and lay them on the floor at my feet.

Now, I'll check if roses are indeed the missing ingredient needed to make more enchanted ink.

Immerse yourself in the other
Fairy Tale Flip Reimagined Books

Start a new Cassie Swindon romantasy trilogy
with Isaac's prequel short story

ISAAC'S CURSE

A short story
By Cassie Swindon

A Linked Trilogy prequel to "Scorched"

The fierce wind flapped the sheet in my hand, so I tightened my grip, shaking out the crumbs from last night's dessert. At least Zeph had licked most of the cake off my abs, so it didn't end up staining the blankets. The morning clouds camouflaged into the fabric, taking the form of a full sail, and I couldn't tell where the sky ended, and the sheet began.

Another gust blew through my loose shirt, the cotton shifting against my skin and exposing the gray and white Mobius loop tattoo claiming my hip. It'd be another sweltering day. I stripped off my shirt and pinned it on the clothesline next to the dancing sheet. Craning my neck to stare at the washed-out, dusty blue sky, I took in the swirls of white and crisp blue stretching through Vayu.

"Isaac?" Zeph's voice gave me goosebumps every time.

"In the flesh." I cleared my throat to get rid of the groggy morning sound and turned to face her.

At age thirty, Zeph didn't look a day over twenty when she batted those long lashes that knocked my breath away. I longed to kiss those high cheekbones and wrap my arms around her slender form again.

"Wes is in trouble."

"What?" Alarm coursed through my muscles to my quickly clenching fists. "What's wrong with Wes?"

"I heard him screaming." Long ringlets whipped her face. "He's outside the dome wall."

My heart stopped. "How?"

"I don't know."

My skin stung as though pricked by needles as I snapped my attention in each direction from the skyscrapers atop the peak to the green treetops that stretched below for miles but couldn't see my son—even with my enhanced vision.

"Follow me." Zeph sprinted down the trail of the steep slope.

I ran after, questions soaring through my mind. The only way my son would have exited the safety of Vayu's barrier was if someone had taken him. How did they find us?

Terror hummed in my bones, and I could feel I was losing control of my calm. My tattoo scorched, summoning my power, and surged a pulse through my body to my fingertips. But I shouldn't manipulate the air this close to the dome—too dangerous. We could be exposed.

Panting, I found my pace next to Zeph, hitting shade at the tree line. Sweat dripped down my neck. My sneakers skidded over loose pebbles, and dirt kicked onto my shins as we descended. Only half a mile left. My calves burned, and my feet thumped on the gravel so quickly, like flying instead of running. When the adrenaline hit this strongly, the sensation of wings always overcame my body, putting me in a focused trance—heightening my sight even more. Immediately, I spotted every angled curve of leaves and the indents on a beetle crawling up trunks as I sped by.

Zeph pointed straight ahead where I knew the invisible perimeter of Vayu met the rest of the world. Wes had once termed our dome "The Bubble." Outside the barrier, a pair of his blue sneakers laid next to a tree trunk. My heart rate quickened.

"Isaac, what if—"

"Don't say it," I shouted over my shoulder as I passed her and pumped my arms faster.

Knowing I was about to transfer through the wall, I squeezed my eyes shut for only a moment and braced for the electric-like pulse. A sharp shock pinged in my tattoo and zapped my whole body from head to toe. Gasping, I landed on the other side of the dome seal, sprawled flat on the earth — Zeph already out of view, protected inside the shield. At least the dome was still functional, and whoever had taken Wes hadn't destroyed the future of our entire city.

Outside of Vayu's seal, I always felt different—vulnerable. The thrum of my powers sliced through me. My sight telescoped in. Exactly one mile to the east, I could see a group of deer grazing. One point two miles to the south, a car curved around treacherous, steep roads. I couldn't see who was inside, but they were moving too fast for a lazy Sunday morning drive.

Some son of a bitch stole my kid. Out of practice, I begged that my abilities were still strong enough.

Widening my stance, I inhaled a deep breath and raised my arms straight to the sky, desperate for help. My heart rate quickened as I summoned every ounce of energy, making an intense pulse surge through my blood. Suddenly, a gust of wind rose and chased the car in the distance. *Form a blockade.* The wind followed my command, soaring forward at my will.

About a mile off, the gust snapped an evergreen trunk in half. A loud crack echoed up the mountain hillside, and the giant tree landed with a thud over the country lane. The zooming car slammed on its breaks and slid to the right on the shoulder, jerking to an abrupt stop. A woman jumped out of her vehicle and raised both arms in exasperation, but now that the car was at an angle, I squinted from afar and searched the backseat. Wes wasn't in there. *Damn it.*

"Oh my god, seriously? What did you do?" Zeph's blue eyes studied me.

I jumped and swiveled on my heels, unaware she had merged through the Bubble too.

"I couldn't think of anything else." I pushed both palms to my temples with such force I swore I could've snapped my skull in half.

"No, literally, what did you do? I can feel your energy, but you know I can't see that far like you."

"Uh, nothing."

She cocked her head, bent down, and reached into Wes' shoe. "Look, there's a note inside."

"A ransom note? Is it someone from Draven? I'll give them anything." I grabbed the flapping piece of paper from her hand and read Wes's sloppy ten-year-old handwriting.

Went to see Mom. Don't be too mad. I'll do extra laundry tomorrow to make up for it.

P.S. You didn't tell me the tattoo would burn me. You LIAR!

I stared, re-reading the last line a dozen times, then finally dropped the paper to my side. Looking over at Zeph's stunned face confirmed my assumption.

"He already tattooed," she whispered in awe with such certainty, paired with knit brows.

"It's not possible. He's too young."

"You know better than anyone that this has happened before. Not everyone is seventeen. Maybe he's as strong as you."

"I was twelve, and *that* was unheard of when we were kids. He's only ten."

Zeph massaged my shoulders like she did last night before she snuck out of my room. "Then maybe Wes is stronger than you."

I could only hope she was right because I couldn't consider the alternative but muttered it anyway, "Or a Draven monster wrote this."

"No, it's his handwriting," she said calmly.

I started walking down the trail, needing to find a car … and a shirt. "Anyone from Draven could've threatened Wes to write it."

After she scurried after me, Zeph laced my hand into hers. "If someone took him, they wouldn't leave a note, and no one from Draven has any use for Wes."

She's right.

"But Wes wouldn't leave. We're a team."

"Maybe it was one of his pranks," she said.

"No, he knows better than to leave the dome."

Zeph sighed. "When his tattoo formed, he was in pain. Do you really think he'd want to show you that weakness?"

"Pain isn't weakness."

"Well, then maybe he's mad at you."

I didn't know how to deal with my son already maturing —I wasn't ready, and neither was he.

"So, you never told Wes about the tattoo scorch?" she asked.

"I didn't want to scare him," I mumbled and moved faster through the woods. An eerie sensation crept over me that we were being watched. I checked over my shoulder. No one. Shaking my head, I continued, "Zeph, a ten-year-old shouldn't have to know all the responsibilities that come with our powers."

"I know you want to protect him, but the last day for that was yesterday."

"No, I will always protect him."

She laid a strong hand on my bare chest, yet with less assertion than she did in my bed last night. "In our world, Wes is now an adult. You need to respect him as one."

A laugh escaped my gut. "You're kidding, right? He doesn't even clean his toys. Toys, Zeph. He is a child. And he decided to run down the mountain alone, without shoes. Why on earth would he go barefoot?" As I side-stepped around her, I nudged into her shoulder a little harder than I should've.

"Ouch. Isaac, come on, I'm on your side." She hustled after

my long strides. "I care about Wes too, and you know I'm better about making decisions when it comes to his well-being. You two can still play pranks all day, but he also needs a firm hand with structure."

"First, we need to find him to lay down any rules." I pinched my beard, trying to contain the wind howling in my heart, not wanting to be held back. "I'm sorry, Zeph, but *I'm* his parent. Maybe you should go back to Vayu."

Time stood still. She tilted her head, holding the long pause between us like a cage of tornadoes threatening to escape. "You don't want me to meet Wes's mom, do you?"

"What? Don't start that again. This isn't about Rajitha." I stared ahead with each continual step, catching a blurry charging station for cars in my peripheral. Maybe the Ordull owner would have a tourist tee-shirt of Mount Evans. I couldn't show up at Rajitha's half-dressed, or I'd get myself into another mess that Zeph would never forgive me for. Sleeping with Rajitha had been too risky. I couldn't let her find out who I really was or about my Magik. The information would only put her in danger. Ordulls couldn't find out about us, Mystiers, which is why I never should've fallen for her in the first place.

Zeph stared at me suspiciously, eyes narrowed.

I cleared my throat before saying. "Plus, you and I are just friends, right? That's what we agreed to."

Her jaw dropped. "Fine. But when you find Wes and have trouble choosing what to do, don't complain to me about it." Zeph turned quickly and jogged back to Vayu.

Alone again, I raced towards the charging station, hoping I wouldn't have to interact with too many Ordulls. Past the trees, over the bridge, and across the street, a squirrel fumbled cracked nuts between its teeth and climbed up the side of the brick building. Despite the distance, my gaze darted through the dirty windows of the shop. No touristy shirts were inside. Damn.

I tapped my solar-powered watch, realizing it was the first day of a new month, so the charging station would be closed anyways. The screen flashed the date, "Red Moon 01-81T," with a bright image of Wes on the front. His gray eyes were replicas of mine, just like his long blond hair pulled back in a high bun mirrored mine. That devious smile matched the one I wore, but his skin tone was darker, more like Rajitha's.

The clouds shifted overhead, turning darker by the second. Local weather forecasters would be frantic about the drastic change. But, I didn't care until Wes was by my side again.

Rain splattered my bare shoulders and trickled down my arms as I headed closer to the road and quickly spoke into my watch, faking a casual tone to my voice, "Hey there, sunshine. You awake?"

Rajitha's sweet voice was peppered with sarcasm when I heard her comm float from my watch, "I thought you only sent that at one in the morning?"

I kept jogging. At least I knew if Rajitha was calm, then she didn't know Wes was missing yet, and I wouldn't be the one to tell her.

I stopped at a crossroads. One headed straight down the mountain, and the other path led to winding paths, eventually ending at Rajithas's. *Which way?*

Rain soaked my hair and drenched my workout shorts. *Focus.* In an instant, the storm mellowed, and the pitter-patter of droplets plunked into the puddle by my shoe. Through thousands of tiny gas molecules, I stared ahead, primarily nitrogen and oxygen with a small amount of argon. *Where are you, Wes?*

Wind howled, and the storm started rapidly again. That

wasn't me. He might be close. I could feel Wes's unsteady energy. Afraid. Determined. Proud. Hesitant. Angry. His emotions flickering faster than a lightning bug. Protectiveness whirled, and my tattoo throbbed, urging me to stop restraining my potential to find him. But I hadn't been training. Magik was too risky to use.

A littered bag plastered to my face, directing me to go down the mountain. I stepped toward Rajitha's house, and more trash catapulted into my body. A fast-food cup smacked my ear. After it dropped to the ground, my shoe crunched the cup underfoot, splitting it in half. A projection of straws hurled and stabbed into my cheek like arrows into a target.

"Wesley Isaac Nilson, I know you can see me. Stop throwing trash at me."

But why couldn't I see *him*? Was he truly stronger? No one at Vayu showed my intense. abilities, which is why they relied on me to run the teen training program.

The wind whispered, tickling my ear: *You didn't tell me about the pain.*

A chill ran through me from the secrets compacted inside that bluster of wind. What kind of powers did my son possess?

"Wes, come here." I scanned every tree branch, unable to spot my son. "Wesley, now!"

Then silence. Autumn leaves swirled down into my hair. I pulled one out of my high bun and tossed it to the ground. The energy encompassing me didn't allow the leaf to hit the trail but kept it dancing by my side, weaving in and out of my knees like a game.

I searched for seconds, minutes, what seemed like an hour, growing more desperate by the moment. Then I felt it again. A presence. Someone nearby. But not Wes's energy. I turned on my heels. Nothing was there. Just space.

Goosebumps prickled my arm. Maybe someone from Draven really did capture him, and this was just a trick. If so, I was running out of time.

My watch vibrated. A still shot of Rajitha's smile and dimples covered the screen, but right when I clicked accept, her voice screeched, "I can't ever rely on you. What did you do? Wes just busted through the door, all scratched up, and looks like he's been in a wreck. What the Abyss is going on?"

Relief blanketed my soul for just a moment. My chest rose and fell fast as I picked up my pace. "He's okay, Rajitha. We just had an argument."

In my mind, I could see her eyebrows crinkle in that adorable way as she was looking out her window.

My breathing turned heavier with each fast step. The road turned narrower around the cliff's curves, and I had to watch my footing— so close to the edge. "We went for a run, that's all."

"In this weather?"

"Yup. He likes the … uh … wind … But we started talking about his karate class, and he got pissed and raced off."

She snorted. "He's faster than you?"

"Apparently." Panting, I swallowed down saliva. "Rajitha, I'll be there in five."

I picked up my pace, grateful that Wes was safe. Luckily, I wouldn't have to deal with a threat anytime soon. My feet pounded the wet pavement, splashing through a puddle

Rajitha's horses came into view first, all umbrellaed and miserable under a tree. As I rounded the bend, a trail of flapping flags led to a view of my sanctuary. Rajitha's cozy, wooden cottage was sandwiched between two windmills. She'd never believe me that the view from her front door wasn't just trees and mountains, but skyscrapers atop a peak, protected by an invisible shield.

I finally reached the path of stones in her yard, starting

from her quaint mailbox, painted all shades of blue, leading to her front door, also painted blue. And I would know because we worked on it together. Wes was a toddler at the time and had knocked over a bucket of paint, and I chuckled at the memory. His baby feet tracked little footprints all over the front patio, and we didn't have the heart to cover them.

As I stared at the prints of baby toes, faded by the sun, my hand hovered over her door. A calming, weightless sensation floated around me like a scarf dancing in the breeze. A tumbling crash exploded inside, followed by a short shriek. I burst in. Wes was chasing after the cat, who darted away, toppling the chess pieces off the coffee table, knocking over the telescope, and scaling up the toybox.

"Dad, Mrs. Puff is scared of me now." Tears streaked down his face as he hopped up and down in place in front of the astronomy charts, desperately trying to hug the cat so dear to him. I remembered too well how animals first responded to my power when it was uncontrolled. Nature always knew.

Rajitha exploded into the room, holding Wes's meds. "Here, hun, your pill will calm you down."

"I'm fine." Wes swatted it to the floor, making the canister roll across the hardwood and land by my shoe.

Rajitha shot him a look, then one just as deadly to me. "Isaac? Can you please …?"

"He doesn't need these anymore." I threw the bottle across the room, and it sank into the trash.

Her jaw dropped. "You're not a doctor." Her thick auburn hair fell in waves over the white silk robe with a slit open just high enough to show the black lace hugging her curves.

I bit my lip. "Trust me, babe."

"Don't …"

Her eyes lasered into mine as she sped forward, tugging me into the kitchen. I'd consider that an open invitation any other day, but now wasn't the time for playing games. Once on the other side of the door, she pushed me against the bay window, her hand pressing against my rain-coated chest. Her fingertips grazed my beard, and the cyclone of passion lining her eyes veered me off-topic. A smile crept up while imagining her body trembling underneath me— always leaving me thirsty for more. But no matter how submissive she was in bed, the hammock, and the shower … she was a fierce momma bear when it came to our Wes.

"What is going on? Tell me right now, or I'll …" When she paused, her nose scrunched up in that perfect shape. "Don't you DARE smirk at me like that." She slapped my hip near my tattoo, sending a jolt of fierce power through my veins, and for a brief moment, all I wanted was to fuck her —hard.

I gulped and rubbed my beard, then let out a deep breath. "Let me talk to him. It's been a rough day."

"No shit. He's acting like a lunatic, and our cat seems to think he's some alien. Now, tell me what happened."

"Nothing. Wes is fine. You know, angsty mood swings."

"I know you have good intentions, but if something like this EVER happens again, I want to go back to court. No more equal custody." She stepped closer, pointing a finger in my face.

Wind whipped against her windowpanes, making her shudder. "And is it Armageddon or something out there? What is with this bipolar tornado freak out? One second I'm hiding in the bathroom with Mrs. Puff, and the next, the air is as still as a statue, and our son busts through the front door."

I crossed my arms and leaned against her counter. "Is that a hypothetical question, or would you like me to educate you about weather patterns?"

She threw a dishtowel at my chest. "Don't be a smart ass."

A smile poked at the corner of her lip, giving me the invitation, I was waiting for.

Stalking forward, I hovered so close that her intoxicating honey scent momentarily distracted me from all the other thoughts spiraling out of control. *Just one kiss.* Her pouty lips hovered under mine, sucking all the air from my lungs. Rajitha rubbed my earlobe, then ran a long fingernail slowly down the side of my neck like the edge of a dagger.

Her hands found my chest. "You haven't come over in weeks." It was a dare.

"Dad!" Wes hollered from the living room.

Rajitha pushed me away. "Go put on a shirt. I have an extra for you in my bottom drawer."

I winked. "Waiting for me to move in, huh?"

"Shut up. Don't even get me started on that. I have still never seen your place." She left to console a weeping Wes.

A kettle whistled, sending steam rising. I passed my hand through the heat, collecting the power and harboring it for later. Would Wes also be able to manipulate steam the same way? I had researched for years to find answers as to why I matured at age twelve and eventually gave up since there hadn't been enough information recorded in our Vayu database to reach a conclusion. *I need more answers.* I grabbed a pen from Rajitha's counter and scribbled a list:

1. Where can I find other ~~mixed kids~~ hybrids?
2. Do all hybrids have powers?
3. Are any hybrids stronger than their Mystier parent?
4. Are they all hidden in their dome, or do some live with their Ordull parent?

I cringed from the static distraction humming in my mind. Peeking up, I saw the television was on, just muted. No wonder. It flashed a news story that read about an increase in earthquakes. An interviewer held a microphone up to a brunette girl with streaks of red in her hair that matched her red crop top. She stood in front of a car, and the ribbon on the bottom of the screen read:

Kyra Kozelski fell into a crack caused by an earthquake after performing at local pub.

"Dad!"

"Okay, bud, I'm coming." I turned off the death machine. That tv had the same toxic energy as all the other electronics in the house. Once it was off, I my mind cleared, and my powers strengthen. Taking a quick moment to make the day easier, I also unplugged the toaster, microwave, and coffee machine, breathing an immediate sigh of relief. As I swung the door open into the living room, Wes's little body smacked into mine in a full embrace.

"Why does my cat hate me now?" He buried his head into my stomach as I rubbed his back.

"Can we have a minute to chat alone?" I asked Rajitha.

"Wes, hun, what do you want?" She glanced at our boy.

"It's okay, mom, this is man stuff." He sniffed and rubbed his eyes.

She eyed me carefully again before we retreated down the hallway. Watching her form had me wishing it was already past Wes's bedtime. I'd have to come back tonight.

"Dad? Why didn't you tell me the tattoo would hurt?" He sat on the edge of the couch, but it was so old the cushions absorbed half his body.

I kneeled in front of him and pushed the blond, rain-soaked hair from his eyes. "I'm sorry, bud. We can talk about everything, but not in front of your mom."

"It hurt so bad." He lifted his shirt a little and showed me his Mobius loop tattoo, gray and white like mine and in a similar spot, diagonally below his belly button, close to his hip bone.

I peeked behind me to make sure Rajitha hadn't seen and rolled his shirt back down, then whispered, "I know, bud. I should've told you. But it won't happen again."

His shoulders softened as he slouched further into the couch. "Are you sure? There's no way I'll get another one, right? Don't lie to me again."

"Well, there's one way, but we don't need to talk about that yet. You're too young."

He sat straight; his eyebrows knit tight. "You told me I wouldn't get Magik until around when I'd be driving."

I smiled. "I guess I need to teach you to drive. Think you can reach the pedal?"

He huffed. "This isn't funny, Dad. I even disappeared."

My heart stopped, and my body froze in place, unsure what to say next when a thousand questions ran through my mind. "What?"

Wes nodded. "You told me all about wind control and weather and stuff and the great eyesight. I mean … when I was running around, I could see super far away, like a superhero. But you never told me I could disappear."

I brought him in close and hugged him to my chest, terrified of what it could mean but so glad he'd have an advantage.

"Ew, Dad, you're all wet." He pushed away.

"Tell me exactly what happened when you said you disappeared," I whispered while Mrs. Puff sniffed the air and tentatively snuck closer.

Wes held out his hand and flipped it over slowly,

inspecting his tanned skin while speaking. "In the forest, when I looked down, my body wasn't there."

"Okay … Um, did it hurt?"

"The tattoo or the disappearing?"

I held his hand. "I know the tattoo hurt, and that was probably scary. But, when you disappeared, what did it feel like?"

He smiled. "Like everything made sense in the world, and I was free-floating."

I knew that feeling. I leaned back and studied him, whispering to myself, "Where can I find answers?"

"What did you say, Dad?"

"Nothing, bud. I'll figure it out …" I rubbed his messy hair. "Now, remember, you can't tell Mom, and from now on, she can't see your stomach. It looks like your swimsuit will cover it, so you should be okay at the pool."

He saluted me. "Yes, sir." His boyish grin turned devilish before he skipped away.

At least he had his energetic spirit back, but I needed to learn the answers to why he matured so early and if this had happened to anyone else. The old wooden clock chirped at nine am, warning me that I didn't have much time.

The breeze shifted, making the windchimes outside strike a faster chord. After a quick glimpse out the window, a small silhouette stood far off in the distance, leaning against an Evergreen. Rajitha didn't have any neighbors. Who was out there? My heart rate quickened, and a jittery sensation crept up my legs. What did they want?

Without taking my eyes off the person, I prowled back to the yard and crossed my arms—claiming what was mine. That should send a clear signal. The guy didn't move an inch but whistled a high pitch call. A brown Labrador dashed out from behind a tree and ran straight toward me, ears flopping and tongue hanging out the side. What on earth? Its paws thundered over the dirt road, casting up a cloud of dust. Once it was a few paces away, the dog stopped and lay down. It carried a little backpack vest wrapped around its brown torso. A piece of paper flapped out the top pocket. I glanced at the silhouette, and he waved.

The pup whined, so I grabbed the paper and unrolled it to read:

I heard you're the Library Keeper of Vayu.
I need access and am willing to make a trade.
It's about The Link.

Jadox Griffin, from Draven

My shoulders tensed, and a tornado of leaves swirled at my feet. Fear coursed through my gut, and I glanced through Rajitha's window to the sight of Wes jumping on the couch with a smile on his face. Everything could be taken away if two Mystiers linked. I couldn't let this happen again. History couldn't repeat itself. Ordulls would try to eliminate Mystiers— again.

I'd have to check security measurements around our library, the beating heart of our city, but first, get this man as far away from Wes as possible. I rubbed my beard, trying to calm my racing nerves, but that didn't work. I released the energy I had captured from the steam earlier and let it stream through my veins.

"Dad!" Wes ran out the back door, through the swarm of tiny mosquitoes, and straight into my arms. "Mom said we can go parasailing next weekend, and she said you can come too. You'll come, right?"

Crap.

I crouched down to his level and glanced around his slender body at the mystery man still standing against the tree, waiting. "No, bud. I just got an important work … conference … and need to stay at the library for a while."

His smile disappeared. "But we can start …" he leaned in and cupped his hand to his mouth, whispering, "… start training my Magik, right?"

"Soon." I kissed his forehead and tied it to hide my shaking hands. "But keep it our secret."

He mimed, zipping his mouth shut, gave me a thumbs-up, and ran inside. While he ran, his body flickered in and out of view, disappearing completely then reappearing.

Shit! I can't leave him. But, if I don't, he might not have a future. Or any of us.

A breeze fluttered over my face, giving me strength. I stepped toward Jadox.

I know what I need to do.

See the next short story in this series, "Jadox's Spell," then "Kyra's Ruin."

THE LINKED TRILOGY
CASSIE SWINDON
SCORCHED
SEVERED
SHATTERED

CASSIE SWINDON
SCORCHED
THE LINKED TRILOGY
BOOK ONE

ALSO BY CASSIE SWINDON

Break the Stone

Hunt the Storm

Stop the Clock

(This Golden Chains trilogy has 6 prequel short stories on www.cassieswindon.com)

Scorched

Severed

Shattered

(This Linked Trilogy has 3 prequel short stories on www.cassieswindon.com)

www.ingramcontent.com/pod-product-compliance
Lightning Source LLC
Chambersburg PA
CBHW070547310726
48982CB00011B/1487/J

* 9 7 8 1 7 3 7 3 4 6 9 5 1 *